Pam St...

PENGU...

# THE WELL
## DRESSED EXPLORER

Born in Brisbane, Thea Astley studied arts at the University of Queensland. *Girl with a Monkey* was her first novel published in 1958. Since then she has published nine novels, three of which won the distinguished Miles Franklin Award: *The Well Dressed Explorer* (1962), *The Slow Natives* (1965) and *The Acolyte* (1972). In 1975 her novel *A Kindness Cup* won the Australian Book of the Year Award presented by the Melbourne *Age*. *Hunting the Wild Pineapple,* her first collection of short stories, won the James Cook Foundation of Australian Literature Studies Award in 1980.

Thea Astley recently retired from the position of Fellow in Australian literature at Macquarie University and is now living and writing full time in Queensland.

£2.20

## ALSO BY THEA ASTLEY

*Girl with a Monkey*
*A Descant for Gossips*
*The Slow Natives*
*A Boatload of Home Folk*
*The Acolyte*
*A Kindness Cup*
*Hunting the Wild Pineapple*
*An Item from the Late News*
*Beachmasters*

# THE WELL DRESSED EXPLORER

## Thea Astley

Penguin Books

Penguin Books Australia Ltd,
487 Maroondah Highway, P.O. Box 257
Ringwood, Victoria, 3134, Australia
Penguin Books Ltd,
Harmondsworth, Middlesex, England
Viking, Penguin Inc.
40 West 23rd Street, New York, N.Y. 10010, U.S.A
Penguin Books Canada Limited
2801 John Street, Markham, Ontario, Canada
Penguin Books (N.Z.) Ltd,
182-190 Wairau Road, Auckland 10, New Zealand

First published by Angus and Robertson, 1962
Published by Penguin Books Australia, 1988
Copyright © Thea Astley, 1962

Offset from the Angus and Robertson hardback edition
Printed in Australia by
Australian Print Group

CIP

Astley, Thea, 1925-
The well dressed explorer.
ISBN 0 14 009882 8.
I. Title.
A823'.3

What will You do, God, when I die?
I am Your jug, (when I shatter?)
I am Your drink, (when I spoil?)
I am Your garment and Your trade.
With me You lose Your meaning.

After me You have no house in which
Words close and warm greet You.
There fall from Your tired feet.
The velvet sandals which I am.

Your great cloak falls from You.
Your glance which I receive upon
The warm bed of my cheek
Will come, will look for me a long time—
And at sunset lay itself in the lap of strange stones.
What will You do, God? I fear for You.

Rainer Maria Rilke

THE WEIGHT of her on his shoulders was almost too much for him.

They circled the room, the boy on all fours, and he was on the point of collapsing to his elbows with the hiccuping laughter and the pain: the pain as she drove her heels in and said "Giddap, jumbo!"; and the laughter as he turned his pale straining face to one side, to glimpse her leaning smile. "Giddap, jumbo!" Abruptly the scream in his tendons dissolved in a supersonic agony and there he was, sprawling on his face while she lurched forward to topple over him onto the dusty playroom floor. A glimpse of navy knickers and plump thighs. Jumbo. Disentangled, they rolled on their backs, coughing and spluttering out the last of the tomfoolery and the images of their burlesque into the breathing-space of an armistice.

Wet afternoon. Muddy light at full tide hid scrawls of dirt charitably passing off vagueness as cosiness, here under a rain-gabbling roof, here behind window slashed and slashed by the wet flat leaves. The girl jumped up and began slapping and beating the back of her skirt, then went to lounge against the window, her elbows set on the sill as she picked with stubby nails at the flaked paint that blistered in a miniature child-sketched sea of ochre waves. The observed heart-shaped leaves were swashing and clinging and lingering against iron and glass. She breathed a rough circle of mist onto the pane and drew a face in it, rubbed it out with her red palm and began again.

7

Behind her, still stretched out along the knotty pine boards, the boy sleepily reviewed his fourteen years. All about him they hummed like tops, they were stacked up in rusting piles along the work bench, in boxes of bent rails, in marbles scuttled into corners, in carved initials up the length of a doorjamb, in the old comic piles, the book, strangely persuasive, smuggled in from Scaler Wayne. ("Hey, Brewster! Take a geezer at this! Yum-yum, eh!" "Gee, Scaler, can I take it home for a bit?" "Two bob to you, son." And the mouth slit-grinned, meaning it, and George felt the coins should have gone in there instead of into the stringy, kibed hand.) The spatial texture of four thousand odd days lost its silky quality. A rain puddle formed in his mind. Plop plop plop. The guttering dripped with memories. Guilty pink set sunwise on his amiable forehead remembering his cousin's crushing weight and the pleasure of it, the ache in the neck. He rolled on his side to look at her—unlovely, fat and vital, fringed, short-pleated, shod in strap-buttoned patent, sailor- (no ship named) bloused.

As he watched she poked her tongue out as far as it would go and, wrinkling her nose, became so hideous that the boy giggled.

"It's your mother," she said coolly when her face resumed its shape. "She's run the window up. I bet she wants you, George."

Conscience sat up in the dust. Scaler's book lay under a mound of paperbacks. George's flickering timorous glance collided at this point with his mother's muscular voice plunging right through the rain and wind layers. "George-" (dogmatic) "-eeee" (rising querulous). Again. And again. The girl made pantomime gestures with a beauty of their own. They semaphored through glass to corseted anger at the kitchen door.

"You'd better go," she advised the boy. "She looks pretty mad."

8

"You, too."

"Not me. They weren't calling me. Besides, I want to catch up on my reading, haha."

George squirmed pleasurably and unlocked the door with also a finger-to-lip warning from fat curly locks who rolled her bulging dapple eyes.

"You be careful," he said, and a year's specific rhapsodies pumped along his thin body. Outside the closed door he waited a moment under the overhang of the shed roof. Beyond the Hotel Pacifique a river steamer and a banana barge swung against the wharves; and beyond that, the training wall, a black glistening scab, curled across the river. In a treacherous tumult of aquamarine and pearl, river mouth emptied storm waters beyond the point. Sallow dunes. Dun cliffs. Smeared shapes of windy trees, piccabean and cedar rambling down from the Terranora forests.

The boy's ape toes that could shy a pebble for forty singing feet squelched through grass slush, dragging the mud lusciously between to rise in eight tawny joys. Mostly he stamped his foot deliberately along the narrow path, with his head down to watch, dragging reluctantly in the rain, sensing his shirt nailed to his body by hundreds of droplets. Irrelevantly his mind said "One more day," and then, happy disciple, he shouted the same words aloud, his streaming face grinning awkwardly as his mother flung open the back door.

"You're more than stupid, George! Change your clothes! And what on earth are you and Susan doing there all this time? Why didn't she come? We're going to have tea before your aunt goes."

Face was so like face. Puberty had not yet defined the boy, so that it would have been ridiculously easy to disguise one as the other if only the frizzy hair both sprouted might be lengthened or cropped; for the same blue eyes, in each case prominent and dispassionate, the same girlish mouth parted

9

into an illusion of smile by the same large teeth, shouted their relationship.

"I'll get her," he said. Doom smirked like Scaler Wayne. A nervous tic. Perceptive Mrs Brewster, with nothing further to add, rushed between rain streamers, a fanatical disciplinarian, while George, biting his plump lip, sidled past her Torquemada eye and trailed wetly to his room down the hall.

Faith without good works is dead, said Grandpa Brewster's departed voice in thick felt tones above the redly varnished furniture, and nudged a whole chorus of echoing texts into utterance while George stripped off his shirt. He delighted in watching himself in the mirror, practising a variety of smiles and sincere looks he kept for certain teachers. Now he used the "no homework done but it was certainly not my fault, sir" gaze of unwavering gravity, genuineness leaping out from the eyes like two trained boxers. If the words did not convince at once, he made certain that his eyes felled his questioner at one truthful glance. There was another pimple starting near his nose. He attended to it absent-mindedly, observing rather his mouth as he practised the "Oh sir that was a boomer" smile he reserved for the abstruse witticisms of the Latin master. ("*Must* you do Latin, Brewster?") He would need that, he reflected, pretty often before the next summer term collapsed in a chaos of prose and scansion and unseen translation. Making his eyes sparkle more, he did it again. They simply shone with youthful alertness and appreciation. He was ravished by his own boyish enthusiasm. "Oh, sir," he breathed aloud, "oh, sir," admiringly, "that *was* a boomer!" Faith and good works, but especially faith, he signalled back to Grandpa Brewster. I have enormous faith.

To test him, the back door slammed on his thoughts and he heard, with a stopping of the heart, his mother propel Susan into a silence of accusing aunts and mothers, of rain-witnesses, of discovered unlawful property, of very innocence that shouted vehemently from his pale round fourteen-year-old face with its frightened eyes. These rolled at the horror of it. He pulled on a clean shirt, brushed his hair and prayed briefly.

Years ago his parents had discovered God. It was an event quite undiluted with the spontaneous bliss of one who finds the Ultimate Father Image, but rather a soured exultant we-knew-we-would occasion that instantly encased the relationship in a spiritual rigidity that absolutely precluded warmth and love. God did not like people who dropped in. One made appointments well ahead. Sunday hung like a millstone around the neck of each week. George, stifling his yawns in the family pew, wondered whether this stern, this unapproachable Maker, were not also coming to dread the seventh day as much as he did, and he would knot his hanky and writhe and furtively play with string in his side pocket while the minister, so his mother insisted afterwards, must surely have been directing the message solely at him. But they discovered God again in another church and some time later again in yet a different one; and by the time George was eleven they had found Him with such increasing frequency that they had practically exhausted all Protestant sects in their small beach town and were being forced closer to Rome or the exotic. Which? No. The query, the cynicism were not George's. He was the most uncynical boy and remained that way all his life. That his parents were not cynics could hardly be more obvious, too, endlessly pursuing divine love as they did in the face of one manifestation of divine dislike after another. But it was not, to be honest, disappointment with the Divine. Usually some trifling difference with a minister, a question of parochial politics, a sense of imposition at church fêtes, workstalls, bottling fests, and a violent, hateful, losing battle against class consciousness and snobberies rounded them up and set them seeking lusher pastures.

Yet like a life-giving artery the unchanging rigour of puritanic

11

home-discipline pumped George along, a microscopic corpuscle. In vain he sought red-blooded companions. In vain he attempted to clamber up the sides and take to the plains. He shuddered and shuddered as his mother's voice summoned him. One glimpse of his cousin's face was sufficient to warn him. His mind gasped a longdrawn ooooh of pain and he plunged his moist hands into his pockets. From the stuffy serge hole where he had followed them, he heard his mother's conviction and self-righteousness.

"Your father," she said across the vine-patterned carpet, "will deal with this."

In front of three sorts of biscuit and two of cake they sat around the dining-room table. Cadenzas of giggles were starting in Susan's chest. Her mother, a spreading woman in watered silk, after asking rather piteously "What is it, Lila?" two or three times, submitted to a firm "My dear, I could not possibly now," and ate robustly, dropping crumbs all over the best china, her skirt and a rough circle of carpet. With dignity Mrs Brewster nicked into a sandwich, poured tea, caused George to pray as he had rarely prayed within his mind, and commented brightly but coldly on the weather while the boy counted the biscuits with angelica efflorescence, those budding almonds and those with preserved pineapple. Now and then he felt his cousin's foot press clumsily onto his; but there was no reassurance. Flesh demands more than mere flesh. Various relations were reviewed and dismissed by the women. Dress patterns and recipes paraded. The rain came in squalls against the iron roof and the room grew opaque with the sombreness of parlours that hold sagas of framed photos, of albums, of cushions, of two generations' yellowing linen, glassware, vases, lace curtains. Dusk oozed up from corners straddled by the moulded calves of sideboard and easy chair, Cut cakes, like cut flowers, wilt and grow forlorn.

"We must be going," Aunt Esme Brewster said—but it

was the discomfort of a conversational pause that urged her. "It is only a block or so and we have our coats. I mean we won't get wet, not very wet."

"If you must," George's mother said with a glance at the pendulum clock that swung a gleam regularly across the wavering dusk. "If you must." She sighed. Weighty thighs swung sideways. Bodies struggled from chairs. Ladylike vehemence jostled and battled from confinement into a cascade of chirruping politeness down the hall, past the hatstand to the damp veranda. Mrs Boyd borrowed a jam recipe from her sister. It is more graceful to receive at this point in an afternoon; and, sliding into her soggy raincoat, she thanked Mrs Brewster twice, with her inquisitive eyes sliding backwards and forwards from boy to mother.

Furry rectangles of rain-patch lay all the length of the wooden veranda. A tecoma bush by the front gate had scattered statements of colour over the lawn.

"Say goodbye to your cousin."

Susan presented a white round cheek which he smudged briefly with his mouth while their eyes slanted across each other for a moment. All the goodbyes became entangled and lost. Rain-knotted wind drove suddenly through the open hall door and flung a last goodbye at the house which did not open its heart to it.

Then Mrs Brewster, her blue eyes bulging with a godly displeasure, led her son inside and closed the door. George's mind closed with it. He knew nothing, his face assured her. After a little, his eternal innocence soaked through, convincing him too. It was a *liber ex machina*. Together they stood over its enterprising pages, George with an assumed wonder that gradually became real, his mother with puzzlement and then an outraged perception which informed her she had lost this round. Under her brittle external religiosity she had enough genuine religion to want to chuckle; but belonging to a

13

sampler-stiff, precept-bounded community where movements were as predictable as cross-stitch, she tightened her mouth. The mental confusion caused by the careless obscenity of spring fertility, summer trees, sulphurous sun-settings and risings, of the rapture of greens and ochres and russets, troubled her son but not her. In each house each evening the fluted glass mantles of blue or red or lemon-tinted glass glowed above conformities of every kind while outside the very earth shifted emotionally, throbbed and shook against the channel walls, the bay; and the long tides of grey and white ate at the heart as well as the land.

Scene—beach scimitar. Time—moment of shells and salt and foreign weeds strung out along rocks. To the right, Rainbow Bay climbs towards the point. Two boats, lying on their tipsy sides straight after Rimbaud, are close up. Canvas rain clouds flap above the sea. Backstage left, a boy moves across, his face concealed from the reader, for the moment, as he skims smooth grey pebbles and chucks driftwood into the lemonade-green water. Streaks of white light converge on the moving surface. Sun rises with vague effect and air shakes and wavers. Startled by gull cry, boy turns, stares and blinks at all our faces.

Placing one testing foot on the nearer boat, George rocked it gently, looked about, then hopped in and lay along the damp sand in its belly. Today. He lit a cigarette and watched the tell-tale smoke float beyond his wooden horizons. Today. Today. Tobacco no longer made him sick and he inhaled, performed geometric miracles, with his legs braced against the boat's flanks, clipping it rhythmically against the hard sand. It was the second day of the school holidays. Six weeks curved sweetly into the infinity we all recall of blueness and heat, of sticky ripe fruits and sweating grass, of camp-fires and voices after dark from the lost faces when words seem to matter and afterwards do not, did not. Mouth-organs blown lingeringly in starlight, starlight lingering in the mind's eye. George exploded this poetry in a whoop that raced away from him with frightened flapping white wings. The gull wheeled. The whoop boomeranged. Whacko candish! In an hour, warmth, brownness, silliness, slenderness, the aching conclusion of his adolescent body, would wander into the ragged garden of the Krugers.

Two summers ago she had begun holidaying with her grandparents in the bungalow next door. One morning he had come suddenly on her squatting on the top rail of the dividing fence. She was regarding him obliquely through forward falling hair.

"Hello," she had said.

Because girls were stupid, he hadn't answered at once and the silver gut of half a minute stretched taut while she stared until he felt uncomfortable and had to look back.

"Hello," he replied grudgingly. There was another palpable silence in which the summer drew their words from them like ichor.

"My name's Nita." The hair was pushed back from an alert eye. A smile tiptoed across the licked lips. "I'm staying here. What's your name?"

He watched the sharp little pink tip of wet tongue flicker across the tender skin.

"George." The tongue withdrew. Nothing. A smile. Nursery dogged him.

Nettled he said, "How old are you?"

"Eleven."

"I'm thirteen."

She should have been impressed but even now he could remember her sudden silly giggle. It was as if a bird beat unexpectedly across a blank sky. The magpie fluttered onto a fence post near them.

15

"Shoo!" she said, slapping her arms at it. "I know lots of boys bigger than you."

He was humbled and flung a stone at the water tank. Clunk! Got it! But still she peeped at him through her black hair in a superior wordlessness that fretted his mind although girls were stupid. She stood with her bent waiting knee, weight propped on her left thigh, brushing back every now and then the thick mass of hair that kept dropping across her eyes. George stood a beer bottle at the base of the apricot-tree and, standing back at the end of the garden, began pegging away as if she didn't exist. The bottle shattered finally into toffee slivers, but she was gone by then—he could hear her singing flatly and muzzily from their kitchen—and he was furious and then empty and hung about the yard all afternoon waiting to catch sight of her.

That was how it was. Puppet George. Puppeteer Nita. She planned. He submitted joyously. All through those holidays and the next they swam, scrambled along the wharves and the training wall, lay on their bellies poring over a shared book, cadged lollies and cakes, and watched, both of them, George fall hideously—oh, dreadfully—in love. Days ripened and dropped into their laps. They bit into them and the holiday juices ran over smiling lips and teeth. On the very last day as they sat on the training wall, their scratched legs pendent above the treacherous tide, Nita, in the late afternoon's loneliness, leant across swiftly and put her mouth against his face.

This particular kiss sang in him for a year.

During the tossed nights of wind-scud in July the silly soft thing prowled round his mind. It almost cost him his mid-year examination, for he day-dreamed continually of the next summer, and the next summer dangled unreachable as heaven, although his parents were constantly beckoning him there along Chapel paths. In one place he learned of a God of love. In another, of a God of wrath. It was very confusing. One thing

16

remained constant in his woolly mind: he was in love—but not with God. He dug out her name with the end of his compass on the inside lid of his desk. Scaler caught him inking it in. "Woooo!" Scaler had yelled. "Gotya!" And was merciless for a week. George was pleased, grinned stupidly, grew out of his clothes, began pimples and ginger down on his cheeks and an uncontrollable cracking in his voice when he became excited.

Some harmless can was kicked and scuffed the entire length of road between Bay and Heads. A final violence whacked it rustily against the arthritic lemon tree at Krugers' front gate. Wind bent the tree's agony against unpainted pickets where George, hands in pockets, pulled up abruptly, not only shy but horrified. He couldn't even remember her face. Love is blinded, he reassured himself, thereby coining his first witticism, and could hardly be expected to remember. Sea writhed in pain along foreshore; wind battered papers and leaves; leaves scratched his bare ankles. Her face? gasped his mind. Her face? What is her face? And he tried to transfer it from last summer to this, but it floated tantalizingly vague within the leaf walls of a tree-house, it laughed featurelessly from the crest of a dune, and

"Hullo, young man," her grandfather, Carl Emil, said from his long-armed canvas deck-chair on the veranda. "She iss nod here yed. Nod yed." A spendid Teuton, all pipe and check shirt, a mass of consonants. Twenty years before he had skippered one of the top-sail schooners that handled the cedar trade for the south from the forests in the Macphersons. All day, his rheumy eyes reflecting the purple currents beyond the river bar, he would sit on his warped veranda, nod his shiny, white-fluffed dome to neighbours and suck on his cold pipe.

George's own head waggled in embarrassment while his heart resumed its rhythm. "All right, Mr Kruger," he yelled out. One corner of a lace curtain raised an enquiring ear. He blushed.

17

"All right. I'll come back after lunch." And was so relieved—he could not have said why.

The long, long, ritual of baked dinner. His father, a thin extremely nervous man with a red face, carved, passed, called for a blessing on the loaded plates, and ate without speaking. His clicking false teeth castanetted merrily. Since Scaler's book had been shown to him and then burned, his eye sidled often towards his son and examined him with a sly amusement not altogether congruent with Methodism. As his mother splashed acid enquiries. George dropped his nagged head above his plate. Leave the boy. Yes, leave me. Leave me. I have chunky muscular legs. I have a newly discovered and perplexing lust. If, he told himself with a bubbling inner irony, if you could only follow one of my twining, disgusting, delicious, unleavable desires, you would leap back from the baked pork and apple with shouts, with cries.

His father was smiling into the custard jug.

"Don't wander off, George. I'll want a hand with the old sofa. I'm going to re-spring it."

"Just into the yard?"

"We're not finished yet."

"I said the yard, just the yard?"

No one answered. There was a tyranny of pudding to contend with. His father removed a solid gold watch from an inner pocket, flipped back its cover and abstractedly glanced at its hands.

"Half an hour," he conceded his son.

"Gee," George complained. "Gee." Yet once through the back door and charged with the electricity of freedom, he ran whistling to the paling fence section past the playshed and, concealed from his parents, perched on the lower rail, his arms dangling over, (silly ape), the sharp top edge cutting him. He was one gigantic pulse.

She was there, squatting under the Brazilian cherry in the

far corner of the yard, playing with one of the cats. Both of them were purring. The girl rubbed herself along the cat with slitted eyes, her head buried in the furry ecstasy of the vibrating animal. Brown limb. Tortoiseshell. Stretchings. Purrings. Eyes closing, closed. The grey afternoon sky leaned over.

Of course he remembered.

You might remember yourself? Time apart was a waste.

Subterfuges of an indifferent kind led his face to hers again and again but courage eluded him and his joy scuttled back to a corner. Obsessed, he thought of nothing else; while she, an experienced pertness of thirteen, would fall off to sleep thinking, "Silly slow old George. I'll have to make him do it. Silly slow old thing."

If only he had known.

Once in the third week both families went for a picnic, bristling with tablecloths, sandwiches and thermos flasks. They hiked right along Greenmount to Kirra Point and high up from the grumbling sea sheltered between great humps of rock. Funfair dolls—aunts, mother and Grandma Kruger—sat uncomfortably straight-backed with their legs tucked under their skirts, dwarfed by their striped cart-wheel hats of straw, their bandanas tied beneath chin, while the children lay after lunch in a slow baking access of desire upon the burning sands. Watching each other they traded slow smiles, the obvious pair, although the Mesdames Argus watched and watched the unseemly proximity of sunburnt limbs and peeling noses. George examined her carefully. Her juvenile shoulders were coated with sand; there was sand even at the tips of her lashes and the mesh of forward tumbled hair. Her small hands dug and trickled fulvid rivers and dug again; and during a moment when he sensed his relatives to be half-blinded by blueness and whiteness he leaned closer with his mouth a breath away from the down of her shoulder and whispered,

"Let's go back along the rocks."

In her eyes the yellow beach gleamed momentarily. "You'll have to ask."

"I know."

She wriggled impatiently, "Well, go on."

"Wait a bit. Wait till my mother smiles, will you?"

There could have been an eternity. The four adult faces were serious with town gossip. Mr Brewster was the Postmaster. His wife was given an unfair advantage.

"Go *on*!"

"Mum?"

No head glanced towards them. Unkindly, the wind showered them all with sand spray. They were whipped by hairs.

"Louder, silly."

George called again and his mother looked down the sloping beach with her hand shielding her eyes as she frowned at the blinding sea.

"Can I show Nita the rock pools round the point?"

All shadow and light, gradations of reaction lost, faces like theatre masks turned to them.

"Why?" asked his mother's concealed voice. "She's seen them."

"Not this year," he argued reasonably.

"It doesn't matter," Nita said skilfully in her clear young voice.

The sea held its waves suspended; whole half-miles of surf trembled without crashing into the valleys; George's hand, on a journey to an itching ear, was caught by time.

"Just for a little while, then. Don't go too far."

Crash went the waves; George's forefinger curled into his big freckled ear and hooked vigorously. Nita, clever minx, pulled a pretty scowl that completely deceived Mrs Brewster.

"Come on," she whispered to George. "Quick before she changes her mind."

South, the beach slanted away where rocks massively piled between cliff and water concealed miniature worlds of chasm and sand-slide and trapped seas. The original washed in streaks of violent blue along the coast and all its wild white gardens blossomed and fell and blossomed and fell unendingly. Like the spring, George thought. "I bet they're still watching us," he said aloud.

Nita looked at him through the mystery of her hair. She had long ago learnt the potentialities of silence with boys. And looked beyond. She put one hand up to her dangling mane and flung it back behind a thin tanned cheek, plumped out for the moment by her smile. It was a smile packed with half-promise.

Sidling and dawdling, eventually they interposed volcanic outcrops between themselves and the adults. Around the point with Greenmount curve isolated to the south they found a natural cave screened by pandanus; and there, Nita, placing a rough palm in George's, said without preamble.

"I'd love to go in without my clothes on."

Delectable horror squeezed in his stomach and then released it like a sponge. He could do nothing but smile in the craziest manner, his prominent upper teeth clipping at his lower lip.

"Oh, George!" she exclaimed, annoyed but trying to conceal it. And impatiently she leaned forward and kissed him for the second time. Instantly he looked all about to see if they had been observed. They had not. Goggling at her, he trembled, and in the fluctuating seconds before and as he placed his arms around her body he was aware of the most minute things—the sudden collapse of the sand under pressure of his feet, spray on one knee, a slowly undulating fringe of weed in the pool on his right. Never would he have a moment quite like that again—but he did not know it. All his life George was silly enough to believe primary magic could be held and repeated at will; and like so many people benignly silly, he was often lucky. But this was one of those shimmering bubbles of perfection. The hemisphere

21

of sky, taut as blue rubber, ballooned over its purple and yellow base on whose diameter George and Nita swayed with all the loveliness of weather pouring onto them. His heart soaked up not only love but the idea of love—more than that, really, and his romantic tippy-toe being was almost a-wing. He wanted to shout and soar and yell and skim away in a distance.

"I love you," he mumbled almost angrily against her cheek. "Oh, I love you."

"Silly George," she said affectionately, satisfied. That made five. She was keeping score.

When those holidays ended, he consoled himself with letters, paper wonders which she answered only irregularly in a half-page of screwed-up writing that revealed as much as a squinting eye. Nevertheless, George was enchanted; his heart almost exploded through school serge on the rare day he saw her scribbled address on the envelope and his heart's insane thundering reassured him that romance was tangible. When they met again, he was nearly fifteen and because he was more or less shy with girls, all the year's hungry frustrations centred upon this. Anticipation was more delicious than actuality of course, but actuality itself became progressively more delicious with each summer. They kissed—only that—at every possible moment and in every conceivable place until they were almost drunken with an abstinence that tortured them in their pro-longed lip barterings beneath the apricot tree, beside the water-tank or in their tree-house still strong against trade winds. He told himself there would be nothing like it ever again—as there wasn't; and she helped convince him of that, although she made no effort to prove the matter to herself. After all—George was the victim of love, not she.

At sixteen his disease was incurable and he was resigned to a pleasurably protracted malady which he vaguely hoped might never be eradicated. From a knicker-bockered thirteen-year-

22

old with a curious but still innocent eye, there had been an interesting metamorphosis to a surface sophisticate with a gravel voice, a pedantic cantankerousness for the exact word and a ponderous turn of phrase which he developed to that nice point where it served to render others envious and admiring rather than to make him appear ridiculous. Past Master Brewster watched the development of his only child with something of the sneaking pride and fear of a duck that has hatched out a roc—albeit a baby one. But his mother, well-balanced and shrewd as a monkey, observed and merely nodded, listened and was amused, and gave pithy directives which George obeyed as smartly as a soldier.

They were still seeking God—but they were older now and not nearly as energetic, and had come to rest temporarily in a small but unusual sect of lay preachers who moved about the district in which they originated, preaching on the Sabbath in small-town main streets. On their lapels they wore a pin which combined with a curious lack of artistry a cross and shoe, while on their right arms a reticent navy band proclaimed in restrained Celtic lettering that they were God's Travellers. Despite the derision such devices might have attracted, they were simple people of an exhilarating practicality in their goodness; they gave in preference to receiving and Knight Templar George was lacerated by a psychical conflict between his romantic idealism which approbated the work of the Travellers and a newly developed snobbishness that sent him haring after intellectuality rather than spirituality.

School holidays had released him from bondage to a Lupercal of preliminaries of loving to which he brought a zest that normally accommodated his spiritual and intellectual exercises during the year. He had never been a popular boy at school in the sense of being a leader, but was liked by the girls, whom he amused, who giggled joyously at his heavy jokes and whom he flattered outrageously. Yet notwithstanding this, other males were mere acquaintances or close acquaintances but hardly ever friends. Scaler Wayne, now a runtish messenger boy of nearly seventeen had the crafty and fox-featured mind of a jockey who knows every race is rigged. He tolerated George that George's father might tolerate him. Scaler not only liked girls, he was an experienced performer who boasted intolerably and almost farcically, enjoying the peculiar fruits of a fascination which slit mouth and shifting eye have for some women. Although George disliked him, scatology and lewd reference made a living textbook of the fellow (falling open at the well-thumbed places, reader) and George, who was by now helping his father in the office, would join him at lunch-time in the Post Office yard and listen pop-eyed and hungering to his amorous exploits. This derived expertise found its solitary mental application to only one fantasy; yet when Nita appeared, warm and brown and sly at the beginning of the holidays, his courage sagged.

She did not tell him but she went out with Scaler, too. Scaler was fun. He talked fast. He chewed. He chain-smoked. And sometimes he produced a flask with a few inches of cheap wine which they drank in turns for the marvellous sense of sin it gave them. Only a few months before she had learned, also, to say "You're marvellous, Bobby!" "Frank, you're marvellous!" Looking up through her hair.

She looked so at George one pellucid Tuesday as they sat on the back steps of her grandmother's house. She looked so and she told him he was wonderful but he simply stared ahead in that abstracted way he had sometimes and groaned. Irritably she pinched his arm.

"Oh, what?" she asked.

"Nothing. Oh, nothing much." And groaned again.

"Don't do that. It's awful. There is something. Tell me at once."

"Dad's been transferred. We're going away."

24

"Are you? When?" She caught her breath—relief?—and expelled it suitably against his shirt.

"Next month. Near Newcastle. I won't see you after this, I suppose." He was unburdened but the day gasped and the leaves shivered against the tank in a *frisson* of green two-hued.

"Oh, George!"

Satisfactory, satisfying tears brimmed, broke down his pale cheeks and when he put his big curly head down on his knees, damp patches of a salty grief gummed his shirt-sleeves to his skin. His heaving distress which he did not attempt to repress brought her generous arms about him, and in the secrecy of his down-bent agony he smiled into his own arms with his wet streaked face absorbing love and disaster like a sponge. The knot of their shadows rocked its sorrow blackly across the stoop.

"But I'll write to you, George," whispered consoling Nita. It was a rash thing to say.

"Will you?"

"Oh, yes. Yes. Every day." The lie might as well be magnificent. There was an obscurity about this situation that befogged Nita, so normally capable of standing, hands on hips, waggling a metaphorically sardonic rump. After a cursory glance at the back windows, George kissed her clumsily, made inept by fear.

"I'll come up and see you as soon as I can. I mean after I've saved up. You won't have forgotten me by then, will you?" he added wistfully. Only recently he had learned to be wistful, discovering that older women were thus charmed into a maudlin state. It only partly charmed Nita, however, because she was a narrow-eyed realist who could recognize an opportunist like herself. Pressing his hand tenderly she entrusted herself cunningly to silence while her mind sorted over the possibilities of his departure. They accompanied their sorrow

25

to the beach, the three of them dawdling way out of town to the long coast north of Kirra vibrating with the major chords of summer. Not far behind the dune-line, in a hollow thick with banksias, they found a place so brimming with the potentialities of love this should have been the moment for all its blazonings, for trumpets, for pennants; but something, even at the peak of a rhapsody of kisses, held George back. He took Nita's small sweet waiting face between his hands and, drowning in it, saw both of them as twelve and thirteen in the magic untouchable hinterland of childhood; and, although he knew she was awaiting some lustier definition of love, he could not; but swinging his body away from hers, sobbed with this added disappointment into the papery grass. Immersed so in himself as mourner, he did not notice after a minute that she had slid quietly from his side, concealed by the loudness of his grief which, though it shuddered forth in only an occasional sob, was a brassy clangour within his mind. When he opened his gummy eyes on the tiny world of sand enclosed by his arms and then on the wider one of grove and dune, she was gone, hidden by the trees and racing away from him in a puzzled hate towards the road.

He sprang up, intending to race after her; and, even as he rocked and staggered in the loose sand, intention died.

That evening it was Scaler who escorted her to the hotfoot dance in the local hall and who squeezed her hard in the shadowy lobby between dances. George did not discover this until a week had gone by, when his clenched jealousy punched him this way and that through the last seven lurching days. But it did not cure his love; and the late afternoon of liquid violets and blues when, trudging his hurt across what had once been their favourite walk, he came upon Scaler possessing his beloved under the scanty shelter of a possum-tree, also failed to scarify his heart. For a while he thought and rather hoped he was going mad, perhaps with the unadmitted idea that violence might return her to him. But the last days, the last few days, each one pendulously long, sticky, clinging to him, unrolled to the last formal goodbye. He gave her a brooch that cost more than he wanted to pay and she bent her shadowed face over the trumpery box a moment with a "You're sweet, George." He squeezed back the words he had intended and the clattering train hissed and puffed away while he sulked and rehashed his losses all the way to Brisbane.

Mosaic of recollection all through the south-bound night. Mother and father left him alone and he huddled under his travelling rug on the narrow bunk of the coastal steamer, eating sandwiches from a wicker basket. Even after a day at sea her face rose and broke and rose and broke on every wave whose green veldt became the sweep of uncut grass in the back block behind Krugers' where imperiously she had forced him to carry her on his back as he crawled on all fours in his pretended hunting-ground, collapsing at last in the poured-down sunlight to find her heat-dewed legs a heart-beat from his face. Fragmentary sketches—precociously adult at dances, teetering on her older sister's borrowed heels, all sex and frills. And in the tree-house. That most of all, in the first summers, belly prone on the plank floor gorging apricots that they stored in a box and chucking the stones into the green air to startle birds like fish. Like a fish George leapt and pulled and tugged on the line she held now several hundred miles away, and at last in sleep skimmed waves to be with her on a northern shore, plunged and rose to that captor hand and woke to find himself far down the coast.

Hunterville's dirty shellback clung to the beach. An industrial crab with urban notions. Mr Brewster became a section head in the central office but could not persuade George to follow him there. The year was 1920. People still wept openly on the Twenty-fifth of April, sang at pianola parties "There's

27

a long, long trail," notched in their belts in the baby Depression and pressed their fingers unbelievingly and joyously on the nipples of their electric wall-switches. For a while there was a craze for crystal sets. Senior Spaceman Brewster, with his long sensitive nose a quivering antenna between the heavy black ear-phones, barely heard his son. He was tuned in to a new god; and his son in his first long trousers, too cheap and too smart, and the sleek beginnings of a deadly small-boy fascination for women, went to work in a bookshop where he sold light romances and texts and stationery every day of the week except Sunday and Thursday afternoons. For a while he spent most of his freetime concocting long passionate letters to Nita who answered with an off-handedness that brought him to despair. His conjectures, his jealousies, nearly drove him insane and her very indifference made him howl for her like a dog. He coddled his heart-break with tripper memories: beaches, flannels on courts, picnic parties, train tickets up the coast, giggles in overloaded buses down the coast, the squeals of the mixed bathing groups.

And Enid.

Enid had twenty-two pairs of shoes.

Years later that was the first thing he remembered about her. If you probed assiduously he would recall her extensive collection of dresses and suits; and, much later, after tremendous effort, a broad pleasant face of willing bovinity came onto the screen. She tried so hard to make him forget Nita and he was an acquiescent participant in her physical endeavours even though much strenuous discipline produced no noticeable spiritual freeing. They first met, two shy pawns, over the book-counter. She was older than he by a couple of years. Her wide, rather stupid eyes, gazed frankly at him across a pile of glossy love stories.

"By Stella Harvey."

"Who?"

28

"Stella Harvey. She wrote *Torches of Night*. Have you read that? It was terribly sad. I mean, all her books are terribly sad."

"No." George shook his lion head. "No, I can't say I have heard of her. I don't think . . . could I recommend someone else?"

He could indeed. He went to the back office where he kept his lunch and whatever he happened to be reading.

"I can lend you this," he said, not quite knowing why he was acting in this way, but hungry for gratitude. He gave her a Colette novel and her sheer surprise borrowed it. Later she was to translate with a fanatic's adherence to the text—yet even love loses something in the translation—the passion and delicacy of the book for George. Alert to take a point, he quickly realized the possibilities of a planned course of reading and began with discrimination to select for her various erotic works which could prove useful exercises for them both. But technically they never became lovers. George could never really explain why; only that they pursued love's course to the point where both were nearly ill with desire when, like a tenuous feathering on water, Nita's image in an admonitory evocation seemed to prevent his consummating the act.

Peculiarly, he was never troubled by any sense of infidelity; for very early George had learnt the sweets of practical rationalization.

At the end of a year Mr Holtby, the gnome-like glaucous-eyed bookshop proprietor, eased his soul into its seasonal cloak of charity and gave George two weeks' holiday on half pay; but George, who had had enough of counter-jumping and the gentle friendlinesses of elderly women, decided to find another job. He resigned ("thanking you for the practical help and advice you have given me"—polite George!) and his mother took him by train to Brisbane for a month. There was to be a convention of group leaders from the Travellers. Mrs

29

Brewster, who had been energetically forming a subsidiary group in Hunterville and had been forced by social pressures to hold prayer meetings in a hired hall, was almost pining for the free-beating rhythm of two hundred souls whose prayers were for a recognizable common purpose.

"Why don't you see Nita on the way up?" his father suggested across the piles of pressed shirts. There was sufficient concern in his voice to make George glance at his mother.

"Yes, why not? Would you like to?" she echoed, the mind behind the words marvelling for an instant at its own charity.

"*Would* I?"

For a day, a mere taste of rapture, his mother broke the journey in the downlands town, submerged by waves of female cousins who filled the hiatus with twelve months' gossip while George waited trembling at a corner of the sleepy main street staring at the entrace of an insurance office from which his darling would emerge. The watching and expectant eye apprehends with shocking clarity the physical resolution of the long-cherished dream. Reality bounded over the lip of expectation. She had grown up. In a minute they were hand in hand eye in eye. She still giggled. She was still silly. She still wore her plum-brown hair to her shoulders, only now it was curled and she had put the faintest covering of rouge on her mouth.

"Oh, Georgie!" she gasped, looking up at him in the same adorable way. He could only breathe her name and press the soft pads of flesh that formed her hands.

In the foreign country of her home where she took him for tea, strategic ogling china ornaments inspected him more vitally than the parents who gave uncovered yawns between politenesses. There was a German weight-clock, a bunting divider-curtain in the hall and a pink and green Japanese lantern in the corner of the room. There were photos everywhere but mainly along the lid of the piano—a yellow brown walnut monstrosity with candlesticks, senile ivories orthodontulous in spots, and a dance-hall timbre that he endured before the meal when Nita's older sister pranced through a jiggling waltz.

"What are you doing after tea?" Fat Jean flung the words over her waltzing shoulder and rolled her sexy eyes. "There's a dance on at the Masonic."

Nita giggled, and afterwards in the front room, as George struggled into his coat, she gave him one of her oblique smiles.

"I don't really want to go to the dance, George. Do you?"

"I want to do whatever you want," he whispered obligingly, his aorta pumping out the flood of his passion at a faster rate.

"Let's just pretend we're going there, eh?"

"Your sister? Jean? What about her?"

"I'll fix that," she said. They shivered and said their good-byes into the steamy kitchen where Jean's smirk and suddy hands caused a blush to grow over him as his fingers slipped on hers.

"What did you mean," he asked softly as they stumbled against each other in the blind night of the garden, "saying 'let's pretend'?"

"You old silly!" she laughed, and he sensed the air of her mirth on his held-down cheek from where it chased all over his shuddering body. Nor would their steps find unison, she with her high heels mincing, he with his reined-in stride. A corner. Darkness cut and battered by the wind and tree-arm. Wind whistled like a lout. Oily light glowed from a house across the street and farther away the shape of the township printed itself in unsteady yellow points along the sky rim as she led him around the block and into the empty grass paddock behind her house whose long backyard, lost in violences of shadow, moved into marriage with the paddock and its privet clumps. But there, in a natural room formed by branches and leaves, he kissed her anticipating mouth before she could explain his intention to him and she in her turn drew him down into the long green hairy garden. No accusing image of Enid danced across his passion-clouded mind and at the peak of his self-loss only the vaguest perplexity shadowed him at her expertness.

The next day's train tore them apart.

He hardly saw the capital. All he saw was an ecstasy, as he ploughed joyously into an eclipse of sensibilities where a visionary light blazed about one thing only. Before they were to return home he persuaded his mother to stay for yet another night in Condamine on the return trip. On that occasion he did not return to the hotel until a whimpering dawn-light washed over the downlands and his mother, inspecting him across the breakfast table, read the loss of innocence in his bland blue eye and tightened her lips over questions shouting inside her.

Brave with love and boosted by parental influence, George went to work as a copy boy on the town's morning paper. "With opportunities," explained editor Rumbold, "of advancement to full-time reporting." Blowing a Santa beard with juicy wet mouth but failing to twinkle. The candles had all been taken down. His storehouse of clichés was packed full and he broadcast them riotously and unfinished into conversation.

"Yes, lad," he advised the young man," this will be a full and rewarding career if you learn discretion as well as daring. Fools rush in . . . You know?"

"I know, sir," George agreed.

And spent his days speeding up and down the unsafe stairs with armfuls of galley sheets; or stood beside one of the linotype men watching the metal slugs fall out as he gulped a cup of coffee. Remote, and divine in this remoteness, the literary staff (apart from Rumbold) was composed of three men: two reporters, and a sub-editor who also acted occasionally as night editor. There was, too, a typist, all bun and glasses, who handled the telephone in the downstairs office, ordered sandwiches, argued with creditors and public. Early displaying all the symptoms of an ulcer, the sub glowed greenly under his eyeshade, nibbled shredded lettuce sandwiches and pickles, that later tortured him as he writhed at his table behind stacks of proofs flung up like a sandbag barricade. From here he snarled all afternoon. The reporters were grey young men who wore snappy clothes, tightly waisted. Between them they had fifty years; yet displayed awesome *fin de siècle* ennui whenever George bounded upstairs with his corrected copy.

"Thanks, laddie," unbearable Symes would say, weightily patronizing. "Keep feeding the hungry presses—and masses." (Masses! Hunterville!) And he would prop twin shiny shoes on another chair and laugh with an irritating affectation of sophisticate whimsy. But Billings, who was more naïve, would pull a sheet out of his machine and, ignoring George, read out for the other some paragraph of pearl-sheen prose. "How's that?" he would ask, rather anxiously, his thick eyebrows raised. "Does it get the feel?"

"So-so." The protruded lower lip. Symes licking a cigarette paper with delicate critical tongue. "Only so-so. What you need is a greater element of shock, a more sudden presentation. Something that jerks the reader out of his cut-velvet lounger. The public must be startled into belief—not disbelief and criticism. I think this might do it. Cause criticism, I mean."

Then . . . "Run along boy," Billings would order, his eyes cold. "Shake it up, now. We're half an hour behind as it is."

But after six months George would not run. He developed a saunter that pointed him out as a self-fancier to be reckoned with. He read more and more. What had once been only a veneer of education was gradually becoming real. The mid-year made him a cadet who reported minor court sessions, church socials, interviewed trade union organizers, visiting pugilists and people rescued from floods, fires and mine shafts. His copy was always prompt, neat and well-written. Rumbold, blowing through white tendrils of beard and resting his mottled hands on his grey worsted paunch, would nod and grunt.

"Good lad, good lad. If a job's worth doing it's . . . You know?"

Bubble-laughter in George's chest fizzed up to his pressed-together lips but he would frown and say "Thankyousir" and then go back to the room he now shared with Symes and Billings; where, having lit a cigarette, he would swing one sharply creased leg over a corner of the desk while with retinae reflecting the reluctant listening faces of the others he mimicked Rumbold grotesquely. Rumbold with piles, in agony between the tables in the downstairs office. Rumbold with clichés, in agony between copy sheets. Rumbold, dyspeptic and burping at a staff party. Rumbold . . . "You're starting to look like him!" Symes would say nastily. "There *is* a God!"

Cadet Rousselle Brewster learnt also to drink, a pleasure he largely time-tabled for the two umber evenings a week on which he did night-shift; and it was on one of these, rosy and grey with diminishing sun, that he again ran into Enid whom he had carefully dodged for a month. Since his holidays he had used one pretext after another to space out their meetings, telling himself that to taper the affair off would be the kindest thing. Then as Nita's very absence increased the strength of her hold over him, sensuality, existing now merely in the mind, was deposed by a spiritual bond during her absence which illuminated and made far more magnificent than actuality the love he felt—or thought he felt. Guilt suffused all his sketchy reunions with Enid who was baffled by a puritanism of behaviour, an indifference, an abstraction. At first as the shame in his eyes slid away from the spurt of embarrassment and reproach in hers, he wished he could crawl into an oblivion, but natural, self-preserving charm collected his wits and a blend of bravery, whisky-induced, said,

"Hello, Enid." A desperate adventurer, he took her arm.

"Please, please don't pull away. I've been wanting to talk to you."

"You never wrote," she accused. Her usually pleasant face was ugly with frustration. "You never called. Whenever I came to your place you were out—or your mother said you were."

"How dare you imply my mother lies!" Quickly he snatched at her own weapon, turning it on her with fake anger.

"Oh, I didn't mean that. I didn't mean that."

He relented, confronted by this depth of wretchedness and a humility of abnegation that he could not really bring himself to falsify. Taking her suety arm that he had caressed with shut eyes as an artificial stimulus, he pressed it automatically.

"Believe me," he assured her in his deepest, gravest tones, "believe me, my dear, it would never have been fair to you. You know I'm thinking for you, don't you?... Don't you?" he persisted when she turned her fat hurt face away and blinked mistily across the waterfront.

The old magic started working. Eyes limpid with belief met his and the wrinkles of doubt vanished on their pool.

"You see, Enid," he said gently, gently, "I couldn't possibly get married for at least six years. I've no money, to be brutally frank. No money at all. And it simply isn't fair to ask anyone as attractive as you to wait so long."

"I wouldn't mind, George," she ventured, timid and brave.

"No. I simply wouldn't do it." He went on as if he had not heard her. "I hope I am not all that selfish. In addition," he added, hesitating before the *coup de grâce*, "in addition, I must be absolutely honest with you, Enid. I've always been absolutely honest with you, haven't I?"

She was entirely confused, "Yes," she said.

"Well, to be utterly truthful, there is someone else." Hearing the cliché, he thought, O God I've caught it from Santa! But he was to develop a natural taste for the device and the self-exoneration for use now was the first step towards the lush

35

journalistic pastures where they grew thick as daisies. "No, no," he explained, brimming with utter truth, glowing with candour, "no, not since. Before. Someone I've known for years. She has expected me—oh, you see how it is?—to marry her for so long."

"Yes." Enid nodded glumly, not seeing at all. A flicker of intelligent resentment at having been used raised a lightning weal in an atmosphere of duplicity for an instant. "But all those times—" she began to protest.

George looked across at the lamenting sea, spilling a repetitive grief along the foreshore. Wind shook its rattle of papers and leaves. Irrelevant and innocent memories came of the brown grazed knees of childhood, kneeling on jetty up Tweed by the government wharves, and the passion within turned upon a line and hook and the fish flashes in the swollen green tide. He unhooks his first catch, a bream undersized, and, trembling, drops it in the basket. Its dead eye catches the sun. His chest clutters up with pride so that he wants to yell victory into the summer blaze. She takes it from him like a bunch of roses. Fish on plate. Girl leaning sideways. Enid stooped against pain—is it?—near the sea wall of this other town in this new time, and he said,

"Oh, Enid! I know. Don't make me feel a bigger bastard than I am. I know. Don't hurt me like this. Surely you don't deliberately reproach me to hurt? If the positions were reversed, do you think I would do it to you?"

She did, but did not say so. Flying cumulus tumbled across the sky. He wanted to cry and he wanted to get away from her, believing his admission sufficient excuse. But she was hurt and intolerant (so he thought) and ran from him through rainstorms of weeping into a clear dry limitless landscape none of the light romances had even suggested, while George walked quickly to the Dominion and gulped a double whisky. His man-of-the-world was shaken up but practically took his mind off the matter by re-reading the typescript of an article

36

he was drafting on the shire improvements effected in the last ten years. It was amazing how quickly he put her pain out of his mind. There was a sort of mental washing of the hands, a trembling cadence of a sigh and another double Scotch.

That night as he drew back the coverlet on his bed, an unusual disquiet trickled coldly over his heart. Kneeling beside his book-table and clasping his hands, he sought comfort with eyes squeezed tight.

"Please God," he prayed, "make her happy. . . . Without me," he added thoughtfully.

Vari-coloured months of letter-writing. Hundreds of thousands of words conveying love, annoyance, grievance, trust, jealousy, despair.

"Is it a tribute or betrayal," George wrote, confessing to his diversion with Enid, "when I try to seek your face, your mouth in another?"

At her end, Nita showed the question to her latest boyfriend and laughed delightedly. She found writing a bother and the intervals between her scrappy replies grew longer. At his end, the appearance of a letter jolted his vulnerable heart and intervening days were piled with anxiety that floated like air about routine work. After one particularly long-drawn-out and difficult period, he received a note that made him gasp in his agony.

"George Darling," she wrote in her curly-cute hand, "I hope you are well, I'm not and I am worried sick. I mean I think I am sick—and I have to ask your help as you are the only only one. Can you please come up next week-end? Please, sweetheart. I wouldn't ask only I know I can depend on you."

Ever lovingly, she remained his Nita.

At first he crushed the paper into a ball and flung it across the room, only to rush after it, pick it up, smooth it and press it to his perplexed heart. Almost automatically he packed his

37

best pyjamas and his second-best shirt; and, having folded her letter and kissed his despair away on it, he told a glib lie to his parents about an assignment, and vanished on the Friday train.

The re-read, re-folded letter yielded no more than its surface of drama but he still re-read and re-folded it in efforts to extract the last droplet of love. It did yield a strange address in her memorized town whose geography he had learnt in a score of nostalgic fantasies. But when he arrived he seemed to recognize nothing. One knows a place by corner stores or pot-holes or tree-clumps or a certain angle between main-street and spire, between monument and pub, with something that is between love and hatred, a genial tolerance. A wind cut across the wheatlands. It rippled the edges of his fear as strangers fumbled with his questions as he fumbled with their answers in a cold town. At last he discovered the place where they were to meet and she came to him palely late in the lost light with her face raised against the wind.

"What is it?" he asked brutally abrupt, still hoping he might be wrong.

"Not here," she said. "I can't talk here. I only have half an hour for lunch. Couldn't we sit down somewhere?"

Her hand clawed its taloned way to his and instantly—oh, idiotically—excitement ripped him apart so that he almost groaned. Fat rumps of horses tied to the hitching posts along the main street quivered at the flies. Exploding cars started from harbours by the centre islands. There were stinks of cooking food and a grinding reek of beer and manure piles. The ugliness gripped him by the tender gentle throat, and choked him. He said, "Here. Let's go in here. One place is the same as another, I suppose." And then, half-obscured by varnish shade and fug, "What is it?" he repeated.

The reply spilled out and he shook with distrust and hatred.

"Are you sure?" he asked, and asked again, and again.

"I don't know. I think so. It's nearly a fortnight now."

38

He glared at her as she began to cry, ploughing her knuckles into her eyes like a small child. He was moved by no tears but his own—and now he could think nothing of her problem, only this strangling jealousy.

"Why?" he persisted. "Why?" But she didn't know why. They had been dancing and had a couple of drinks and she missed George (her ploys made him look like an amateur) and it had just happened. Please to believe her. Please to help.

"Is he here? Does he know? Why won't *he* help?"

He was gone, she confessed, a traveller for a soft-goods firm and much older than she. She thought he was married, anyway. George's mouth screwed up. Goose-flesh crept out suddenly on his shocked limbs and he shuddered, looking down at her forlorn face and drooping shoulders. Tribute or betrayal? Superstition caused him blame the failure of love upon his own deceits, and in this narrowing down of accurate reasoning, he fastened on almost any satisfying fallacy with joyous false security. It braced him for the future suffering which such illogicality would surely inflict on itself. She was still talking, but two minutes ago he had ceased to listen and the sun along the training wall was so direct, he felt himself half-sleeping as he noticed the line curve away with the tide-pull. Her hat flapped back on its chewed strings, and her pointed face, golden with light, was suddenly all he could see. While he watched, she licked her lower lip, It was the sight of that sharp pink tip of tongue that weakened him.

"All right. It's all right," he comforted vaguely. "I'll do whatever I can. Don't worry, little pussy."

Nita, watching her pointed nails, heard the pet name with sly rippling relief, and she stroked her narrow brown arms folded across her lap. Behind the shelter wall of her slim body pulsed the knot of ganglia she called her heart. Its tick was empty as a clock's, but she whispered.

"You're so kind, George. I'd die without you."

39

"I don't know," he said, poking this way and that at the food on his plate. "I simply don't know what we can do. I mean I just can't marry you for a while. There isn't any money to live on. Why, only last month I had to explain—" He broke off, horrified, at the crumbling brink-edge of revelation.

Nita looked up at that point and caught his eye. She was not deceived and the mutual recognition of infidelity only brought them into a closer and stronger relationship. George, detected, absolved, knave with knave, smiled his slightly buck-toothed smile of warm boyishness.

"Don't worry, pussy. You might still be lucky. We'll wait a bit and see what happens."

She was lucky and wrote to tell him so the next week. In his delirium, George wrote back recklessly that he was coming to join her there, that he would resign that month and apply for a reporting job on Condamine's tri-weekly news-sheet. Days he saw like sun-bursts, splashed carmine with joy, molten claret-coloured days transparent with light, deepened with reflections of days ahead, the grape beyond the grape.

## [II]

FASTIDIOUS in light grey, Mr Brewster had dominated for ten hours a tiny compartment in a box carriage travelling west, for three weeks a front bedroom in a private bungalow and for eighteen days a silky oak desk and swivel chair in an upstairs room of the Condamine *Hub*. "The Hub of the Downlands," a carven pediment stated dogmatically. By swinging in his chair, his interested blue eye could dominate a perspective of scenic planes—central town square of benches and pepper trees, the upper half of a war memorial, a gentlemen's lavatory, half an acre of park and the awnings of shops on its far side. A wretched terrier, prancing like a silly tripod on three of its legs, paused by a paper bin in the square. The abstracted half of George's mind absorbed each rippling fragmentary action on his day's surface, while the other half, that half prancing in black sateen shorts and boxing gloves, danced across the canvas jabbing and feinting prettily at the object in planetary opposition.

With the gloves on—yes!—he continued to type:

—"unusual terms of reference for such an Act of Parliament. In addition, thousands of unemployed will be an interesting swinging vote according to the climate of governmental policy. Our legislators must realize that it is they who wield what could be their own instrument of execution." He read this last sentence aloud and sucked his teeth lusciously.

"Yum yum!" he said. "This boy will go far." Pinning the three sheets of his article together, he went along the corridor

41

to the sub-editor's room where Ferguson, a tiny Scot with beautiful violet eyes, waited like a lady spider.

Outside, the perimeters beyond perimeters of undramatic and wavering coloration of lilac and umber, streaked and barred square miles of grassland that wandered to the shallow hill rim. If the reader had leaned over George's shoulder where he hesitated for thirty seconds of sky-filled time, there would have flowed away before his eyes streets of timber and iron houses capitulating soberly to dry air, dry country. Everything about this town had that attitude of submission to climate; the high tin hips of the roofs could well be supplicating a capricious rain-god. Angry trains bunted the town four times a week from the coast. They snarled and nuzzled their way east, puffing smoke at the flies. Ritualistically George waited until the last steam-trail evaporated from the mid-day train, until the trickle of awkward passengers dispersed along the street; then he tapped and entered Ferguson's cubby.

A lifetime of ruthless training had gone into Ferguson's quirk of never raising his eyes to junior staff. Rolling a cigarette without looking at either that or George, he continued reading the copy in front of him. Having made his cigarette, he lit it, picked up his blue pencil, crossed out an entire sentence, read to the end, scribbled across two "very's" and one "quite" printed "too long" at the bottom and flipped it back into his re-write basket. Still not looking up, he reached across for the next typescript, said "Leave it!" to George and went on reading.

"Oh, you bastard," George said softly to himself in the corridor. "Oh, you rotten, rotten bastard." And went for solace to Ronnie Shead, the shorthand writer who took down the news telephoned by Country Press. He worked with a stenographer in an annexe to the downstairs office where the pair of them huddled like moles. Shead extended this image in a dark hairiness of splendid vigour; a blunt round face with

42

aniseed eyes that he rolled tentatively at Miss Trumper. Miss Trumper was a timid creature, with an inborn tendency to burrow beneath her desk when addressed. She wed this beguiling shyness to a body of amazing flamboyancy. Such disparity amused George tremendously. The implied challenge of her behaviour demanded that he persevere with compliments and small attentions until there was that meltingly dim acquiescence of glance which was all he ultimately wanted.

"How's tricks?" solicitous Mr Shead inquired.

George made tiny circular movements with one hand, a royal wave.

"So-so. I don't seem to be terribly popular with the gentleman upstairs."

"Have we one?" cracked obvious Mr Shead. "Who? Duckworth?"

"No. V. J. Ferguson. He chills me off. Is he like that with everybody?"

Shead popped a eucalyptus lolly in his mouth and commenced crunching and reeking.

"He's okay," he mumbled, "when you get to know him."

George sighed. He preferred to charm instantly. Perhaps, he reflected, he would never hit it off with his own sex. Nor, frankly, did it seem to be an ability worth working at.

"Maybe." George leaned confidentially across the table, a shade too close to Miss Trumper's electric black hair. Her instant withdrawal was not in the least artificial and George, understanding this, drew back in a rush of hurt feeling. The glanced-down female nose need not necessarily imply disdain, he assured himself, though admittedly he had been somewhat late in discovering this. Perhaps the fact that Nita never glanced down hers with those lambent willing eyes bred the earlier deception. Miss Trumper's shiny chin and nose bent shyly over her typescript. "Has anything come in?" he pursued.

She nodded at the heap of copy at the end of her desk and

43

George gathered it up, riffling through the top pages for items of importance.

"Thanks, Miss Trumper," he said courteously. "I'll take them up to Mr Duckworth if you're finished."

Miss Trumper's petal lips opened frantically but no sound came out.

"Go 'way!" said Shead grinning. Eucalyptus toffee fragments clung to his teeth. "You frighten the kid."

But not everyone. George congratulated himself that Duckworth, the editor and part owner of the paper, a barrel-chested big-bellied bully of fifty, had taken a fancy to him. For apart from the two or three dinners he had enjoyed at the editorial home—largely, he was sure, that more work might be squeezed out of him by the semblance of friendship—he spun in a flurry of loving, dingy café meals, diamanté gifts, cheap wine and all night parties that culminated in bursts of passion which at times both bored and nauseated him. Yet his interminable desire for Nita, now a musky reality of flounces and cheap jewellery, found its continuance in the magic he projected from lost visions of shared summers.

The Duckworths lived in an impressively added-to house on the east side of the town above the river where fawning willows tottered up from the waterway to flatter the ant-eaten bleached timbers. Imelda Duckworth, an aggressive long-legged woman with a rubbery red mouth, had fossicked for years among the junior reporters on her husband's staff, the sanguine old-timer, turning up the occasional small but pleasing nugget. The frustration of having worked out her last seam two years ago focused her prospector's eye on George, upon whose bland baby face late hours had sketched an intriguing map. Here is the island, children. Here the land-locked harbour with the treasure hill beyond inviting the seekers. Here the cay, the reef, the intimations of tropicana—the cabbage palms, the desolate plantation, the branded tree. Primary tactics included invitations to the house, to tennis clubs, to study groups (Know Your History, Know Your Painters, Know Your Music) but later, when the lubricatory effects of whisky had established for her not only Nita's existence but also his relationship with her, and she had, with the manners of a procuress, made her house occasionally available to them, polite affectations vanished; and, one singularly humid April evening, she climbed into bed with them. George made of this in later years an uproariously funny story, but at the time used to confess with fetching *naïveté*.

"Lord, was I embarrassed! Didn't know which way to turn."

Yes. Love satisfied lost little of its yearning. This astonished him. For the two years he worked in the town he was obsessed by Nita in a way so forceful that he could only imagine it was the constant representation of his childhood and the hot salty holidays along the Tweed that were now being played over and over and over. He took her in his arms in a hotel bedroom but his mind's rapture raced down slippery dips with her in the shaggy park near the river or fished with her along the breakwater. She was cuts on his knees and rambles up bracken slopes towards Razorback, was coastlines of white afternoon with sea of malachite, was cricket played on footpaths, and school satchels, long slinging bouts of tennis, was burrs and heat and cold wind and bicycle pumps and rows and examinations. Sometimes the sheer vastness of the areas to which she provided reference overwhelmed him. It was as if there were nothing else in his life at all.

With her? Not the same. He tortured himself with hopes that it might be; but, after exasperation yielded to resignation which recognized nothing outside his own insanity, he discovered that she was not even faithful to him. He could never prove it but the fat weevily hints dropped by her sister were convincing. Listening meant a kind of death.

Obliteration was in work. He learned a great deal about the

45

newspaper game and soon became well known in the town. Duckworth demanded a high standard of reporting and a reasonable polish in style. George could handle a political or race meeting, a district show, a concert, a stock report with all the skill the Downlands *Hub* required and a little to spare. The first year he was there, State elections and economic uncertainties caused by the short boom and the resultant depression bred a turbulence of anxiety among the grazing men of the Downlands that Duckworth was careful to play down in his editorials. The Queensland Government's Savings Bank had been taken over by the Commonwealth the year before, injecting a wild confidence into the primary producers which was to prove misplaced.

"I know I'm working class," he explained to Ferguson one night over drinks, "but I can't damn well show it. You've got to remember that this paper is largely owned and backed by one of the biggest graziers in the south-west."

"Who? Sinclair Dawes?"

"You shouldn't be asking, Brewster. It's your business to know these things. A good journalist finds out without waiting to be told. That's something you must learn to do."

George squirmed, humiliated before Ferguson, but Duckworth took a great gulp of whisky, belched and went on. "We can't possibly promote Labour votes. We'll find ourselves out of a job. That's another thing you'll have to learn—loyalty to your paper. That comes first of all. If you don't agree with policy you'll have to shut your mouth. If it gets too much for you there's only one thing to do." He looked hard at the young man.

"Well, for God's sake, Bert," Ferguson exclaimed, "plump for the Nationalists and you'll cut the sales all over town. Condamine isn't chock-a-block with landed gentry. It's counter-jumpers and shopkeepers and labourers—and you know it."

46

"I know. I know. You'll just have to watch every bloody story like hawks till September. And I'm deadly serious about this. I stand to lose a lot if Dawes's nose gets put out of joint."

Idealism? Loyalty? There was still much of the young man who had carried round tracts at the street-corner meetings of the Travellers, still vigorously interested in the right to express unpopular opinions openly. "Where's this vaunted freedom of the press?" he complained to Ferguson.

"Rationalize," the other advised. "Rationalize. This is a country where every man has an economic obligation to look out for himself. Things might seem bad now but I can tell you this—they're going to be a bloody sight worse in another eight or nine years and then there won't be any room at all for false notions about promoting public good.'"

"I think that's a rotten way to look at it. If the newspapers of a country don't peddle a few ideals or try to insist on the application of social justice, then what the hell use are they?"

"Fancy notions'll get you nowhere in this trade. Nowhere at all."

George scowled and, sulking over this one at his desk, produced a survey of election campaigning in the outlying shires so biased for the Labour speakers that Ferguson blue-pencilled the lot and sent for him.

"Look, Brewster," he said, "I don't know whether you're trying to be funny but the next bumper like this will have to go before the old man. Now. God Almighty, I've warned you! Don't make a pimp out of me, too."

"I didn't mean to put you in an ambiguous position, Viv."

"No. Maybe not. But you will if you do it again. Now listen to me. Next week-end at Stanthorpe, Henry Wilkie is talking and I want you to go down and keep those bull-headed notions of yours right out of the picture and give me a decent account of the thing. There's no need to sink all your

47

principles, but just gentle him along, will you? Just gentle him along."

A small suit-case and Nita accompanied him. A lie concocted some days before placated her parents. Separate rooms at the same hotel salved the proprieties. One takes from these journeys a flickering glance at space-time which refloats years after the one spot of wild light on the water flask in the rack, the lesion on the leather seat across the aisle, the apple core skulking beneath it. Not so much is the intensity of the other person needed, but the adjuncts, those properties, that poetic *bric-à-brac* which locate for ever and ever a mood, a place, a time. Classic bredes of stringy-bark and telegraph wire moved southwards through a plumbaceous twilight where the long-drawn, milk-can-punctuated stops at whistle-sidings held the delicacy of pen sketches on a watery paper. They pulled into Stanthorpe in a dewy darkness and, after having early dinner at their noisy pub, explored the main streets as far as the School of Arts. These tumbling timber towns! Their strangling courageous ugliness was something that lashed the onlooker with love, that caught him by the heart threatening urgent nostalgia in distant places. Lovely ugly country, thought George. Lovely ugly.

Outside, lost shapes in the badly lighted street, a crowd swayed and pulsed until the front door was flung back by a shining-pated attendant. The locusts swarmed, eating up the seats, five hundred of them at least crushed onto benches, sitting and standing on window sills. Mainly men, but there were a few women with bright-eyed pyjama-clad children snuggled into their sides or squirming on lap. A restless yeast bubbled and seethed while on stage a chairman fussed about a table draped with a flag on which stood a water-jug and glass. Nation builders of fly-specked seriousness watched bleakly from the walls, impassive even when there was a stir in the wings and three men strode onto the stage.

48

Waving a Press ticket, George shoved and elbowed through the packed crowd near the door with Nita clinging like a little brown shrimp to his arm. At the front, half a dozen chairs had been labelled "Reserved".

"Is she Press, too, mate?" a voice called as they sat down. Nita giggled.

"Pressed," she whispered, batting her silly lashes.

Sentences trailed away unfinished. Isolated clapping broke off in embarrassment. A child howled persistently at the side and was smacked, screamed more loudly and was dragged from the hall. Through these sublunary disturbances gusts of phrase plucked at the straining ears of orchardists and wheat growers.

". . . no necessity to introduce such a prominent man as the Right Honourable Henry Wilkie . . . well known for his progressive spirit, his interests, I may say, his multiple interests in the district and his tireless work for . . ." George turned to a blank page in his marble-edged notebook and put the tip of his pencil to his tongue. All about him the hands beat their automatic response while, under the shelter of that drum, ironies and cynicisms were exchanged, coarse-grained protest or approval.

Henry Wilkie rose, a big smooth man in a big smooth suit, too smart and expensive for the times. As he surveyed the hall and instinctively recognized antipathy's hungry glinting eye, he regretted coming, but he was no coward and urbanity formed a half-smile on his mouth as he picked up his papers from the table, shuffled them into place, and took a sip from the glass. He held the room by silence at first and then for some moments the mob listened quietly enough to his opening remarks. George scribbled busily, and in the margin he had left for audience reaction, wrote "favourable."

But Wilkie was too plausible.

". . . places Empire first. It is something to be proud of

49

that loyalty to King and Empire had been placed at the fore-front of the Nationalist Party. There will be a Nationalist victory next Saturday and our party pledges itself to encourage enterprise, the introduction of capital and to remedy industrial troubles." George wrote quickly. The hall was listening attentively.

". . . with every possible hope of reorganizing the primary industries in the whole of the Granite Belt. We aim to subsidize the orchardists and see them through the bad seasons; to form a Growers' Protection Board to deal with marketing problems during slumps. This is largely a fruit-growing district, one of the best, if not *the* best, in the State. Our first interest must lie with the orchardist. At present, and only at present mark you, it is not really possible to make definite statements about conditions in the dairying industry, but we hope, when your confidence has returned us to Parliament, to take some sort of action that . . ."

"For Heaven's sake!" George whispered. "How long can he go on saying nothing!"

"Wot abowt Chidwell?" someone yelled from the side. "He said the same thing las' time."

The speaker continued blandly as if there had been no interruption.

"We are hoping, too, to increase unemployment relief . . ." Multiple layers of prejudice, the dingy skins on some old painting, Wilkie told himself as the automatic words spouted forth.

"*Wot abowt Chidwell?*"

"In fact we guarantee an increase in unemployment relief to all married men with three dependants."

"Wot abowt them with two?"

"We aim to draw up special work pools in this area to enable employers to make the most fruitful use of all available labour force."

50

"WOT ABOWT CHIDWELL?"

Wilkie paused. He removed his glasses and polished them busily with a too clean handkerchief. Someone spotted it.

"He's a regular Gussie!"

"WELL? WOT ABOWT CHIDWELL?"

"Wot 'e ever do an' all the promises 'e made three years back? Lotta ruddy twisters an' liars!"

"I wasn't aware," Wilkie said, holding time's trembling little paw, "that Chidwell failed to fulfil his election promises."

"What about the pensions?" screamed an elderly woman down front. "He lowered 'em, not raised 'em like he said."

Wilkie resorted to urbanity. "The lady just now . . ." Voice pitched above heckling bursting like hail. "I said the lady just now accused Mr Chidwell of failing to honour his promises. I put it to you"—(shouting) "I put it to you that no man in face of the economic conditions that existed at the time could possibly have increased pensions with trade balance the way it was. In that year" (he referred to notes) "our excess of debits over total credits was £4,123,000. If the good lady in front of me" (half derisive bow) "is an expert in political economy, perhaps she could explain this."

"No talks. More facts!" another voice yelled hoarsely. "Facts."

"Yeah! That's what we want!" A chorus of "facts" swelled up.

"This is the stuff," George said to Nita. "Newspapers' life-blood and I've got to hush it up!"

"Shut up, will you!" Wilkie was shouting, his control ebbing away. "Shut up and I'll give you facts. Figures *are* facts, ARE facts, I tell you. The Labour Party has made use of every vile election practice there is—corrupt franchise, stuffed rolls, and a distribution of seats which prevents the true expression of the will of the people." (Shouts of "We're happy!") "I have in my possession a pamphlet printed at the

Government Printing Office and marked No. 3 in which it was claimed that Old Age Pensions and Invalid Pensions amongst other things had been secured for the people by the Labour Party. The truth is, however, that Old Age Pensions were introduced long before the Labour Party held office and long before there was any likelihood of their holding office. The factories and shop legislation was on the Statute Book of Queensland before there was any Labour Party in the State. Another thing for which they claim credit is the note issue, but the note issue in Queensland was first commenced by Sir Hugh Nelson at a time of financial stringency and the issue of notes taken over by the Commonwealth. They also claim the Eight Hour Day without real justification and that they have brought in free education—but that had been done many years ago by the late Sir Charles Lilley."

"Tell us more about the Eight Hour Day!" someone heckled.

Wilkie went straight ahead with his advantage. "This election is being hurried because the Government wants to get the elections over before the actual truth concerning finances is revealed. The Government and its supporters are far from easy in their minds. Why? I'll tell you why. Because when the Auditor General's report is made public it will be of such a nature that if published before any election it would politically kill the Government. The Nationalist Party will appoint a Minister for Labour who will act fairly, justly and sympathetically towards all classes of the community. Economies *can* be effected without resorting to retrenchment. You ask for facts. I give you facts. During the last few days Mr Theodore has been working himself into a frenzy shaking his fists and threatening British financiers. What good is that likely to do? Mr Theodore complains of unfair treatment but the treatment he has met with has absolutely been brought about by the repudiation and reckless financing of his own Government. You ask for facts! Aren't they facts?"

52

From the back in an unexpected silence a voice alliterated a filthy participle with facts and was dragged out by two policemen. Nita began to giggle with a pretty hand covering her mouth.

"Did you hear—?"

"Sssh." Wave tremors of excitement were breaking on the shore of George's mind. "I think it might be a bit of a roughhouse any moment. Best to keep your mouth closed, sweetie." He took a sly look at her. She was in something red and waistless. Her size-two feet were crossed with idiot demureness at the ankles. Her brown left hand clasped a tinselly black purse. Oh, he loved her! She was cheap and warm and silly and bright and, in the spiritual exchanges, shockingly expensive!

Wilkie shot a desperate glance at the chairman, who pounded the table with a hammer-hand.

"Order!" he shouted again and again.

"Yairs! Order!" called someone from the body of the hall. "Let's hear what the silly bastard has to say."

In the faltering silence that followed, Wilkie, his face aglint with sweat spangles, went on delineating conservative policy. Half a dozen policemen had moved into the hall and the spectacle of dark blue uniform gagged upspringing comments. Beside him he heard the chairman expel a breath, a trembling prayer. Wilkie's confident brown eyes cannoned about the wavering confetti of faces but behind his automatic phrases, his hackneyed couplings of political ideas, he was conscious only of relief when the fight finally flared up just beside the entrance where an overflow of audience had half listened, half argued among themselves. Within seconds it became a general brawl and three rows at the back emptied their male contents into the street's cockpit. On stage Wilkie, appearing to abandon it all, poured himself a tumbler of water and sat down for a minute in a subdued attitude of prostration, rubbing his large blond hands together, while all over the heaving hall men clambered across seats, grinding their bodies in an intolerable transposition of idea.

"I got most of what he said." Efficient George pulled Nita to her feet after he had popped his notebook smartly away, a Nita whose dim grey eyes were fixed on the stage and who was focusing through those dreamy slits the well-fed and prosperous body of the politician. George's elbow bit jealously into her arm. "Come on! We'd better get out of this."

"He looks fine." Nita kept her indolent gaze on Wilkie.

"Oh, God!" George began walking off. The cheap little bit! It would never never never be any different!

Through the tapestry of a sudden melancholic anger he pushed blindly to a side-door, finding with a shred of surprise that she was still behind him as they emerged in a cantankerous garden at the side of the building where wattles argued and writhed across the scrubby dark. Crowds excused his squeezing arm about her waist when he swung her towards him in an embrace that held more jealous rage than love. Because of the surging disturbed mob, he urged her to go back to the pub while he went round to the front of the building in order to get some on-the-spot colour. He watched for a moment as her slight body took on the camouflage of dusk; then he ran along the side as the shouting, grunting circle crashed and broke its whirlpool edge into the struggling bystanders. A picnic of a fight! The frustrations of a score of Sunday-school outings were secreted in over-willing humans who found in that slap-up free-for-all excuses to revenge long-nourished antipathies. A split lip was the expressed justice of a five-year-old calumny, or a punched jaw requited an observed illicit kiss. George tried to keep on the fringe while police flung their way to the central point by weight.

"Mug copper!" yelled the brave concealed voices, and the fight lost its original focus, becoming instead brawl of law with citizen, where no one really knew what the fight was about.

"Hey, y' ruddy Nance!" a hulk on George's right roared out. "Git out or fight!" And he threw a giant fist across the air and smashed its burrowing flesh into George's, who reeled against the man behind, almost vomiting with nausea and fear. But already the farmer had forgotten him and was dealing blows indiscriminately, as George, tossed forward angrily by the man he had crashed into, staggered across the road to the shelter of a shop awning where he leaned against a backdrop of faded soft-goods, shivering, cuddling his throbbing cheek and trying to light a cigarette. He saw the crowd split apart. Two policemen bent over a man on the grass. It was a series of black and white slides. Cries for a doctor sobered them up. Spent feelings, ragged and meaningless as election pamphlets that littered the grass, coalesced in the subsidence to a social temperature.

Wilkie waited behind. There seemed no point in exposing himself and deliberately challenging a stray temper. One of the policemen strode down the aisle knocking the overturned forms aside with his thick calves. He stood below stage with ten lumpy knuckled fingers fanned out on the footlight screen and said,

"Give us ten minutes, Mr Wilkie, and one of the boys will see you home."

"That's decent of you, officer," Wilkie said. He smiled. Even one vote made a difference.

All the way to the pub in the dry spring night the unknown quantity of love's problem fretted him. Under jangling leaves he moved in checkerings of moonlight and shadow of poignant insecurity, stroking the swelling rise of his cheek and jaw. Foot followed foot. Tag-end to the shocked state of surprised heart or surprised flesh was that which analyses the simplest safe action with overbalanced joy. Recognition, anticipation of simplicities came in regular drum-beats of defiance and proof and subsequently trust and love. Nita. Nita. Nita.

But she was not returned.

The door of her room opened on a fathom and a half of grey air with aquamarine bed and melted mirror, ghost of water-jug, bones of chair. Fish-heart leapt in spasms of suspicion. Spring thrust a grief-green foliage on every branch which he broke aside with hands, pulled, pushed his way through to observe his tired face staring dislocatedly back from a mirror whose faults already elongated his forehead or shortened his nose. He switched on the light, dipped the corner of her towel into the belly of the jug and touched it to his sore flesh, while he swallowed saliva of jealous fear and with a dread perception anticipated years and years of scenes duplicating this one with an executioner's precision and impersonality. Brewster the sad lover. Brewster the wronged husband. But Gay Dog Brewster, however, sponged his eyelids to a glistening joy and went downstairs to the bar where, standing so that he could watch the hall, he gulped two neat brandies.

"Could hear it up here," observed the barman, a skinniness with big yellow false teeth that he shifted gently and affectionately under his tongue.

"What's that?" George asked, absently. There she was now. Gleam of red in the street light, movement and darkness and. . . . No. Wrong girl. "What's that you say?"

"I said I could hear the brawl up here."

George indicated his asymmetric face and smiled wryly.

"They get y', mate?" He was pulpy with concern. "Who started it?"

"Well, it began as politics but it was anybody's fight at the finish."

"That's it. That's the way it goes." He looked unhappily at the clock up on the wall behind the bottles. "Wish it had been a bit earlier. There's lotsa blokes'd do with a bit of a drink

56

right now to straighten 'em out after a bindy like that. But I don't dare try it on with all them coppers."

"Have one with me." George slid a coin over the greasy bar.

"Thanks," said the other; and, "Here's luck!"

Their eyes followed the moving bunches of people along the path outside for different reasons. A well-fed, multiple-chinned man thanked someone they could not see and moved in and then out of the light from the doorway.

"That's Wilkie," the barman said. "He's stopping for a few days while he canvasses the district. They say he's a good bloke when y' get to know him."

"You'd think he'd need a drink after that, after the roasting they gave him."

"He don't drink."

"No?"

"Nope. Never touches the stuff. He's stopped here a few times. I orter know. Doesn't smoke, neither. Wonder what he *does* do?"

"There's only one thing *to* do," George's genial leer was distorted by swelling. It emerged as irony to the barman's surprise, who could read a face better than he could read a book.

"D'y' reckon? There's never a bit a scandal about him. I think that's what gets the boys' backs up. He's just too bloody good to be true. Now take old Mulloy who was member ten years back. What a character! Drank like a fish, had a string of women chasing him from here to Brissy, but every election day he packed the polls all right. Ever hear about the time he launched *Triton*—she was a little coastal steamer went up to Cairns and back—down at Newcastle? 'Stead of smacking the bottle open he nicked the top off clean as a whistle and drank half before he christened her! But people don't mind that sorta thing. Seems human somehow."

George giggled. "There was a chap like that in Melbourne a long way back." he said. "At the opening of one of the Municipal Baths he said, 'I now declare these baths well and truly open,' and dived straight in with all his clothes on."

"Christ!" said the other. "What happened?"

"Oh, they had to fish him out. But, as you say, it didn't seem to cost him any votes." His voice faltered; glass in hand paused; brandy still below his tongue bit like acid and his stomach heaved.

His own heart was standing with that mind-breaking limp fragility in the hall gazing in at him.

The flat tones of the incurious voice.

Even the barman swung towards him a moment and then swung away.

"Where have you been?" George thought he revealed nothing but the surface of those repeated words.

She lied so easily.

"With a friend I met, someone down from Condamine."

"Oh. Man or woman?" Casually and carefully, he warned himself.

"Woman." She smiled. "I'd love a drink." The piquancy of her slim face charmed the barman. One hand pushed absently at the dark brown leaves of her messed hair.

"I was worried you'd get hurt. Someone took a punch at me."

For the first time she really saw him with her tangent of a glance. "Oh but you *are* hurt," she cried, and a bird-soft hand flew to his cheek for a moment of private bliss. His. He smiled content but some lunacy screwed him again even as he said,

"It's all right. I've bathed it. Does it look bad?"

"I still love you."

"Do you? Who was she?" asked his innocent lips.

"Who was who?"

58

"The woman you met?"

"Ooooh . . . you wouldn't know her, George. She works in my office."

"I might." But he knew it was useless to persist. She began talking to the barman as she curled her brown fingers about a glass. Observing her wet mouth, George felt a sticky web of falsehood binding him with wires; but the harder he wrestled, the more tightly bound he became.

In the kapok trough of his bed he held her against his body mimicking happiness while his mind grieved and gloated at once, sorting over the possibilities of her infidelity. Something advised him to pull clear of her before it was too late—but this cancer was inoperable. Moaning he pressed his mouth into the warm hollow of her hand.

"Nita," he pleaded, pleaded, pleaded. "You do love me, don't you? Don't you? Utter truth?"

She was half asleep. His words had only the vaguest connection with her. His malleability did not pluck any long-drawn wail from the gut of her heart's strings.

"Silly old George," she murmered drowsily and he had to content himself with that. He thought it would cost him his mind.

No press article was an immortelle.

The tyrannic, demanded fertility of the tri-weekly newspaper had all the pointlessness of random breeding and made George certain that his craving to achieve a work of some permanence was being dissipated in gaudy utterances no one would remember. He was becoming too glib. Writing on demand was a clever trick—Rumbold had told him that and he had proved it for himself—for given an hour's notice he could turn out a polished two thousand words on anything at all. Ambition, kept in the container too long, curdled, turned sour.

After six months during which the mould that Duckworth

demanded his men should pour themselves into was shaping George's outlook into a disgusting middle-class pretentiousness, the staff was jazzily invigorated by a new man. His name was Ivor Lippman. He was older than George and now senior to him as reporter, had a talent for florid extension of facts, domineering and slightly depressive good looks, a maniacal laugh and an insolence that seemed pathological. A certain pathos lingered on between insult and insult. Lippman drank excessively, sketched briefly brilliant, cynically under-reported stories that he left, a mass of written-over typescript, on Ferguson's desk, disappeared for sometimes two days and then reappeared unapologetic and offensively assured.

He blew George in and out like a paper snake.

"No brutality, Lippman," Ferguson said grinning. Who saw through him.

"You're miles ahead of me, old man." Lippman shrieked with laughter and glueing two bulging eyes on the sub-editor, pinned the tip of a plump forefinger to his chest. "Too cerebral."

"I don't trust you," Ferguson said coldly.

Lippman laughed with delight. "Rightly so. Rightly so. And does Mr Duckworth, he wisely also, share your lack of confidence?"

"I don't discuss other people's opinions. I don't know what he thinks about you—but I'm warning you—no bloody nonsense. Brewster's no sweetheart, but he's a capable man. Don't rattle him."

"He has some essence of saintliness," pondered wise Lippman. "I want to dip the most reverent of toes in it. Can't you see? No, no. I'm not being facetious. Contrary to what you think, Ferguson, the saint has a morbid fascination for me that the sinner entirely lacks. Consider the humdrum, the sheer boring nonsensical humdrum of petty venality. Now against that put, even for one delicious second of eye-searing time, the blinding sanctity of the martyree—if I may use the term. The pre-ordained self-wishing martyr."

"That shows how little you know of Brewster."

"Not so." Lippman's pudgy face, padded out with theory, bent closer to the other man who would have recoiled but endeavoured not to. "The man is a monumental mutt. But only because of his Gadarene-like destiny against which he does not fight."

"These rickety arguments!" said Ferguson, suddenly amused. "What do they prove?"

"To you, apparently, nothing."

Ferguson's face wriggled in disgust. Across the street a slattern group of shops lounged around the corner pub. Palm perpendiculars made allusion to a lazy tropicality recalling a lost world.

"No. Not a thing. But I like him around."

"Sentimental, eh?"

"Sentimental nothing. He makes me laugh sometimes. He has the makings of a first-class drinker. Where's your saint there?"

"He's busy looking for God."

"God? By chasing a little gold-digger all over town? Do you call that looking for God?"

"If you can't see it . . ." Lippman shrugged his heavy shoulders in a kind of caesura.

His pavonine strutting blazed its colour spots. The next week as he was sitting at a table not far from George and Nita in the Brown Down he ogled her furiously for two courses and then, with a visible swagger of his hips, came over to them.

"For coffee," explained specious Ivor.

"It's manners to wait," protested George banging an un-original drum. O stupidity of bounding heart! Under blue flare of the wall lights expectant sheen in Nita's eyes pulverised him with lightning flash. He swooned away in his jealous sea hearing Lippman laying out his trumpery talents for display and sale. For by now the very limen of his relationship with her was the two-syllabled stress of her name, the ambiguous pleasure of seeing her sharp-eyed brother Peter Emil pruning the park trees, the nostalgic evocations of a grass on which they had lain or a corner where they met or any diffident scent that recalled her own.

But leaf-face was charmed of course. Lippman pressed the finger-stems of her farewelling or welcoming hand a little longer than even Browning would tolerate, while, numb with annoyance, George sought infidelity everywhere in nuance of word or glance, and paid the bill for the three of them with caustic deliberateness.

After this, Nita began to call on him at the office, a practice he had always discouraged. Now he was certain she did it in a duplicate connivance that brought her face to face with Lippman flamboyantly being pressman. When he discovered them talking with a natural intimacy in the downstairs lobby, his emotions would stagger and almost fall. He became convinced she was seeing him privately, for Lippman came to work some mornings with such a patronizing good cheer George thought it concealed a guilty heart. In a frenzy of brooch and necklet, of bracelet and ring, he sought a final purchasing. She took—and gave—her body in an uninhibited and nymphean way and all the time risible George teetered on the crumbling verge of love's dementia, duped, he was sure, but never knowing.

At parties at the Duckworths' she would vanish for an unexplained hour, and the garden, so sanctimonious by day with its simplified parterres and demure shrubs, became a diabolic maze into which, one splendid drunken August evening, George lurched and ripped aside the secrecy of every shadow crouching below every bush. He did not discover her. When he returned to the smoke and the garrulous pianola, she was handing round coffee and throwing salty laughter for luck over one fragile shoulder. George clung to a door-post and his eyes punched at her senses until she turned with her pussy mouth curved up into its triangular smile.

"You bitch!" he said across the packed room. The word cut through conversations like a saw. From this split love's resin flowed out in its final wound. Waggling his head from side to side, shaking off both his thoughts of her and what he had uttered, George tottered out again to the road and vomited his soul up.

They made it up of course.

But although his apologies grovelled and abased themselves and although she forgave him instantly in the way that seemed most meaningful to her, he never trusted her again and she, having learned his weak spot, played on it with an artlessness that amounted to venom. They still giggled together, got drunk, made love. Their resilience was superb. Yet she became confirmed in her infidelities and privately George wrote away to a Sydney paper and applied for a job there. He took Duckworth into his confidence.

"Aren't you happy here?" the big man asked. He had grown a moustache like a hyphen in the last couple of months and it gave an amusing hesitancy to his face. "You're doing well. I'm pleased with your work." He belched, staring straight at George with narrowed eyes. "You'll be a pretty small cog down there, I can tell you."

"It's more experience," George said stubbornly.

"Well, I've never wanted to keep anyone who didn't want to stay." Big blustery potentate. "But it seems a pity just after I'd cured you of all those damn-fool notions you used to cherish when you came. Still, if you want any letters of reference, I'll write them for you. One bit of advice I'll give you, though, and don't be offended. Stick to simplicity in your writing. You tend to be ornate. You'll never get on that way. Simple clear-cut prose, big catchy cross-heads. Now come back after three and I'll have a letter for you in case you need it."

Not since he had left high school had George felt so much like a grubby-fisted child. Duckworth? Sly relief. After that party with Dawes and his wife bang in the middle, it would be a damn' site better if he did go. The girl, though. Pretty bit of work. That evening could have finished him, too. It was just luck they hadn't been caught. Still, he'd stay away from that particular field for a while. It simply wasn't worth the trouble. Drawing his typewriter closer, he wrote lengthily and fulsomely on Brewster's work. "God!" he murmured to himself, generous patron Duckworth, when he re-read it. "I wish that were being said about me."

This letter, plus another from Dawes, had an ecclesiastical or royal magic, not because Duckworth was so highly regarded as a journalist, but because Dawes had many investments in Sydney as well. George, unsuccessful in his first application, was recommended nevertheless to a smaller and less important evening paper that could promise him a position as court reporter. The very day he got word, he packed his two cases, lived on a ration of shirts until the Friday and told Nita only on their last night together. Resentment at first drew her pussy-mouth into a down-curved line revealing clearly that she needed George to play romantic pat-ball with. Accordingly there was a measure of desperation in their ultimate embraces. With a fatuous romanticism she gave him a pair of her panties to remember her by. In return he fished in his case and handed her socks which, during the next months away, he envisioned her as wearing over her size-two feet—feet lovably lost in male-smelling wool with overtones of leather.

"Write every day, won't you?" he asked, turning the ring on her finger in a golden circle. Appetence would be roused once they were apart, he knew. She was the clear bell of his childhood pealing across the drier plains of adulthood. For answer

64

she nuzzled into his side, put her nose into his armpit, tippling with her tongue (the clapper of the bell?) on his salty skin. He hugged her to him savagely as thanks for this.

An abrupt agony gripped his heart, causing him to catch his hissing breath. He lay perfectly still and the pain receded, yielding to a terrible nausea.

"Oh, I feel ill," George moaned unexpectedly in the heart-thick darkness. Releasing her, hearing their flesh unstick, he bumped his way across the room to a table on which a water-jug and basin stood. Nita, cosy in George-smelling sheets, listened to the water bubble from jug to glass to throat; heard the gulp as he attempted salvation. if he were to vomit she would not have minded, understanding the body so well as she did in all its animal manifestations. An orphan tenderness would have longed for this that she might practise one final sincerity upon him. But this was denied them both, for he tumbled back into bed where he lay motionless, sensing the blood draining away to his feet and a sickly sweat breaking on his forehead.

She nestled more closely.

"Don't," he said, "don't. I feel terrible."

A snowflake pattered in his breast. The lightness and synco-pation of its movement terrified him. Nita, aware of his stiffened attitude of fear, sat up in bed tiger-pelted with moonlight, and examined his face.

"I'll get dressed and get someone," she whispered.

"No." The word came as a gasp. "No."

She clutched his hand between hers, and the moonlight lay between dressing-table and wardrobe in a bright gash. This is years, is a lifetime, thought George as the pain, the now faint pain, melted and the snowflake became once more a vigorous muscle pumping out love and loyalty and small dishonesties.

"It's gone," he said at last. "I'm all right now."

"But what was it?"

65

George dragged an arm across his face. "I don't know. A dreadful sense of horror, of panic."

"Weren't you really sick, then?"

"Of course." He was momentarily indignant. "I felt ghastly. But it was more than that. It was a wide space full of nothing. I was alone. It was the aloneness, can't you see? The aloneness and the pain. Without it the pain would have been nothing."

The girl began a rhythmic and unexplained sobbing. Tomorrow they would be apart. She was sorry she could not feel really unhappy and cried partly because she had lost her minor tragedy. But he thought she was weeping for him.

"Oh, darling, darling," he murmured. "There. I'm all right now."

## [III]

A FANATICISM to please attaches limpet sacrifices and abstinences to the body in love. Although tantalizingly free amid the enticements of nearly a million people, for months George pursued the solitariness of loving. Eventually the joy to be extracted from conscious immolation would wear thin. Eventually he would hold the gossamer of sacrifice to the light in a letterless week and see beyond, other mouths, eyes, hands, feet. All would smile in their special way.

In the meantime, the *Voice* with its staff of ambitious men and women kept him working at pressure. Echoes from the printed news had an amphoric quality after the small-town gossip items that were tinny notes on a high C whistle. There were days when he could hardly keep pace with the engagements listed for him by the chief of staff; and there were those when he hung around a slack city-room, smoking and swapping yarns with other cadets.

All types of god required propitiation. The closest deity, the chief reporter, was a fat man of about forty, a spry satyr sprouting indecorous jokes and a surface affability that concealed a testy intolerance of inefficiency. A serious mistake brought this god's wrath in one resounding thunder-clap. No one, so the stories went, had ever made more than one mistake of any gravity. His name was Archer. The editor, a brown bear with sombre eyes, appeared seldom. He moved in a climate of such aloofness that George, accustomed to the easy familiarity of Duckworth, hardly dared good-day when they made their rare encounters. His blind-seeming eyes roamed everywhere. The pallied face with its semblance of half-interrogation swung from speaker to speaker at the morning conferences, allowing each an opinion but frequently vetoing the wishes of the majority with one mildly interpolated preference. No one liked him. Everyone respected him. Only a few really knew him. Thirty years before as a cadet he had changed his name by deed poll from Goldberg to Gowanloch. Now he was successful he would willingly have changed it back again, but effort made him tired. He had extensive peptic ulceration, a much younger and extremely beautiful wife, and two sons at a Church of England public school. Although he appeared not to notice newcomers to the staff, he followed their work and behaviour in detail for at least three months until he was certain they had established steady work routines.

The squalor of the city courts fascinated George and another reporter working on the rounds with him. Drunks and prostitutes, shop-lifters and pimps lost that two-dimensional quality they had had when merely subjects of tiring jokes. Their squabbles with presiding magistrates like bubbles of vitamins invigorated their minds, flavoured their writing. Hilbery and he began a happy friendship that was to last all their lives. They drank together, and in a type of delayed adolescence that lasted three or four months, .played practical jokes on other junior staff, posted twelve feet of sausages, each sausage stamped and addressed, to the chief sub-editor. All the next day they hung about waiting to hear if they had been delivered and how he reacted, until someone, suspecting their anxious enquiries about McIver, told him. When the sausages were brought upstairs by a grinning copy boy, McIver smiled briefly, ordered them to be taken to the canteen, cooked and served in the newsroom. He strolled down for a few moments at the four o'clock tea break, beaming when he saw Hilbery and Brewster seated before mounded plates. "The lot, gentlemen," he said courteously. "Or night-shift for a month." Prophylactic? Cathartic?

Ache eased with these distractions.

In three months he was no longer a mere emotional incumbent, and, during a lull in the fever of his feeling for Nita, had a short-term sweetheart named Beryl who was one of the telephonists in the overseas cable-room. She was older than he and her experienced approach to love-making was quite terrifying. On the first occasion he took her in his arms to kiss her, she bent backwards in a gravity-defying manner forcing him to support her entire weight. Noticing the simulated bliss of her closed eyes, he wanted badly to laugh. Those parted, hungry, blindly seeking lips! Something adult in George giggled critically, saying "Oh, my God!"; but he kissed her all the same and feigned rapture, too. Yet she was a minor sweetie-pie. Between their touching faces he would be aware of Nita's etched in before he could switch off his conscience. Squeamishness was aggravated rather than mollified by the suspicion that probably she, also, was at that moment easing her own base itches in someone else's arms.

"Ooh, she's an awful bit of lah-de-dah, old boy," Hilbery said, watching her mince away from the newsroom. "You couldn't be serious."

"Don't be silly!"

"Well, why bother?"

"Oh, God, you know how it is. Downland's a long way away."

"But surely you can play about with something a little classier than that. She does remind me of the gay ladies up in Darlinghurst Road."

"Tosh!"

Yet George was pricked sufficiently to drop her, and in a kind of ambiguous reward he received two days later a fat letter from Nita full of hints about marriage. Sister Jean was getting married next month to a farmer from Killarney. Wouldn't it be fun if they could all be married together? "Would it?" George asked himself soberly, sitting on the depressed edge of his boarding-house bed. "Would it really?" He glimpsed plump sexy Jean with her cheap dresses, her brassy cosmetics, and shuddered. An ideation of his marriage had lain mystically in his mind for years, shadows of delicacy, of beautiful words and romantic plighting, of flowers, of eagerness. There was no substance—only these flimsy concepts that held no woman of flesh but a quick rainbow laugh in a treehouse or flying limbs on a long beach, the drowsy quality of summer, the mouth's softness, the warmth of four grubby hands. Now the moment was on him he groaned out an agony and wrote back to her.

"Not yet," his letter pleaded. "Not yet. In your woman's heart I know you will not for one moment suspect there is any reluctance in my love for you. Darling Nita—on the contrary! But, to be brutally frank and put it in a word, I simply haven't the money to keep us. Try to understand this. Try to believe I am saving every penny I can to bring our magic closer." At this point even his pen faltered as he recalled expensive nights with Beryl. "Let us try to look forward a year, say. No more than that. Just a year. It will pass so rapidly, so unbelievably rapidly. After all we are both terribly young, too young, I may venture to say, for family responsibilities. Try to see this, my very dearest."

She punished him by not writing for three weeks and drew from him half a dozen letters of impassioned contrition but no weakening on the question of immediate marriage. As letter followed begging letter, Nita stuffed back the doubts she had held about her lover, replaced his inexpensive diamond on her finger and, bidding a temporary goodbye to Ivor Lippman, went south to Sydney for a week's holiday. The seven days were so crammed with love-making that by the end of the week, George in a reaction of self-disgust and weariness during their last day, disloyally longed for her to go. Years afterwards the one bright flash from that time was her laughter under the green trees of a harbourside park where they strolled along the afternoon paths. He had shown her the inscription on a drinking fountain erected by a temperance organization. After the train carried her away, he went to a coffee stall outside Central and had two cups. All he could feel was relief. The week, looking back, was a nightmare of black underwear.

This seemed to mark the end of a movement. Pace now—*andante maestoso*. Four half-hearted months later, with no premonitory shiver, he opened a letter from her telling him she had been married to Tommy Wayne. Scaler! George held the shocking ugly paper away from him. He pulled another magic lantern slide across the light. There was Scaler, on their last jaunt to Brisbane, ogling Nita in a city pub, with his grubbiness sleeked back, his mind still scabrous. In a good light, a better light than this cruel lemon lantern play, one could observe how the grease-spotted trousers were creased like knife-blades. He wore a natty bow-tie and a panama with a coloured ribbon. Horrible!

For two days George was unable to go to work. With her rejection, all her desirability swam before him. Locking himself into his room with two bottles of whisky and one of gin, he half-killed himself with misery and liquor. The first night he was sufficiently conscious to shout to his landlady to go away, but on the Thursday morning she came rippling with curiosity to his closed ten o'clock door and tapped endlessly on the panels.

"Mr Brewster? Mr Brewster? Are you in? Are you all right?"

But he lay in his sickness, breathing noisily, Mrs Lutherborrow took out her master key—its appearance needed

71

little invitation—and opened the door on a stench and squalor that assailed all her proprietorial senses. Festoons of bedclothes, crumpled papers, three bottles, two of them empty, and a basin into which George had vomited not only bile but eleven lost years. Mrs Lutherborrow was disgusted and pitying at once and did want to do something for the young man whose face in slumber was not in the least swinish but pathetically and movingly ill. She moved among storms of writing paper. There seemed to be a lot of letters flung about. Behind his bed the half-open window was blocked by a dark blue holland blind which she raised. Bright ruthless morning rushed at them; and George, rapt, sundered from pain, stirred and mumbled a name she could not catch as she bent to shake him gently. But he rolled away from her hands where the wedding ring was almost embedded in the fleshy finger and she, still filled with charity, took his disgusting basin away to empty it—and a letter as well, for such goodness of heart must have a simple reward. Her motions to replace the basin and return the raped letter to the heap fretted at his wakening eyes. A gold-washed kangaroo pinned to her floral bosom gleamed in his eyeballs, was so huge it reared through a dream of the grandest despair and boxed him awake to lovelessness and sewers of taste and conundrums of thought.

"You're in a proper mess!" sweet-and-sour said dispassionately. Words floated thin match-sticks in a gutter-tide. "You nearly needed a quack, that's what."

"Ooooh!" He groaned and groaned.

"Can I bring you a cuppa?"

"Oh, no. Nothing thanks. Wait a bit. What time is it?"

"Half past ten." She added thoughtfully—"Thursday."

"Oh, my God!" George attempted to sit up. "Mrs L., ring the office for me, would you? Tell them I'm ill."

"They was ringing themselves for you this morning."

"Were they? What did you say?"

"I said you'd taken to your bed with a heavy cold. That's what."

George smiled twisted gratitude.

"You darling!" he said to her beefy wide pince-nezed face. Rousing his charm.

"Well, you're always a good boy," the other said. Made her feel real motherly he did, always dropping into the kitchen for a snack and a bit of a gossip and not coming the high and mighty. "I wouldn't want to see you in trouble. You're all just like me own boys, all you young men here. But I'd give 'em a ring back if I was you," advised sonless Mrs Luther-borrow, "because they sounded as if they'd like to hear from you themselves. Just lie still and I'll bring you up a cuppa and then you can go down while I clean up this mess."

"You're a saint, Mrs L." He wanted to strike an exact note of contrast with his sinful swill. Her pleased smile proved him right.

"You're not just a boarder. You're me boy."

"Bless you, darling," he said.

"That girl was a fool!" Mrs Lutherborrow said indignantly forgetting herself in her loyalty to Mr Brewster. And then both were in a state of confusion.

Everyone forgave him and after a few weeks of forceful work the wound healed over. It was still painful to the touch —so he would not think of her, and flinging images from his mind became a physical toss of the head which troubled him like a nervous tic. His mother wrote a long consoling letter packed with advice and suggesting he turn to God in his trouble. The inclination to laugh lost itself in recollections of sub-tropical evenings in his early youth, when his father, lean and red, harangued a patchy group of listeners at the border gates or stood, clutching his coat around him, in the winds of July on Sunday nights in Mullumbimby or by a waterfront hall at Brunswick Heads. There was no collection, he remem-

73

bered, a thing which had perplexed him as a child, and seemed to embarrass the grown-ups. Religion that was free smacked of fanaticism.

One dismal evening some months afterwards, when, although the first nausea of grief was gone, yet a heavy depression lay on his heart, his doughy heart, he wandered aimlessly across Hyde Park towards St Mary's. He had never been inside a Catholic Church except for professional reasons and was diffident now about entering a building where he felt he had no spiritual right. But once he had opened the black padded door and had seated himself unobtrusively in the brown dusk, he began to find a peculiar comfort in exploring the technicalities of silence and stained glass. Sanctuary glimmer of candle and lamp, the twilight-adumbrated gesture of suppliant before icon, the calculated mystique of gothic nave held him like stout Cortez confronted with the Pacific. Tears squeezed easily from the sponges of his eyes and he sat on and on, tippling on a liquor that was new. Three old women and one young man lit candles at a long brass candelabra, then knelt to pray. Why? He could hear the susurrations of one soul, frantically fervent, importuning God over and over, and, between the saliva and the breathiness, some words came again and again, as if rote meant result—as perhaps it might, thought weary George. As perhaps it might. He slipped out of his seat, but no one even glanced his way and he staggered spiritually like a God-drunk into the dusk of College Street and the hobo-flowering park, touched to his romantic core.

Essentially he was a man of impulse and acute and sudden enthusiasms. But brevity and impulsiveness have their own sincerity. He read Newman, disguising the book in a plain jacket, in case Hilbery should spot it on his shelves. Then, entranced, he ceased to care, burned the jacket in a moment of impressed faith and an intellectual snobbery which informed him that many first-class minds were also seduced by the philosophies of the Roman Church. Not only was he drawn by the consolations which apparently it offered in a never-ending flow to the penitent, but also he became more and more convinced by Newman's arguments for the existence of a divinely established church. Sense of sin oppressed him. With characteristic reaction he was inclined to look back on his relationship with Nita as a period of complete degeneration.

"In a sense she ruined my life," he used to say later on. "She had a capacity for lust that overmastered me. And yet I loved her with all my heart. That was what was so terrible. She made me love vice just as she did."

"But was it vice?" the other would ask. "Sleeping with a girl is ordinary enough, surely?"

"It was more than that." George in his new-found wallow of virtue would sometimes sound specious, Yet he was not, in this. "It was the things she made me do. And liked doing," he added truthfully.

"Like what?"

"Oh, God!" George held his big curly head in his hands. "Don't make me say."

He read Augustine, seeking the redemption of a libertine, and, excited by his journeys into spirituality, he gorged himself on Thomist philosophy and eventually caught up with Bergson and Maritain. He felt justification for believing in an inspiration that demanded acceptance of right and wrong. Truly, at one stage, he had come close to finding the world useless, for he could accept neither materialism nor philosophies of scepticism, so that living rendered itself absurd. But although George thought God had vanished from his mind, his heart would not abandon Him entirely and his greed for spiritual peace led on his curiosity.

"What do you think about religion?" he asked Hilbery. An exquisite embarrassment possessed him.

"Nothing, old boy. Just nothing. Policy of non-interference."

"No, seriously, John. Don't you think it's an essential for peace of mind?"

"Not for me."

"Really?"

"No. I have a moral code, but that's a different thing entirely. I don't need to go to Church on Sundays to know what is socially acceptable, to know the things one should not do."

"I suppose not."

"Look!" Hilbery leaned across the table in the canteen. "You've taken a terrible tumble over that girl. Put her out of your mind. Get another girl and you'll snap out of it in no time. See if you don't."

"It's more than that. I *want* a religion. I want to feel there's a reason and purpose in existence."

"Well, there used to be for you," Hilbery said cruelly. "Girls. Don't kid me, Brewster. You are aware that is all that is wrong with you."

"Oh, shut up!" George drank his coffee and stared out at the city buildings across the street. Hilbery picked up the bill to placate him.

"Well, you've a choice of half a dozen sects. Why don't you settle for one and try it? How about something off the beaten track. Latter Day Saints? Mormons? What about something eastern? Get right away from all our Christian bigotry. Just fancy, falling for the Lord on the rebound!"

"Profanity is stupid. I've tried half a dozen anyway. My parents dragged me as a child from one church to another."

"But a child isn't capable of judging whether a thing like that has merit," Hilbery said, sorry for him all of a sudden. "Maybe you should try one of them again."

"Have you read the account of Maritain's conversion to Catholicism?" George asked. "He said 'If the truth were concealed in a dung-hill, then he would have to accept the dung-hill.' "

76

"No one could accuse him of bias!" Hilbery said. He dabbled a finger in a coffee stain and made a pattern of spots. "Are you thinking of throwing in your lot with Rome?"

"I don't know. It certainly interests me. Perhaps because it's the only one my parents never tried. But I would hate to think it boiled down to anything as simple as that."

"What *do* you want, then? The blinding Pauline flash on the way to Damascus? It's the intellectual fashion. The Chester-Belloc-Brewster. Imagine! But I'd shut up about it round here. There's plenty of anti-Catholic feeling on the paper and it won't do you any good with Gowanloch. Did you know he has the personnel officer vet prospective blokes about their religion?"

"Yes. He vetted me at the time. I wanted to tell him to mind his own damn' business."

"But you didn't?"

"No. Would you?" His mouth set in a glum curve.

Satanic Hilbery, shoulders arched, leaned over and whispered wickedly, "See that girl in the far corner—she's a new cadet with the social pages. Doesn't that take your mind off your soul?"

George turned. Across the room sat a dark large-eyed young woman of about twenty. The remarkable feature of her face was the ridiculous length of her eyelashes which, on her perceiving the men's interest, she instantly flapped. Curls, like her round face, held laughter trembling to expose itself.

"Vital?" Hilbery suggested.

"Monkeyish," said bitter Brewster.

Nonetheless. . . .

She proved no suitable therapy.

Miss Klein ached for marriage and threw her whole behaviour's purpose into seducing George while he, struggling against the seductions of fluttering eyelid, provocative attitudes

77

and finally open request, said "no" with a firmness that surprised him, a cruelty that baffled her and a religious self-justification that certainly deceived no higher spectator. "One pop," he confessed to Hilberry," and I know I'd be done for."

With a prim adherence to the technicalities of morality, they made love, George almost swooning with the temptation to submit to Sadie's invitation. He would have to keep away from her for weeks at a time but on those occasions that he did take her out, he availed himself so readily of her kisses, she was soon aware he was making use of her. Her efforts to seduce him intensified. What sort of a morality was it, he asked himself in his more honest moments, that could make pretence of continence like this? But he did not give in—not for a minute, and she began to feel that perhaps his determination to maintain a level of chastity was because he ultimately wished to marry her. She was wrong.

Nor did this diversion keep him from the problem that really ate at his mind. As he sampled the classic periods of the *Apologia*, he became more certain that the spiritual ingredient his existence lacked, the very thing which could give him an assured happiness, was to be found in a highly organized system of worship.

One evening in the thick winter cold, he went during his tea-hour to the presbytery which stood in the Cathedral grounds. He called briefly into the Cathedral and afterwards an ecstasy of dim chancel and lost gothic raptures lingered about him as he asked the housekeeper if he could see one of the fathers on a personal matter. Sceptics had warned him of Rome's gluttony for souls, so that he was entirely unprepared for the seemingly uninterested man in black soutane who finally came to the parlour where all, even the humans, were angles and sharp problems of emotional geometry. A flattish religious picture shone in the light. Polished table glimmered hard. Doorknob was sphere of white. For a moment as the other man's mild and appraising eye mapped the possibilities of insincerity, he was sorry he had come and began drumming fingers and clearing his throat.

"My name is Beckett," the priest said, and smiled a little wistfully at the private joke of which he had grown so tired. "What can I do for you?"

This suspension of his problem or perhaps some expectation of deliverance held George without words. Head moved in a sideways agnosticism.

"I'm not sure," he replied finally. "Perhaps I had better say first that I am not a Roman Catholic . . ."

"Catholic," the other corrected gently. George apologized.

". . . but I am extremely interested in the Church. It interests me more emotionally than intellectually, you understand. And I find that is insufficient. Not what I really want. For it to be solely emotional, I mean."

He hesitated, trapped.

The priest looked at him with some amusement and curiosity. Here was a plump, curly fellow, with a good-natured mouth and fairly empty eyes. He sounded important—or rather—he wished to sound important. Forgive me, Beckett prayed inwardly. My lack of charity is because I am so much older.

"Yes. I see." There was another measuring pause. "May I ask you your name?"

"Oh, forgive me." George was intolerably ashamed. "I'm so sorry." (He always protested too much!) "I must be rather upset to have lapsed so. It's Brewster. George Brewster."

The priest nodded. "Yes, Mr Brewster. And so you—you feel you are interested in the Faith? That is hardly a problem, surely."

"Oh, but it *is* a problem, can't you see? I want to understand *what* it is that attracts me so powerfully."

"There you would do better than all of us," Beckett said.

"Understanding is not the requirement. It is an act of faith. But let us leave that point, for the moment. May I ask what your occupation is? I mean, is it something that would have brought you into contact with Catholicism?"

"I'm a journalist." Where was this hunger for souls he had been warned about? By now, according to all the legends, the other should have been tremulous with the achievement of the missionary, pinning scapulars, medals and indulgences to his grateful though cautious breast.

"We always believe you pressmen to be hard-headed and with little time for mysticism. There! The danger of generalization is brought home to me." He laughed very gently at his little joke but his eyes remained entirely calm.

"That is an unfortunate reputation we have, Father." He used the form of address uneasily—but it was a first hurdle cleared. "Perhaps I'm not a typical pressman."

"Tell me," Father Beckett continued, his mild eyes fixed on the other's face," has there been any special thing which has perhaps prompted your interest in us?"

George loitered with a few stray ideas. Nita, Nita, Nita, shouted conscience. "No actual incident. No. I've always been interested in religion. My parents tried many when I was a child. Rather like wine-tasters. And of course being a child I was only allowed sips. So you see I know little about it."

"Were you baptized, Mr Brewster?"

"I doubt it." George pondered. "When I was born my parents were interested in a Church that believed only in adult baptism and by the time they left it, I should imagine they had forgotten all about it. I really don't know."

Beckett smiled sadly, his long white face apparently impassive. He observed Mr Brewster's twitching fingers. Neurotic? At twenty-three? Four? "Go ahead and smoke," he said. "No. No, thank you. I do not."

There was a silence charged with awkwardness until George, who could not bear social pauses, spluttered some vague and tangled statements about his reading which was bringing him to an appreciation of the Church even if not a conviction of its truth.

Beckett listened without comment and waited so long before he did say anything that George found himself wondering if perhaps he should repeat his remarks.

"You know it would be better if you received some formal instruction in matters of doctrine," the priest said at last, "not to convert you as it were, but merely to let you know a little of the working of the church. Reading and interpreting for yourself isn't quite the same thing as hearing doctrines explained by one who has a working knowledge."

"Oh, I agree."

"Well, then, do you think it would be possible to visit the Cathedral regularly for, say, a month?"

Would enthusiasm be out of place? George wondered.

"Gladly," he agreed. "Would you be giving the instructions yourself?"

"We'll see," said Father Beckett. "I'll write to you at your paper and fix a time three weeks ahead. I'm going to be away for a while at a country parish. Unless of course you are anxious to begin right away. But I think it will give us both time to think things over."

Astounded, George preserved an acquiescing calm.

"Even though you doubt at present whether there will be an intellectual conviction," Beckett continued unexpectedly, "faith makes anything possible."

"Well, of course!" George was inclined to laugh a little. "Any first principle accepted—then believing anything is possible. But it's accepting that premise of divine authorship!"

"You say you have been reading Maritain and Newman?" Beckett put his pallid hands together and measured finger against finger. His eyes were inexpressibly mournful. Thin strands of yellowish grey hair clung to his skull and drooped down his weary forehead. His lips were firmly pressed together from the effort of guarding against violence for thirty years. In fact even the passion he had felt for God seemed to have subsided to a less wearing domestic love in which he moved comfortably without testing the strain of miracle or personal rapture. Quiescence spun about him downs of intellectual softness. He was content in God and almost cynical of the ecstasy of others.

"If you accept a God and the theory that He revealed Himself in Christ, then your main problems, in fact your only problems, should be whether a Church was established and if so which one it is today."

"That would be a fair statement of my difficulties, I suppose." George hesitated at revelation. "It's a moral harbour I need as well. I want peace of mind."

The priest regarded him curiously.

"There is nothing else to want."

"Nothing?"

"Nothing at all. Peace of mind is the ultimate. We—we give our souls for it." He stood up but his thin body offered only a whisper of reassurance. From a glass-fronted book-case along the wall he took two volumes. "I'm going to lend you these. I want you to read them and tell me what you think. Try to examine them for spiritual content rather than sheer intellectualism. Not . . ." he added with raised hand as he saw the protest begin to form on George's face, "not that I wish you to avoid arguments of an intellectual appeal. Not at all. I just think perhaps you may be more unhappy than you are perplexed philosophically. Or perhaps that is the same thing."

"What makes you think so?" George adored discussing himself.

82

"Oh, I have seen puzzled and unhappy people for a great number of years, you know. There are many indications."

"Such as?"

"Don't press me." Beckett smiled. "I may offend you—and it is too early yet. We are not even friends.

Ah, the delicate acid of asceticism ate an image into George's reflecting mind and he sensed a schoolboy rush of admiration for the man before him. He went out into the city's dazzle with one part of him expectant and the other disappointed.

It was, after all, Father Beckett who undertook his instruction. George found himself looking forward to these weekly meetings at the presbytery with as much enthusiasm as if he had been meeting a new girl. Once he said this to the priest who only laughed, liking and understanding the young man better with each encounter.

"You needed a holiday from the world," was all he said.

There was a large proportion of argument as well during the hours they had together, argument which the priest enjoyed as much as the journalist. But in the end it all boiled down to a blind act of faith, and George was beginning to realize this without the other's even insisting that he face the fact.

"What's up with you?" asked an impatient Miss Klein. "Are you ill or something? You seem to have lost your zest."

"I'm just about to find it," George replied, regarding her fluttering lashes with a great deal of distaste.

"Well, that will certainly be a change," she said, misinterpreting happily. They were out together on an assignment to report a play's first night. George was given occasional reviews of unimportant theatre and made the most of every chance to turn in some of the fine writing that Duckworth had so despised. They stood to one side of the foyer watching the last arrivals. Miss Klein had made her narrow scribble over three or four pages, notations of name and dress guided by special concern for indications of income in appearance, poor little rabbit. George was looking prosperous in an overcoat that made his broad shoulders seem massive. Her heart sang like a cash register. During the play, which was flat and heavy she was conscious only of his arm and shoulder hogging most of the chair rest—and loved him for it, subscribing to all the gush read in the women's papers: men liked women who needed protecting. Her willing and humble limb was finally elbowed off its support entirely. George barely knew she was there.

It had rained while they were in the theatre and when they came out into the sloping light puddles, drizzle like silk saturated the air. Asphalt gleamed a spilled wine. Gutters ran wine. A drunkenness of expectation caused the young woman to misjudge the abstraction on her companion's face. When he accompanied her to her tram and there propelled her absently towards the step she turned a protesting countenance that whispered,

"Aren't you going to see me home?"

Jerked back to this present from divine infatuations, George could not for the moment orientate himself to the expectancy of her rosy mouth. Hideousness returned. Carnality rushed up at him and in this place of peace that he had stumbled on he said,

"No, Sadie. No. Not tonight." Bending closer to the damp curls he murmured, "I think too much of you. Really I do."

The tram snatched her away before she could demand an explanation and for forty stops she wrestled with those six words attempting to adapt them to the plans she had for him. Rationalizing thus, she felt happiness bubbles rising in her heart. So did George at that moment—but for a vastly different reason.

Having won this victory over the flesh, he was prepared for

further flagellation of the spirit. Self-denial after all these years of indulgence had a ripe appeal. Virtue is infinitely more attractive, he was discovering. Was it only because he could indulge his egoism a little further, wallow in pride? True, there was no humility of spirit in him yet, but that would come as such a refinement of virtue, he could not even think ahead to that point. For many weeks he tortured himself with doubts about his sincerity in the matter: did he really want God? Did he really want peace of mind? Was he perhaps not merely seeking an emotional substitute for something he had lost?

There is a point when the mind, raw from revolving the same, same, same, never-ending question, mercifully refuses to focus on that disturbing problem and darts off tangentially, as uncontrolled as mercury, seeking an anywhere-at-all. That was how it was with him. He could no longer ask and ask, knowing there would be no certain answer, knowing that much would have to be taken on trust. The brain in splints was limping home to a last haven.

There was a new love lapping his parched coasts.

Although he was normally unmoved by all music except of the simplest and most obvious form with tunes as primary as spectrum colours, he began in this welcomed solitariness attending orchestral concerts or chamber music recitals. Time-filling; escape; pleasure in itself. One evening during a performance of the "Swan of Tuonela," he was so moved with a subjective interpretation of his own wilderness that he felt the tears roll warmly and plentifully down his cheeks and, on coming dazed into the city traffic afterwards, was preserved from accident under the wheels of a bus only by the sheer good fortune that guards the intoxicated.

"*In tuis manibus, domine,*" George prayed with much accuracy.

Three weeks later he was received into the Church.

AFTER HE MET HER he was married within the week.

The simulated indifference of the broken heart was still shadow-thin even with two years of other faces in another town. Behind the daily façade of journalistic goodwill, of gay-blade reporter, the ache persisted, the grinding pain in the heart, the worse pain in his pride. His religion, by removing the distraction of other women in his pursuit of purity, unfairly allowed him greater time to reflect on the one he had lost.

Succumbing one pearly evening to the spiritual indigestion brought about by a nostalgic picnic among old snapshots and some letters which had eluded his anguished *auto-da-fé*, he wrote to a name that he had to dredge from a sluggish river silted up with hundred of faces. This one belonged to a brides-maid at the wedding. All the heart-rending details of Nita's betrayal he had preserved in a fine vinegar of hatred and love and regret. He knew where she had honeymooned and for how long. He discovered where they had gone to live afterwards. Then for two years he determined not to flagellate himself and deliberately put her from his mind. But on this night a purring curiosity prowled all about him. He wept a little as he looked first at the photograph of the bridal party which he had cut from the Brisbane paper and then at one taken of Nita and himself in swimming costumes somewhere along the beach at Rainbow Bay. He stared and stared at the first photo, struggling to recall the name of the young girl Nita had described as her best friend, and as he stared he longed unutterably to hear how Nita was. Generous enough to want to know she was still happy, at the same time, being human, he yearned to discover her disillusionment. So he wrote to Alice Welton—Weldon?—Weller, that was it, asking for news of Nita and suggesting that they meet. It would be fun also to see the fellows on the *Hub*, he told himself. Oh, he told himself that many times on the journey north.

He had decided to go through Brisbane—there would be a four hour wait between trains, time enough to explore her new country. He asked for two days' leave from his annual holidays—enormous favour! All night in the coastal train in the jolted half-sleep that possessed him on his reeling bunk, an anticipatory exultation and excitement shook the surfaces of his dreams. When the false dawn streaked across the sooty windows, he woke to a world of grey dew and hill that levelled out as the sun came up into the green stretches of Coff's Harbour. Near the border, sighting a bitsy township where once he had spent a week-end with her in the swollen timber pub, he dropped his face into his hands and sobbed. The conductor coming in then with thick china and thick biscuit was obliged to say, "Wot's up, mate?" but did not stay to hear and George nibbled and sipped, stood with his legs braced against the bunk and door and peered into the mirror. Had he changed beyond what she had once recognized and loved, he wondered? The razor outlined his sober self. His suit adjusted his mind. He put the cup back into the corridor with a sixpence rattling on the saucer and went to the platform at the end of the compartment to watch the fluidity of trees.

Even before he breakfasted he walked in from South Brisbane to the Post Office and found her name in the telephone directory. There it was. T. S. Wayne, 21 Elimatta Road, Bardon. Oh, stupid bounding heart! His sweet lost brown love! He put the pennies in a call-box, only to hear—Scaler's voice?

87

No, her voice! Hers! Hers! What bliss as she said over and over, "Hello, hello, hello, I can't hear you." And then the receiver was placed on its hook and she was gone. Munching a pie, he caught a tram to Bardon, found her street, strolled along it weak in his excitement, and when he neared 21, crossed to the other side with his hat pulled well down, his head averted until he had passed and could look safely back. Colonial 21. Veranda across the front. Steps to veranda. Steeply pitched iron roof. Chocolate brown. White trim. Nothing at all to mark it out from the houses on either side except the fact that as one man looked at it some lost bird of paradise swayed over a forgotten lawn. There was washing on a line across the yard. He could see a dress of hers and, with loathing, a man's shirt. He had only to cross the road, he told himself, to test her as well as himself. Thirty paces to her front gate. Thirty. He swung about and strode up the hill again with his coat flapping. The last photograph of all: a box of a bungalow with two symmetrical cotton-palms and blue curtains at a side window.

All the unforgotten but deliberately unrecalled landscape of Condamine hit him blow after blow as the afternoon train snorted in. To what end, this trip? To what stupid end? He had examined his heart. It was chocolate brown with a white trim—and there was nothing further to see. But he had to go through with it, and gripping his valise he leaned out of the door to scan the score of waiting people. Even the hoardings had not changed. The tap outside the lavatories still dribbled across the concrete. Burdened with a fine trembling, George stepped down into his own despair.

From all these unknowns one moved forward tentatively with the smile of a child. The photograph fleshed itself.

"Hello," said both voices at once.

George could not remember Alice Weller looking like this, ever, ever. Once before they had met and he had thought her colourless, but the pallor of adolescence had deepened imperceptibly to a finer point where a blinding beauty of bone dazzled through the skin; everything, apart from the grey-blue eyes, was harmony of white or cream or gold.

"You look different," he said. "Oh, marvellously different." And gaped. And quite forgot to ask about Nita for the moment. Later on did so as they drank tea together in a café off the main street; asked and was answered. Yes—they wrote regularly. Yes—she was happy. Happy and—still playing around.

"*Is* she?" George murmured, totting up his first satisfaction. "And how does Scaler like that?"

The golden girl opposite him giggled charmingly.

"He doesn't know, of course." She raised clear shadowless eyes to his and his heart unexpectedly side-stepped brown Nita. In profile she was adorable—how had he not seen these things four years ago? Yet despite the tentative approach of a new rapture—giddy George!—he was filled with a hopeless delight, imagining that as they walked down the town's main street towards the park he might encounter his truant world in dark hair, dark eyes, slender limbs. Everywhere this Saturday length of street were faces he remembered, nodding.

"Do you mind," he said during an awkward pause, "if I call in at the *Hub*? I'd like to see some of the fellows. To see if they are still there, I mean."

She shook her head. "I won't come. I'll wait in the park."

But he wouldn't hear of it—she was too pretty to waste. So, a slim silent shadow, she accompanied him up the stairs. She was to be his slim silent shadow for ever, though she did not know it then—but would not have minded if she had, for he appeared so urbane, such a sophisticate when she thought of the farm and the green days that were only green days.

On the landing, Ferguson—so unchanged, so completely unchanged that his same clothes seemed to bear the same

creases, the same frosting of dandruff on the shoulder—
groped with recognition and then said: "Well, for crying out
loud! The prodigal returns!"

He nodded his bitter face at the girl, then looked back at
George. "I wouldn't have known you, son. You've filled out
and grown up."

"Can you have a drink?" George asked.

"Not now. It's a bad time. We've moved along since you
were here. Bring out a broadsheet daily, now. I'm busy every
Saturday getting the Monday stuff set up. Give us half an
hour." Suddenly he grinned and the lovely violet eyes grew
luminous. "Why, darling." he said, "I just remembered. I've
been wanting to catch up with you over the big cross-head you
ballsed that week I was off with 'flu."

"Oh, God, Viv!" George laughed, surprised to sense some
of the old nervousness tickling under his skin. "I remember—
'LABOUR FICTION RE-ELECTED.' I was glad to be going!"

Ferguson laughed. "No end of a stink. We had to publish
an apology next day signed by g-o-d himself."

George remembered Alice and introduced her. Already she
was becoming the natural after-thought.

"Why don't you go on up?" Ferguson suggested. "Most
of the old bunch are still here."

"What about Lippman?"

"Gone down to a Brisbane daily. Place isn't the same without him—it's a bloody sight saner. Go on. Shoot up. I'll be
with you shortly."

There were two men in the room that watched the park.
Hope and Clarence were entangled with a mass of galley
sheets which entangled further as they dropped them to slap
shoulders. When people who have worked together meet on the
other side of intervening years the exchange of memories is
either stilted or a vociferous dramatization of a more meagre
relationship. Here they mulled over only the splendid moments

90

of newspaper *gaffes*, the drinking sessions, the dirty jokes, the inside stories or the town scandals.

"What's happened to Ronnie Shead?" George asked. "And lovely Trumper?"

"Ronnie's still with us," they told him. "But Trumper left. Lippman put the hard word on her and she up and gave notice. Still round the town, still single. Still got a figure. Wow!"

Alice glistened, listened with rainbow admiration and everyone found her charming, even Duckworth who strolled down to see what the fuss was about and asked them out to dinner that evening. Half an hour later, sitting in the freckled shadow of a pepper-tree in the park, fatuously George cosseted a silly pride that she had fitted in so well with his friends, refusing to examine the treacherous idea that her acceptability was based on a negative rather than a positive display of personality. In any case that was all to the good. In journalism—in those days anyway—only one sex had an opinion.

There was no one about. Grass sprawled under trees and idled along between flower-beds. On their shoulders sun burned and faded behind clouds and burned again. He turned to inspect her rather long face under the flattery of a drooping white hat and smiled the smile of a liberated man.

But,

"I know where Nita's living now," he said, prodding the sore place. "I snooped."

Alice only laughed. "Jean is still here," she said. "Would you like to see her?"

Just for the interval her words occupied there was the illogical flare of curiosity mingled with love that surprises any long-lost relationship. Leaves chopped gently at air. Birds related branch to sky and sky to lawn. The milk-mildness of the day rocked tenderly.

"Why?" George asked with a stroke of the genius he had

in his dealings with women. But she was not as urbane as he and perplexedly asked,

"But isn't that why you came, to see how Nita's getting on? Jean would know more than me."

He was silent. "Well, isn't it?" she persisted.

"No longer," he replied, allowing his eyes to glutton on hers so forcefully she was compelled to turn away. The Long Level Look, he called it jokingly, and had practised it in bars, cafés, at concerts, plays, on beaches, buses, "This—" accented pause, "this is the first really happy moment I've had for two years." Thereby he reached unerringly for her most sensitive spot so that her confusion increased steadily. A cripple staggered by on his wooden crutches and sat down in a halo of roses near the fountain. Juxtapositions such as this—the grotesque with the lovely—of enchantment with reality, dark with light, movement with stillness, of hard bench with yielding flesh the hand a finger's breadth from the hand: all achieved silent victories. He tried to probe about her family, her friends, but there she was silent, merely offering a smile of magical candour.

They drank at five o'clock with Ferguson in a quiet lounge at the western end of the town until it was time to go to Duckworth's.

"I'm not dressed for dinner," Alice said, inspecting the creases in her dress. "Will there be anyone else?"

"I don't know," said George. "But you look lovely to me." Three double whiskies reached over to squeeze her hand. The tenderness, however, was not spurious for it was a long time since he had relished such compliance in a woman, such a melting non-aggression.

Ferguson thrust forward an assenting lower lip and said tactlessly, "You can pick 'em, Brewster! And better than last time, too."

Whereupon George extended his tail feathers and strutted to the bar for more friendship and wisdom.

In the wind-streaked dark they staggered jovially to a cab rank where Ferguson kissed each of them elaborately and swayed into the night. Should he in this temporary privacy take hold of the little white paw that lay invitingly on the leather seat between them? Once, just once, he crushed it in his big square ugly hand and let go. He saw her teeth gleam in the darkness. He saw her big white hat, now held upon her knees like a dropped cloud. The car banged and groaned along the dirt road out of town and pulled up beside the gate—Oh, God! beside the tenderness itself of two dead summers. He paid the driver off and asked him to call back at eleven, took the young woman's arm in his and stumbled along the gravel between dark coverts of shrubbery where once he had kissed his agony away on Nita's compliant face. Then the calm that had linked arms with him all afternoon drew away somehow and,

"Oh, God!" he cried softly.

"What is it?" The gentle voice in the dark. The gentle voice in the dark.

"Nothing." He took his arm from hers. Fool to imagine himself cured! His heart was thudding with an excited misery that brought Nita so close to him in this familiar place he could hardly put up with it; and then the next minute light carved out their faces and in the demand for social conformity with introductions and platitudes, a treacherous lull came over the inner turbulence.

Duckworth was much more portly, more hoggishly assured.

How many whiskies, wines, rare steaks, dirty stories, women, had gone into creating the rotundity and genial arrogance that confronted them both? Missus Fossicker Duckworth, horsier than ever, but still handsome in a high-pitched whinnying way, pawed a gin and regarded George insolently. How many junior reporters, golf-club greensmen, bank-clerks or book-makers?

"Well!" she said with heavy satisfaction. And sipped. "Well! What is this? *Recherche du temps perdu?*" (Know your Languages?)

"Perhaps." Man-of-the-world Brewster crossed his legs.

"Or *recherche de la femme?*"

"Don't be hackneyed, my dear," Duckworth interposed. "Our young friend is back merely on a social visit. We've expanded since you were here. I suppose you noticed. Two more machines downstairs and a cubby with a blonde telephonist."

"It's the blonde telephonist that counts."

Mrs Duckworth laughed harshly. That creature he'd brought along! Pallid little thing. Colourless. She looked her up and down lingeringly. A neurotic fury at her failure to capture him sprouted like a weed.

"And what is life like in the big places?" Duckworth was asking meanwhile with a certain amount of jealousy that he troubled little to hide. His living-room was punctuated by small-town commas—golf trophies, local water-colours, photographs. His wife leaned back in her easy chair, crossing her legs so high her skirt displayed two thin but extremely elegant knees that drew George's automatic glance. She sucked on the long black cigarette holder she had only recently begun to use. Down its length as if through the sights of a gun, she would fix her aim at a man and concentrate the bullets of both eyes. George wriggled uncomfortably, transfixed by lacy underwear and a length of thigh.

"Oh, pretty rushed," he said. "I'm doing court work mainly. Some of the tales those Sydney dregs cough up in the petty sessions would stagger you."

"Not me."

"Well, no, not you, of course. But each day is a long procession of prostitutes and pimps, drunks, brawlers, perverts. You get pretty hard-boiled after a while."

94

"My little soft-boiled egg!" drawled Mrs Duckworth, lusciously exhaling.

"But it's the frequency with which the same ones keep appearing. Time and time again. They never learn."

"Who does!" Mrs Duckworth inquired, blowing more smoke to heaven, which ignored her. "We all come back for punishment."

George should have blushed. "I'm enjoying life," he continued in amateurish display of deafness. "I run a special court column now based on that stuff, you know. It has tremendous popular appeal. There's always a sob story somewhere."

"You always were a sentimentalist, Brewster," the older man said. Nothing could be less so than he, who had acquired by fifty the dispassionate approach to self, the selfishness that investigates without an emotional flicker the brand of a tobacco, the label of a wine, the body of a woman, betraying no subjectivity at all. There was nothing to be betrayed. It was with this same technical interest that his bloodshot eye appraised Miss Weller's kitten-soft person curled unobtrusively in her chair. He approved disinterestedly her prettiness, the little girl *extase* of her smile. She didn't have much to say, either, he noted with underlined approval. Better that than those who continually said nothing over and over again.

"Is Murray Parks still with your crowd?" he asked after a moment.

George sucked his false teeth.

"He went off to Melbourne to the *Telegraph* last March. Got married too, just before he went."

"*Did* he now? That's interesting." Mrs Duckworth's face brightened with malice. "And who was the lucky gel?"

"One of the stenogs. A case of have-to, so the newsroom boys said."

"They probably knew!"

"Probably." George laughed. "I can assure you I didn't."

"You always were charmingly monogamous though, George," she said. "All your infidelity was mental. Practical only up to a certain point."

George glared at her. She must be drunk, he thought. But then he hardly ever remembered her being any other way than half-tipsy.

Tattoo of leaves in wind outside on timber. Timber creaking. Beyond the unshuttered glass the rhyming branches flung about the sky. Chiming into their unhappy silence a clock (Toowoomba Men's Finals, 1917) reminded them of their need for dinner, for change of posture. To stand, to flex arms, stretch, ease feet across carpet. Places taken opposite enemy or friend, and with flowers and a trailing arrangement of ferns, a cheese soufflé and a child-like unspeaking radiance next to him, George was lulled again to dinner talk, to risqué jokes to city-room scandals.

"And where's she living now?" Mrs Duckworth asked, also prodding the sore place.

"I don't know."

"Don't know?"

"No."

"But surely . . . My dear," turning to Alice's bland countenance, "isn't it remarkable! He was ker-razy about this gel. Truly. The piece that passeth understanding. I'm punning, of course!"

Duckworth watched his wife unemotionally. He was used to her being a bitch. It amused him.

"Yes," Alice said unexpectedly. "I knew he was. She told me and I had met George once, oh, years ago. Nita was my best friend in those days."

"Ohhhh." The long look. "Then you'll have lots in common."

But all evenings of host and guest in the lists terminate with the souls dragged out like elastic lengths then allowed in

96

that final parting to relax like worn garters. After initial excitement and curiosity, after the degeneration of talk into scurrility, pauses broke out like the spotty symptoms of some minor illness. Hands clasped the minimum of each other at the doorway where in zebra setting, now revealed, now concealed, they waited for the cab to return from town. Sentimental journeys are a pointless business, George was now convinced in this stale interval between the acts. Returning was without even actual pain—only the surd of that agony that once described pinnacles of pleasure. Flatly, with boredom, drink-numbed, battered by gossip, enervated by shovelling words into pits of silence like a navvy, he stared, without actually apprehending, at the wide lonely country road down which within that thought the long apple-pale beams of the car scissored the night. Farewells repeated. Oh, God! he cried within. Will it never end? Certainly write. Yes, yes, yes, anything; a card, a thousand cards, cards, cards and thanks again and again and again.

Eventually he was alone with this golden silence in the back seat of the cab while outside night ran by like water.

This woman bred peace. Understanding that, he edged closer to soak up whatever it was she appeared to give of the tranquillity of a remembered harbour; and she, so potent but so unarrogant, sensing submission, placed her left hand upon his arm. Thus for three miles of corrugated dirt road. In a resurgence of sentiment he closed his eyes pretending it was still Nita, that there had never been separation, that all things were restored to proper places—the clock ticked on in the centre of the carved wood mantel, the family photos marched along the piano, the blood throbbed in the arm, the hair blew across his face in the wind. And opening his eyes as he removed strands of it across his mouth and trapped tongue, he perceived in the dimness that they were yellow after all. And after all there was nothing to be done except walk her to the farmhouse gate in the moon-grey fields and kiss her once only on the pale skin below

97

the blowing hair. She was half-expectant he would want to see her again the next day—and so he did, aware of the expectancy.

Each took into sleep that night an imprint of the other's face—the magnificent leonine head with its boulevardier lilted mouth, the creamy golden features smiling like a child. But head would not turn to head, and in their separate beds each nuzzled the pillow in an extravagance of need that required more than flesh to immesh flesh, rather bone to harry bone.

Affection measured out by the timelessness of hours spent with another may possibly be miscalculated, but the addition of an artificial climate of lost excitement revived in the aspect of a park-seat, a dance-hall, a special boskiness of road, a hotel, a main street, the disposition of shops, brings about a sense of communion long before it is normally achieved or deserved. Entangled, confused, but convinced of the clarity of her elusive calm, he proposed to her in the sunlight hours of the next day, believing as he plunged into her eyes that he would want to be with her for the rest of his life. He was right up to a point, for she began then the idolatry which endured, augmenting itself, for the rest of hers. In between the kisses he was curious enough to ask if she had had other men who loved her. Her gentleness was immutable.

"No post-mortems," she said. "I know about Nita. Let's call it square and start from now."

There he had to content himself, but in those later moments of doubt when he observed her exhilaration at dances and parties he would remember her resistance to all his queries and writhe with jealousy. Still, he rather enjoyed writhing. George was always something of a masochist.

With the snap decision of the brave man or the fool, he could not postpone his release from celibacy or his capture. In the strictest analysis he would have discovered that his nostalgia was forcing him into a marriage with a Nita at second-hand—after all, they had been schoolgirls together—

and here he was in the sentimental backdrop of her hometown, recapturing as much of the fantasy as he could. Unbalanced by love, they decided to marry the next week-end when he would return and take her to Brisbane for some days of that doubtful bliss where two complete strangers accustom themselves to each other.

Their parting on the dingy platform contained promise and anticipation, the recollection of the authentic comfort of kisses.

There was no time for doubt. He refused it entrance, busy with the practical side of marriage—the renting of a flat, the obtaining of a licence, and the suddenly least important thing —telling Sadie. Years later he saw her anger as it really was, but at the time he hardly noticed her disturbance. She was a candle flicker in the enormous light of this novelty.

"You made use of me!" she stormed at his tepid concern.

"I know. I know. Forgive me. It has happened to me also."

"Has it? That's a lot of satisfaction."

"I can't help it, Sadie," he repeated dolefully. "I just don't want to marry you. I never have wanted to."

Revenge branches farther and farther. She fulfilled her rage finally in a wretched union with one of his work associates, thereby repeating the pattern, and became grey and shrewish with a rankling sense of deprivation. Detached George would say vaguely years and years away—"I suppose she hates me now."

On the first evening of their marriage, alone in their beach flat, panic visited his dicky heart as he bent to run a bath for her. She was a stranger. He did not know her. They had hardly exchanged an idea beyond that of mutual love, and what is that when it is only words? Her quietness was beyond his imagining. He was disappointed too by the mildness of her passion; she appeared untouched by his glittering adoration. But the days went by; they became accustomed to each other in a variety of mundane attitudes that are perhaps the essence of married life.

When a week had passed they returned south by train. At Condamine in a snowfall of fluttering handkerchiefs her mother handed Alice three letters that she opened later in the train. Each one contained a marriage proposal. Boosted George! She might be no intellectual, he told himself, but she had been a local belle.

Hilbery was not at first as enthusiastic as he should have been.

"Bit of a risk, old boy. I mean you didn't know a thing about her. You might have ruined your career."

Through George's highly suggestive psyche coursed a shiver of apprehension that he shrugged away in a recollection of physical compensation.

There were astral pleasure grounds. The days stuttered with love.

For four hard-working, hard-drinking years, the best of his life, George worked as a parliamentary reporter in the capital, living there for five or six months every year and returning to Sydney during those periods when Parliament was in recess. He liked to describe himself as a swinging vote. Although he had no real politics he did have a capacity for understanding the political machine and for interpreting the chicanery and lobbying that went on and occasionally being able to forecast budget manoeuvres before they became fact. His gregariousness established early confidence in his good cheer and he was a quick man to seize on the idly dropped indiscretion. With him, constantly adoring, went Alice, content to be background to his waggishness, his ebullience, his flirtatiousness. He held floors with a kind of compulsion, button-holing cabinet ministers and compelling their attention with a piece of introductory scatology—George: "What man doesn't like to talk about it?"—often biassed nicely, if it were topical, to seduce the political ear.

It was during these years that Alice discovered, at first with distress and then resignation, his real need to be constantly admired by women. It appeared to go no further than that but if she had not been tolerant and well-balanced and occasionally amused, it could have formed a basis for grievance because he was so transparent in his popularity seeking, so unconcerned to conceal his party conquests. Yet all the time he swore to others, but to himself especially, that he loved her dearly. And he did.

Their closest friend—or rather, George's closest friend—was a sophisticated divorcée of thirty, a handsome-ugly woman with a masculine mind, a capacity to use four-letter words without giving offence, and two ungrateful children. They had met amid the ennui of small sherries where heads incline and words bent a variety of insincere ways. Too smart in a combination of lilting colours she held three men on the trembling lip of laughter. It was the first time George had ever found himself over-shadowed as a raconteur and his desire for a spiritual *droit du seigneur*—she must admire *him*!—brought about some ludicrous virtuosity of attention. With flattery, with ready laughter at her *mots*, eventually he obtained Mrs Timbrell-West's hyphenated deference.

In Sydney they met again at his home, a bungalow that looked across the Lane Cove River towards Longueville. Her brain and conversation satisfied a part of him that had yearned for years and it became his habit to visit her William Street flat. To friends he would say she had enriched his life. Perhaps she had. Certainly he did not ultimately manage to befuddle her with his flatteries for early in the relationship she made it clear to him that he did not attract her physically.

No shaft bit deeper.

Twenty years later George still pondered this with pained bewilderment.

"She said I simply didn't attract her in that way. I think she must have been crazy!"

101

(Really he was delightful in his innocence!)

"George is harmless," Mrs Timbrell-West used to say amusedly. And the name stuck. Largely because he told his family in sulky aggrievedness. Old Harmless. He felt bound to prove her wrong. Once she flung a glass of beer in his face as they stood chatting at a party on a yacht in the harbour. He never forgave her inwardly but, on the surface, managed by some casuist device to turn the whole incident to his advantage. He could not bear to lose her friendship over a drunken trifle and she, too, began turning to him for help at difficult times, for he had an intrinsic goodwill and was without malice.

His column on the magistrates' courts had given way to a weekly political round-up of aphorism, House repartee, and innuendo. From this he moved to the status of occasional feature-writer on Government policy and was so impressive with his fulsomely knowledgeable periods that editor Gowan-loch decided to send him to the Melbourne paper as news editor.

That night, celebrating with the press gallery boys, George got so drunk he managed only the taxi journey home before he collapsed untidily on the back veranda where Alice, awakened by the thump, found him fast-snoringly asleep and streaked obscenely with illness.

Tenderness overcame repugnance. She settled rugs and pillows about him, removed his teeth in case he was again sick and went back to bed almost bursting with love. When male pride is reduced to frail sickly flesh, the female senses her only moment of equation, or power.

They rented their house with its two young lemon-trees and its eye on the blue water and the next week caught the train south.

Their new home was on the bay front. It was double storeyed and from the upstairs windows Port Phillip's wind-tousled waters could be seen challenging small craft and fawning to the coastal steamers. A fun fair exploded half a mile away, recapitulating the limited wants of muscular youth in horizontal or vertical forms under sidereal phenomena of an electric quality that spattered sickly light over the roller coasters and the merry-go-rounds. Dim suburbs crept out of the ghetto to the eastern beaches where, nagged by the southerlies, houses dragged tile brims over their fenestration and furtively entered the architectural debate of the Thirties.

In the May of that year their daughter was born. George's false teeth ached during the entire confinement with a misplaced sympathy. Together in the evenings they would gloat over the fuzzy-haired baby that was their private miracle. Alice regained her figure, to George's enormous relief, and life went on as usual.

They had no other child. Alice's health became the reason they believed in, but when George, swooning with parental idiocy, gloated over the rubber-bud two-year-old face amusingly screaming "Earwig! Earwig!" at the front gate, or imperiously demanding gifts, he did ponder the satisfaction of having a son.

They began an album. There were hundreds of snapshots—of Alice in the long-legged skirtless bathing costumes of the time; of George, sporty in tennis flannels, boyishly thin; of picnic parties; of relations smiling because they had to; of fatuous parenthood; of Jeannie at her christening in masses of white lace. With those repetitive fixed smiles barely changed throughout the years, what did they really record?

When Brewster took over the news desk on the *View* he found Ivor Lippman feature-writing along the corridor. Five years had streaked grey in his hair; his body had begun to thicken.

"I thought you were in Brisbane," George said.

"Too hot," explained Lippman. "Climate, I mean."

"Well, you certainly look prosperous and *distingué*."

"Part of my genius," Lippman said. He had never really liked Brewster. "I hear you've made the fatal mistake."

George smiled placatingly. "True. But it's a happy mistake."

"Not your little friend, Netta, was it?"

"Nita. No, no. That blew over years ago."

"Just as well." Lippman stared shrewdly at the other man. "She was quite a player, wasn't she?"

"I suppose she was."

"She certainly was." Lippman could not resist malicious emphasis, observing pleasurably that Brewster's face sagged in defeat and dislike of having to recall. He added with delight, "She even made a play for me."

George arched his eyebrows, knowing now the reason for a hatred that had always been intuitive.

"I hope you obliged," he said bitterly.

Lippman tossed his great dark head back.

"Oh, for God's sake! Of course I did! Fancy knocking back an opportunity like that!"

George nodded but the pulse in his throat drummed intolerably.

"Yes. A fellow would be mad, wouldn't he?" He picked up a bundle of galleys and pretended he was looking through them. Lippman tweaked them to one side with a perkiness that invited a punch and, pursuing viciously, said,

"Must have been in 'twenty-three, or was it 'twenty-two? Either just after you left—or just before. My dear fellow, have you realized that makes us brothers-in-law? Or is it step brothers?" Again his curly head flung out its mirth.

Confronted with such specific venom, Brewster was as uncertain as a man who unexpectedly finds that he casts two shadows, one of which is a humped unfamiliar. Despite efforts to avoid Lippman's macabre brilliance, the man jabbed at him again and again. Therefore wretched Brewster attempted a spurious form of friendship—of overt jocularity and too-hearty insistence on shouting the drink—that was more hideous in its unreality than hatred. But the insanity gripped him and he would invite Lippman home for meals, enduring while the other mugged Alice, was impatient or patronizing or arrogant. It was unendurable but he did not know what to do.

Through eyes of stained glass George must regard the world. His breath was liturgical. In those days clerical collars thrilled him almost as much as plunging necklines. A peasant simplicity regulated his attitude to prayer and request in prayer and hope of fulfilment whereby he could hold up a shield in this way and turn aside most of Lippman's brutal thrusts. His entire seriousness took him regularly through temporal obligations to religion, and he made Lenten resolutions of ambitious sinlessness that amazed even Alice. His big miraculous shield of good works did indeed turn Lippman away to the arms of a nonsense blonde on the switch, but with the capriciousness with which prayers are often answered, anguish came trotting delicately down another road, ears back, nose snuffling, hoofs high-lifting.

In mid-May when their ringleted pet had just had her second birthday, they left her with friends and went to Mount Buffalo for a week. On the snow-slopes George was awkward and weaponless, but in the evening, comforted by log fires and the numbness of the other guests, he dominated the room with his gravelly voice, outlining stories Alice had heard so often she was tempted to commit the blasphemy of a yawn. An American couple called Santry spent every night with them at the bar drinking until midnight. Jason was nearly sixty but still of that weathered handsomeness that is apparent only in the later years of some men. His wife, Moira, was half his age, assertive, strong-minded, a splendid skier and an athletic drinker. After their divorce George always insisted Jason had picked her up in a slalom. "Then just held on for a couple of curves," Alice commented brightly, astounding everybody.

Four faces confronting each other for seven days begin slow

private assessments. Observant from habit, George noted Jason's attentions to Alice, first with automatic pride and voluptuous sensation in his ego, but later with a rasping irritation that made him trap words between teeth and lower lip when he would find the American kneeling before her to lace up her snow-boots, or at the run's edge, helping with the greasy straps of her skis. Alice was a riot of dimpled laughter, citrine curls and happy acceptance. Moira pretended not to notice or perhaps did not, drinking more and more gin with her bright mouth streaking the glass rim. She hung limp-sack in George's dancing arms, sensing him searching over her black-strapped shoulder for the pain of observing Jason move his cheek against Alice's or tighten his arm across her back. Worse not to find this of course, and know they had stepped outside to the veranda for glimpses of the snow-fields whitely romantic in the moonshine.

"You like Jason?" George would ask Alice as they shuddered together in the cold hotel bed.

"Yes, of course I like him." His wife's chin would tilt pleasure.

George would grunt. "He certainly seems to like you."

And he would make love to her possessively, and she would console him with a cliché.

"Where would I get another like you?" she would demand of his profile subsided in aftermaths of rapture. Where? Where?

Even after the Brewsters had returned to Melbourne and the Santrys to Geelong, Jason would drive across and take Alice to dinner while George watched with an odd feeling of pleasure. The gentle masochist at home! Patting his daughter, washing up, reading and lengthily getting drunk on Scotch until they returned.

On the fourth occasion she left him with such a transcendental luminosity of feature and indifference to his abrupt

106

pain that he stewed jealously for three hours, observing the clock hands take her slowly through every aspect of infidelity of the spirit as well as body. Accordingly, accordingly, there was no surprise left when, after hearing the car crunch in some minutes past eleven, he saw from the upstairs window of the falsely darkened house, Jason take Alice, pliant and unprotesting, into his ageing arms.

That night they had the first real row of their married life.

He had lain quietly enough, shamming sleep, as she entered the room on the lilt of whatever love-song she happened to be singing below her excited breath, when he snapped the bedlamp on savagely and lit up her private rapture. He scowled without speaking, his eye bulging accusation.

"What's the matter?" She peeled off each stocking like a husk. Still he could not illuminate the imagined adultery. "I had a lovely, lovely, lovely time." The dress over the shoulders, the hair upinned. Her brush plunged into the long masses of it, worried it like a lover.

"What's he to you?" George blurted out.

"Who? Jason?"

"Yes."

"Oh, don't be silly, George!" There was the lightest laugh. The mirror was half in shadow, obliquely lit by the lemon lamp. The gentle voice in the darkness. The gentle voice in the darkness. Recalled in that compelling moment, the bushes black by the timber house, grass and earth smells, the tangled voices of distant party—all his past but not forgotten grief over Nita crushed him now. He groaned with self-pity.

"I saw him," he accused. "I saw him kiss you."

Her brush hesitated against her hair.

"But that's nothing."

"I don't like it."

"Don't you?"

"No, I don't." He was stubborn.

107

"But I've had to watch you often enough at parties."

"That's different. We've all been there. I never took anyone outside."

She nodded. "Still—it's not much fun to watch your husband flattering other women all night."

"I'm not the only one. You've flirted around, too."

"I suppose I have. Yes. I suppose you're right. . . . I'm so tired, George. I'll just take a peep at Jeannie to see if she's right."

He heard her cross to the other bedroom on the light feet whose soles he had kissed only the night before. Recollection rushed like blood to his brain. He got out of bed and switched on the main light.

"Look, I won't have it," he said. "I won't be put off."

"Well, lower your voice," Alice argued coolly, returning to the room, "or you'll wake Jeannie." She closed the door behind her with a gentleness that made George frantic.

"Now answer me!" he ordered.

"What?"

"Oh, God! What's he to you?"

"I like him. He gives me fun. He makes me feel like a woman."

"I suppose I don't."

"Oh, George. Of course you do. Don't be so silly. But it's always pleasant to know someone else finds you attractive."

"How attractive?"

"What do you mean?"

"Has he made love to you?"

"He's kissed me."

"That isn't what I mean. Stop hedging. You know *exactly* what I mean. Has he . . ." George suddenly hesitated, frightened of what he was asking and terrified of the answer. Alice was regarding him steadily with her grey eyes neither cold nor warm, merely observant, the eyes of a fairy-tale character under a

108

spell. "Has he said he loves you?" He adjusted his mind consciously. Now he would never know. Nor did he wish to.

"Yes, he has."

"I see. And do you love him?"

"No. I like him but I don't love him.

The big lump swollen in George's throat would never go away now. He knew it. Years later he reminded himself of this scene and felt the hard unswallowed fact still stuck in his gullet.

"Tell me something, Lissie," he said, he begged. "You know all about me and Nita. How many men have you had?"

"You don't want to hear about it," she said, still standing by the dressing-table, still holding onto the mirror's frame. "You'd only think about it afterwards and worry. I know you."

"I want to know. Tell me. I don't care. I want to know."

She watched him there and a certain dislike she had always known about made her resolve on his punishment. And even when she said it he could not believe it!

He was so astounded that he couldn't move, although his cudgel heart battered insanely in its padded cell.

"Oh, my God!" he said at last. "You're joking."

"No. It's true. I didn't want to tell you."

"Tell me," he said. His ice-cold feet took him back to the bed where he lay sick against the deceptive comfort of pillows. "I want to hear the lot. Everything. Right from the beginning."

Alice's face was a long white oval above her loosely hanging blue gown. She sat at the end of the bed, her feet caught under her as a child might sit, and with a candour that could have been purposed cruelty looked straight into his murdered eyes.

"Go on," he prompted, his lips compressing on the last word as if it were some acrid little pill he must take to save himself. "Tell me."

And she did. Only her surprisingly innocent face remained intact, but for all that, despite every dull adventure she

109

recounted—and they were dull—her purity remained intact, too.

For a long time George doubted if he would ever get over her confession; but, learning to rationalize it and aware all the time of her genuine love for him, he managed to blur those images. They returned with acuteness to trouble him frequently the first year but less so in the second, until by the sixth when he was salving himself with an infidelity of his own, he justified his sin as reprisal and necessity for oblivion.

Better still, Mr Santry stopped calling.

In 1934 Melbourne celebrated its centenary. Schoolchildren received a medal on a patriotic ribbon. The medal depicted Batman and Fawkner defrauding the natives in a pleasantly social way. As if to perpetuate this, retailers all over Melbourne carried on similar defraudation. Pylons and bunting, welcome placards to Royalty, Little Henleys. Jeannie was not at school and did not receive a medal, but one of the children in the house next door let her hold hers for a minute while greed bulged out of her pop eyes.

"I want it," she stated at last.

"I only gave it for a lend," lank-haired Miss Hoffman said. "You can hold it a bit longer."

Jeannie ran off with its shrill guilt moistening her palm. Vi Hoffman roared after her, pigtails streaming straight behind, and pushed and pummelled until Alice walked into their screams and scratchings.

"Give it back," she insisted. "You're going somewhere special and there'll be no outing at all if you're naughty."

"I want it!" Jeannie shrieked.

"Well, you can't have it. It's not yours." Alice bent over the fat hand to pluck the fingers from their sweating treasure. Jeannie let fly a volley of sobs.

"We're gonna go to Luna Park, too," Violet added, unable

to leave it alone. "All the kids get a free ticket and we get free drink and everything." She caressed her medal with a dreamy finger.

At this Jeannie's screams became tortured. Her arms lashed out.

"Go away, bloody Vi!" she yelled. "Go away!"

Absence of razzle-dazzle and roller-coaster, of distorting mirrors, ghost-trains and wind-shafts.

They went instead to watch the long white ship coming into Port Phillip. The wind along Elwood Beach found the standing crowds with their eyeballs rolling like worlds across a vision of blue water, and stung them to watery loyalty. Jeannie took the memory of salt-bent scrub and hundreds of legs with her into adult limnings of the city as she found it fifteen years later. Phrases stuck to tongues all over town—"This is the village for a spot!" and "We dooks the dook!"—along with topical ribaldry that drunks and schoolchildren passed innocently around.

Somewhere special was Saturday, was the Botanic Gardens, was a starched white frock that stood out below blue sash, stiff as a tutu. Jeannie's tiny tight curls glistened. Her little pink parted lips glistened, too. She raced away from her mother across dream grass acres, hid behind flower-beds, drank tip-toe from fountains, smeared candy floss and toffee and ice-cream in a hideous compound.

Colonnades of doric and corinthian trees. Rococo summer-houses. Spanish Mission tea-rooms with impressionist *glacé* edifices. All along the Yarra small craft with flags, gay-girls in mid-Victorian dress, houseboats strung with coloured bulbs. In the distance the geography textbook view of the city with Anglican spires and leaves. Alice sat with her back against an elm and knitted a large shapeless jumper for George, while Jeannie, grass-streaked and pert, harassed a ball down the slope towards the river. Eventually the sun slid behind skyline

111

and crowds in the dusk moved to the water to watch the fireworks begin. Rockets curved red and orange splatter across Princes Bridge. A man (the Duke?) in coloured fireworks, jigged irresponsibly. Jeannie's open mouth whimpered pleasure. Darkness and lovers everywhere. The black air was shattered by laughter and the glow of fireworks hung pinkly over the town. Rain crackers. Smoke becoming mist. For shelter they crowded onto a white houseboat moored to the bank and the rain splashed gently, the fireworks still spluttered, the crowd still groaned its delight.

Jeannie hung over the side with dangling arm and stared at the dark river rising nearer and nearer as more people packed on. Treacly water. She wanted to dip in and trail fingers. Alice noticed the listing of the houseboat's deck with alarm and tried to push her way off again but the crowd pressed her tightly to the rail. A procession of lighted boats went by, their doubled lights streaking across the river. Suddenly, with a disgusting lurch as the crowd swung to the far side to glimpse the procession, the houseboat tipped crazily and the first black wavelets rushed across the decking.

The boat was keeling over.

The wave was the human one.

Bodies welded, massed into shapeless terror as the surge back towards the bank began. It was only seconds, but Jeannie, separated from the greedy clutch of her mother's hand, sobbed and sobbed as she was hoisted across the gap between shore and boat. In the flaring light from the still smouldering fires, her mother found her clasping her sticky rubber ball, glowing green, glowing purple, howling into this enormously indifferent world.

"There!" Alice said. "There! We'll go home." Uphill past the Shrine on the wet grass.

"I wanna sit down," Jeannie whined. "I wanna sit." But Alice dragged resolutely on the resisting arm.

112

"We can't stop, darling," she said. "And I can't possibly carry you. You're too big. You'll have to walk or we'll never get home."

Jeannie whined like a tiny car. Impatiently her mother lifted her up but could only manage to carry her some of the way down the long hill to St Kilda Road and the bridge. Heels caught in grass, skittered on paths. They snapped and smacked at each other, caught, clutched each other's hands and at last came up to the eastern approach of the bridge where crowds wedged in a gently heaving mass.

It took half an hour to cross.

All round, children wailed or had their terror borne shoulder high. Alice would have picked Jeannie up and sat her astride her own shoulders, but their arms were pinned to their sides as they swayed forward, held upright by the even and frightening pressure of many thousand bodies. Alice began counting the pylons on the bridge. They had been erected and decorated especially for the Duke's drive through the city. Fifteen minutes were ground small before the monster that the crowd now was, brought its stinking person opposite the middle one. At Alice's waist level Jeannie's terrified yellow profile lay a rimpled bas-relief against a massive-thighed man.

"Not even crying," Alice marvelled. "Absolutely not even crying."

Contradictory colourings troubled the grain of upturned faces, lamp towards lamp. Fabric of conversation or groan stretched into infinite weariness of propelled bodies, waddling legs, crushed chests, pinioned arms. The monster was silent for the main part. And gradually the city's glimmering flower received its swarm of bees. At eight-fifteen Alice and Jeannie staggered onto the packed safety zone to wait.

From a window five floors up, Lippman and Brewster surveyed the densely packed street.

"You know," George said thoughtfully, "I think Lissie's

113

probably somewhere in that mess. She wanted to give the kid a treat today."

Jeannie cried fitfully for two days afterwards and for several months only threats of a beating could induce her to enter either a lift or a crowded railway carriage. But George with his journalistic glands opened to full throttle executed a timely series of articles on crowd behaviour, crowd control, and famous crowds of history.

"Sweet coz!" Lippman said later as he marked down the week's edition for tabulation purposes. "You can weave 'em, pal!"

"What do you mean?" George demanded, affronted.

Lippman smiled grimly. "Those clichés. Journalistic fair-isle."

## [V]

THE PREDICTABILITY of living was what finally soured George.

Return to Sydney five years later found their house still steep-gabled, still bay-window-shingled, still with the cactus-plant tapping the glass, still passion-vined, still stone-walled. The path ran obliquely as before; as before the feijoa near the fire-heap needed lopping; as before grass scrambled into flower-beds. The only adventurous thing about it, he reflected bitterly, was that the place badly needed painting. Their tenants moved out, they moved in. The small rooms gave George a possessive little hug as he wandered from one to another—and he winced.

But the *Voice* had changed. There were dozens of stranger faces and allusions to foreign territories of experience. He took over his job as chief-of-staff with new-boy tremors that dissipated as the charm of his own room established his never reluctant egotism. Yet even this. . . . Ferries ran with only ten minute deviations from schedule, buses arrived like acts of God. Nine-till-six and nine-till-six and nine-till-six stretched out to a shuddering infinity that made him quake when he contemplated it. Blade-bone pies lost their domestic magic; confession no longer left him with that new-cleansed sensation. There were no sins!

The literary editor's stenographer was a short fair young woman, physically colourless, but kittenish in atonement and with a bitingly witty tongue that attracted a certain amount of amused male attention. When she joined the staff of the

*Voice* she was not long graduated from the University of Melbourne where she had taken an honours course in French and a classical interest in men ranging from one of the professorial staff to a high-school footballer who came to her for special coaching in matriculation subjects. "He was sweet as a nut!" she used to say to George when they had reached that point in their self-exchange at which they were prepared for almost any admission. That point was not reached as speedily as one might normally have expected between two people who were experts at dropping the social barriers between the sexes, for, during the first three years she worked on the *Voice*, she had been the mistress of the literary editor, a sad gentle poet whom she came gradually to hate. The geography of love is not vastly different from that of countries with tritely obvious similarities. But the lushest valley sates; the mind craves aridity and hard-noon baked spaces floating in thin light; and after a season that, too, wearies the heart demanding aspect of lake or bay.

Rees Morgan was a poet rather than a journalist. He wrote plays; he had published a novel that was unsuccessful enough to make him assured of its literary worth. All his life he dreamed childishly of reaching England, a sucker for the ivied turret, absurd pageantry, and, as he grew older, the cultural enticement of words like Wigmore, Covent Garden, Drury Lane. A spare time sonneteer who was prevented by one set-back after another from ever achieving his wish. He made absent-minded love to his secretary and sometimes confused her name with that of his wife. Both of them resented it.

A few months after Brewster returned from Melbourne, Morgan resigned. In a moment of pique he did it in the form of a triolet which he pasted beneath the glass top of his desk; gathered a few reference books that he crammed into his satchel; and went abruptly and successfully to a features and talks department in the national broadcasting commission.

The casual affaire with his stenographer tailed off into oblivescence on his part. You would have had to jerk him sharply to make him remember her name; while she recalled only too acutely the distraction in the eye as they ate together, the off-putting pat followed his impersonal demands on her body.

Brewster disliked her at first. Perhaps he disliked her at the last. But she fascinated him, it was true, with her voice so soft that the listener must suspend all mental errantries to discover in these near-whisperings an excruciatingly funny remark. George began to look forward to the few zestful half-flirtatious moments they would expend daily as he perched on the edge of her desk discussing week-end reviews, And there was more. Marie Schell ran a weekly column in a new Catholic monthly—the *Austral*.

It was the year of the Eucharistic Congress and the *Austral* was expanding publication and attempting to reach a wider public with secular articles by prominent laymen. George's friendship with Father Beckett had brought him a certain amount of notice in Church circles which he interpreted as a silent spiritual applause that was greatly pleasing—never did the definition "the participation of the laity in the apostolate of the hierarchy" have such significance for him as it did in these days. When Miss Schell asked tentatively for his help and this request was supported within days by a telephone call from the co-adjutor Bishop, the irresistibility of his moral and temporal obligations to God became apparent. Fortnightly, and catching the last ferry to the Hill by ever widening inches, George would accompany the literary editor's stenographer to a beer at the Journalists' Club, a spaghetti bar in Castlereagh Street and an evening's discussion of layout and material for each month's issue with Father Bernard O'Neil (One '1', Mr Brewster") at the magazine offices in Elizabeth Street or his presbytery in North Sydney. O doomed Brewster!

In unaware August Alice took Jeannie and two suitcases

away for a fortnight to the farm of a married younger sister at Cobbity. Like a visionary expecting nothing more than repetition of domestic chores even in holiday surroundings, she received her husband's farewell kiss, advised him on the whereabouts of essentials, and departed leaving him enough clean shirts and underwear for the fourteen days.

" 'bye nize Jeannie," George said fondly.

His daughter sucked her new front incisors and narrowed her green eyes at him.

"Be good, Dadda," she said with abominable precocity. Alice and George laughed proudly. Their link had been forged in brilliance.

Predictability and emptiness as well.

Within his house each morning he mooned about longfaced, incompetently frying eggs, muddling among the crockery, dragging back bed-clothes in a messy heap; but evening dressed itself up in the glamour of bachelor days when George had felt that merely by slipping a thin knife between the hours of seven and eight, he might prise open the mollusc onto heaven knows what wonders of pearl-sheen and pearl. Pseudo-bachelordom gave him one of those man-to-man glances encouraging him to drink and dine out—on one occasion he missed the last ferry and Hilbery bedded him down on the floor of his flat at the Cross. Thus, thus the joyous and inevitable progression towards an evening at the climax of the first week, when he and Miss Schell would confer on the next issue of the *Austral*.

He? Quivering celibate anticipation.

She? Amused derision.

"You are the most ignorant man I know," she had told him angrily one night as they argued a point of literary criticism. And he never forgot, even reminding her of the words twenty years later when he met her and her husband by chance in the cathedral precincts after Mass.

118

"Did I say that?" she laughed, not remembering. And her honey of a husband had grinned.

"She always was a bitch," he said amusedly to George, which mollified him sufficiently to invite them back for coffee.

At half past five their conjunction, a hearty hotch-potch of Georgian whimsy and Marian repartee, carried them off for ginny debate.

"I feel a bachelor urge towards the stuff," explained George. Priapus winked a salacious eye. "A friend of mine, a Mr Wine and Spirit Merchant, tells me there's only one other drink that comes anywhere near the gin you get in the States."

Marie tucked a skinny and gripping arm within his comfy tweed and smiled her thin-lipped bitter smile.

"I'm not asking what it is," she said. "I'm only interested in the beverage's aphrodisiac properties."

"Ah-ha!" George squeaked, drawing himself back in a gross pretence of horror, "Wicked girl!" But he was thrilled.

As they drank he examined her shrewdly. She was not a pretty woman. She was too mousey, too nondescript—until she opened her mouth. Five minutes after leaving her he could not have sketched in the outline of her face—except in a vague way as the shape of a lamp is concealed by the glow of its own light. Perhaps it was this very quality that began to fascinate him, for soon he found himself at work watching the opening door, waiting for the uncontrollable shout of laughter her witticisms called forth, seeking and accepting her opinions. But she regarded him as another coconut to be skittled in the shy. As with many really plain women, the need to attract men and prove to herself that she could, was almost obsessional, and in this case where the man displayed blatant interest in racy good looks, the brassiest surface, the challenge was piquant as well.

"How is the Great Australian Novel going?" Miss Schell's lips registered bitter amusement at her capitals.

Such succulent invitation! George wiped his lips carefully on his sixth clean handkerchief before launching his craft.

"It has sweep and range. I've followed the recipe of a writer pal of mine who swears it's a non-fail formula for the family saga type. You know, it moves from sheep-farming in the west to glossy professionalism in law in the big smoke through all kinds of setbacks of a geophysical kind. . . . It's the works— abortions and all. My dear wife is all aghast. 'What will the Bishop say?' she says."

"Nothing intelligent," murmured Miss Schell. George giggled. "Will you let me see some of it. I'd very much like to."

"Not yet. Not yet. The plan is immense but the present execution isn't worth looking at. Give me time. I must say, though, that the characters are starting to take possession of me."

He regarded the young woman opposite in disappointment, relating her to the vivid flashing Sophie who on paper became his ideal, was the deep delicious gulf into which he plunged with verbal abandon. In his mind she had grown to a reality garnered from a dozen women he knew; taking, like some plastic surgeon, eyes here, mouth there, limbs from another. This one gave intelligence; that—heart; such a one, wit and grace. Oh, it was an endless joyous pursuit where the inter-mingling of fantasy and exactness (old stickler George!) was a distracting mania that alone gave rhapsody to his day.

"But enough about me," he said falsely. "I swear that when I've finished a section that satisfies me, you shall see it. And I'll want your honest opinion, Marie, your honest one, mind, for nothing else is worth having."

Miss Schell concealed her irony in her glass and George launched into never-ending anecdotage in his gravelly voice. I cannot, thought Miss Schell, turn big adoring eyes to his, I cannot. But forced herself nevertheless and his insensitivity grasped hungrily at the recognition until her cruelty conquered her and she said "I'm hungry," aiming her statement at the climax of a story he had told her at least twice before.

"If you'll bear with me for one moment," he requested ponderously. "One moment," he repeated emphatically, not looking at the boredom in her eyes. Marie half-turned her small blonde head.

"Sometimes you're a living penance, Brewster."

He was terribly hurt then, rising fussily to his feet. But in the tipsy washing air of the taxi he reached over and squeezed her hand.

"Point to me!" Marie said to his obtuse ear.

"What? What was that?" he asked belatedly.

But she spun her real magic for him over dinner when, with a clinical zest that even her barely audible voice could not mask, she told him of her experiences with Morgan. George craved detail with such a fanaticism for marginalia that she indulged invention and had his blue eyes baby-bulging with a crazy mixture of lust and *naïveté*. They had never been so matey.

"You're bad for me, Marie," he said with relish.

Father O'Neil, waiting in the front parlour beneath polka-dot copies of French impressionism, put a marker in his breviary when the door-bell sounded and went out to let them in. As they stood under the greasy light of the porch he suspected they might not be sober, but was not offended, being at heart a man of genuine and immutable tolerance. He liked people, drunk or sober, discovering manifestations of the godhead in sinner or saint, and preferring, if the truth be known, the sinner, not because of his venality but because, despite it, warm and lovable characteristics would reveal themselves.

"Good evening," he said and with those words the cloak of automatic deference wrapped itself about George and coated his tongue.

121

"You make me ill," Marie complained later. "Can't you speak normally? O'Neil's a man. You're a man."

"He is also a priest," George reminded her with a pious sententiousness that made her shrug her shoulders in an angry rebuttal and despair.

A crop of wiry hair sprang up from O'Neil's sloping skull. He was older than George, powerfully built with wrestler's shoulders. Yet his face had a gentle abstraction and he smiled easily and warmly and laughed spontaneously and cleanly, showing a gap in his teeth without concern. On the other hand Brewster was so intent on irradiating spiritual warmth that its diffusion over so wide an area resulted rather in the impression of a man who was at heart cold. But now, at least, he was all eager gin-fuddled warmth as he ran a plump forefinger down an article he had run out on story-writing for teenage children, explaining polysyllabically and with prolixity. Sad Clown, thought Marie, watching him. Sad Clown. He once conducted a children's essay competition for the *Voice* in which a nostalgic and evocative line-drawing of a flour-daubed, rouge-reddened fellow was there to call forth whatever it might of magic from the child mind. Putting a hand filled with tenderness on George's arm she gave him a friendly squeeze as he monotoned on and on. O'Neil observed this with a patient smile and she explained without malice and much embarrassment,

"I'm practising charity."

"Indeed." O'Neil cocked his head to one side, the wise old parrot, but George had missed the byplay altogether. He was the saddest of sad clowns and she felt she would never think of him any other way.

The presbytery cupped its praying hands about a special stillness, an area of silence that held wildflowers of telephone or heavily-heeled boot. Doors let in the world and closed it out again, and, way down below them in the harbour,

122

some sea-borne craft wailed the calamity of voyaging to the night, moaning above the galactic reflections of the bridge. A duet of yawns.

"If you are too tired," suggested O'Neil, "why not take this bundle away with you and sort it at your leisure? There are still two or three weeks before it has to be ready. In any case I'm not too sure of the article on Fry. I'd like to include it, but I think it's a bit precious. Have a look, will you, George? And there's a two-part essay on the language problem for the Missionary that seems over-technical. You might be able to suggest a cut that won't offend Father Donkersbloom."

"I think I would rather take it. I'm pretty washed up tonight, Father. Baching you know, while dear Lissie is away. This so-called women's work is physically exhausting."

"You think Martha didn't choose the better part, then?"

"Certainly not. I always felt Mary was rather unfair."

"Oh, come, Brewster!" said Marie bitterly. "We all know that the truly feminine woman finds only joy in those repetitive back-breaking chores. They fulfil her. You men have been telling us that for centuries and so it must be right. Isn't that so, Father O'Neil?"

"It is too late for debate, my dear. And the subject is too delicate, I fear." He looked curiously at her strained plain face.

Unintending to detect a thing, he intercepted Brewster's obsessed eye. Like the cleverest doctor he could advance prognosis of sin before its symptoms became apparent.

"God bless you," he said, very gently to them both. "We'll meet as usual in a fortnight, if all is well. I can see you are both too tired to work this evening."

"Not tired. Tight." Marie pushed her thin hair away from the shallow lines of her pale face.

"Everything has its reason." The priest paused. "Would you care to visit the chapel with me, both of you, before you go?

There's time. You won't get a train for another twenty minutes, I think."

Unerringly, the girl thought. Unerringly. He hits on that pulsing nerve with blow after blow of sheer love. Oh, how cunning Christ was to turn the other cheek. The cruellest of revenges. Yet she followed him, while wanting to pull back, and tied a scarf over her hair as she knelt a row away from George in the small room filled with memories of Masses. I should be praying fiercely for strength of purpose, she told herself, when my whole intention is debased. But she said in her mind and automatically, "Help me, God, to resist my sin," and closed her eyes in the shadowy chancel, prickling with the consciousness of George's plump body only an aisle away and O'Neil aware of everything in her mind.

Out of courtesy they waited for the priest to genuflect first and wait in his sombre cassock beside the holy water font. Each action—the bending of the knee, the dipping of the finger, the sign of the Cross made her disgusted with her hypocrisy and impatient to be away.

"I shall walk with you to the gate," O'Neil said maddeningly accompanying them along the gravel. I shall shout my sin in your face, she thought, if you do not let us be. But they examined for a moment or two the south shore of the harbour with its neon gardens, inspected the bland night sky, checked their watches and parted finally near the gateway's camellia-tree with its saucers of milky bloom.

"Pray for me," O'Neil requested, one hand holding back an impetuous branch.

"I often wonder," George said as they walked over the railway bridge, "if they really mean that or if it's sheer habit."

"We can share a cab to Drummoyne," Marie said.

"Yes, of course. But do you think it is?"

"Is what?"

"Is habit?"

"Oh, God, I don't know!" snapped Miss Schell. "No, of course not. That's how they punish you. They really mean it. Just when one is prepared for damnation they fling you shockingly towards their special Paradise."

George drew a cab to the kerb as if he were playing a yoyo. In the back seat he looked at her, not having forgotten her talk at dinner. He was still excited by it. Her bitter profile shone in the lights of shopping arcades.

"I will make you coffee," she announced softly. "I have my mother tucked away in a corner of the house, but she isn't particularly well. And she's deaf, also."

He remained silent. Aspirations of a saintly kind warred with an incipient lust.

"Frightened?" mocked the other.

"Well, yes, I am." Now that the expected had moved into step beside him, reluctance born of a private pride in twelve years' fidelity wound threads about his feet.

"What of?" she asked. He ground out, obliterated her tedious coquetry in a kiss behind Bull Neck who drove impassively around a bus. And when the cab pulled up at a street corner near the water, he paid the man off and followed her into the darkened house through a side door. The premonitory shudder. Cool, brash Miss Schell flung light into living-room and kitchen and began making coffee.

"This is for you," she said. "You may measure out your life in coffee spoons, darling Brewster, but I measure mine in gin bottles. It's quicker." She cracked some ice into a glass and let it stand stewing at a slice of lemon.

"While I'm waiting," George said. And they drank two while the coffee boiled over.

At one o'clock George rolled his drunken body from easy chair and married conscience said aloud,

"Ring us a cab, honey."

Marie giggled. "Why not stay here, boss? It'll hold us both."

"Marie, I don't really want to, you know. I want to be faithful to Alice. There's a certain satisfaction in fidelity."

"Is she faithful to you?"

George examined the tipsy carpet, the tipsy curtains, the tipsy line of bookshelves. Uncertainly they stood still and asked him the same question. Mournfully his head moved sideways.

"I cannot discuss it," he managed at last. "No gentleman ever discusses his wife in that way."

"Well, go on, George," she said prettily, but he missed the point entirely and repeated his words.

She perched her thin behind on his fat knees, hooked one finger in his ear and smiled casually.

"We musn't," George protested. "You know we musn't." He lifted her off and put her back from him reluctantly; but Marie slitted her pale eyes at him and methodically began taking off her clothes. She let them drop to the carpet at her feet, watching him all the time through unsmiling narrow lids. Somewhere a clock raced like a pulse. In a dim muffled bedroom age coughed into deafened pillow, groaned in its sleep at the daughter's nakedness.

"Of course we musn't," she said.

Father O'Neil dreaded confessions, endured them with such agonies of scruple and pain he was tempted to ask the bishop if he could be relieved of parish work for a time and given administrative duties at the cathedral. There was personal penance for him in sitting in the dusty twilight, the semi-grey candle-smelling dimness of the confessional, and hearing over and over between the harsh grating of the slide the same terrible, not-terrible-at-all sins of impurity and anger and dishonesty and malice that affect all human beings. Sometimes, lulled into absent-mindedness by the monotonous whisperings of the struggling soul on the other side, he would not hear and then fret scrupulously that he had not given the exact advice suited to that burdened heart.

Twice a month the children poured in driver-ant streams from the parish school and then there was even greater weariness in store as they hesitated and stammered through introductory prayers and admissions of pettiness that would have wearied an archangel. But that was not so bad as those times on Saturday evening when, staggered by his own frailties at the end of a week, he was forced through charity to endure the insistence of others. The bishop ordered him down the coast to a retreat house for a month and he came back refreshed and concluded that that was all he needed—occasional relief from the world—and was ashamed.

He was sent to a neighbouring parish once to take charge when the parish priest became ill. On Saturday evening at seven he strolled across to the church, vested himself, and went down the south aisle to the confessional Father Gollan used. There was a group of men and women kneeling along the side waiting for him, but according to his habit he walked past quickly without looking at them, sat down briskly in the cubicle and drew back the partition. Slowly they came, poured out their nauseating spotted troubles and departed with his blessing.

Then accidentally and horribly the voice beside his ear with its unmistakable gravelly tones intruded beyond his deliberate impersonality, broke aside anonymity, and he found to his embarrassment he was listening to George Brewster sweating through a variety of fleshly weaknesses. O'Neil had never had this moment before, that of complete certain recognition, and it was something he had always dreaded. He closed his eyes that he might not be tempted to turn by even a hair's breadth towards this supplicant. He kept his hand pressed to his face so that he too might remain anonymous and barely shifted it as he made the sign of the Cross during the words of absolution.

127

"Six Hail Marys," he said in a voice not his own. "Pray for me." He drew the partition gently between them.

In the darkness he drew a handkerchief from the sleeve of his soutane and mopped his face, praying to his God that he would forget as automatically as he always did. Then he drew the partition on the other side.

By some quirk of reaction, a gesture of defence, he found himself looking straight into the face of the next penitent. It was Marie Schell, pallid and unreal in this diffused light.

There was irresolution then that seemed to draw itself out over centuries. The Ash Wednesday sinners dragged themselves along church paths on their knees. One agonizing pace after another.

"Oh, God," she whispered. "Is it you?"

And rose and vanished.

At nine the straggling queue came to an end. O'Neil left the confessional and went down the church to the communion rail. He knelt—unsure what he was praying for, or for whom. He even doubted whether he had the right to pray for the confusion of what he heard under confessional seal. Ikons remained gravely impassive. He sneezed once or twice and was pleased he was sufficiently aware of his needs to realize he had a cold coming on. He went to the sanctuary lamp and checked the wick and oil; he straightened the altar cloth and snipped a weary bud from a flower. These deliberate devices were not such potent thought salvers as he had imagined. In the candle and lily glimmer he sighed, switched off the main light and stood for a moment to watch the moonlight tremble through the stained glass—rose, wine-stained, flavid, blue.

Their spasmodic relationship continued for about two years. There were times when he tried to resist her but went back again and again. He could not have explained why he did, for her body filled him with disgust even as it excited him. They

128

would go for weeks, months, without the need for each other, resolving for the sake of conscience to keep apart, until a hurricane of want flung them at each other like mannikins and as brutally ripped them apart stunned and regretful. Sometimes she would ring him when he had to work back in the evening and his angry refusal amused her greatly.

"You'll come," she would say, laughing softly into the telephone. And he would go. Creeping from her house to lie to his wife, the stench of his behaviour would rise all about him; and on those calculated evenings of husky winter when he had to encounter her clear suppertime eye, he often wished he were dead. He was not made to lie. He did not do it easily or well, but eventually gained a certain facility at pitching cock-and-bull tales about the office that sounded plausible enough.

Marie, strange to say, fell in love with him after a fashion and for a time. She was not aware of the fact until she discovered herself one evening putting her lank ashen hair into curlers and pressing her unsmart clothing with more care. Cynically she stood off and laughed. But it was there, gnawing its ugly crab inside her, this creeping disease called love.

Casualness in George impelled it on its course also, and though she might despise herself she could not repress the jealousy that burnt her when she observed his flickering orbs pinning down a junior typist or overheard his unctuous and heavy-handed compliments.

"Flattery from Brewster," she confessed to Hilbery, "is like being slugged by a hammer. God spare us!"

During the last weeks of August in 1939 the *Voice* was in turmoil with special editions; working schedules were topsy-turvy; during all this upheaval it could have been a gala time for George but he was beginning to tire of the situation. Adultery is one thing. When the mistress falls in love, it is another. Love puts out the tentacles of the wife, and to be embraced by two sea-creatures at once is insupportable. He volunteered to go to Brisbane during the last month of that year to write a confidential report on training camps in southern Queensland, hoping that the two or three weeks in which he was away might serve to separate them. Always a fearful man, he was terrified that office talk might be growing. Often he would ask himself if it were really the pull of his Faith that sponsored reluctance. He did not know. But one embarrassment piled up after another. Each occasion of sin meant confession and the resolution of not sinning again.

Brewster had no conception of the military mind although he had once been obsessively interested in the citizens' militia. An examination failure prevented his progressing to commissioned ranks—and he could simply never see himself in the rôle of a private. He did not particularly admire officer class, but what it stood for sparked off snobbish approval, for he had the early underprivileged man's adulation for the privileged.

"I have always been able to get people to do what I want without raising my voice," he used to say. It was true, largely because as he grew older he was maturing as a bore. Quick-fleeing obedience had its attractions for the underling about to be transfixed by a story. But the monumental dullness of the military man planted in him a sense of genial superiority that overcame any sensitivity he might have had about appearing in their company out of uniform.

In Brisbane he stayed at the best hotel, which cringed under the shattering hourly blows of the town-hall clock. He spent the first week travelling hundreds of miles in staff cars and jeeps, wrote his articles in the second, and got them away to the features editor with a chummy note. Rubbing his plump hands together, Mr Brewster, now welcome at two messes and a familiar figure in three city bars, settled down to a week's holiday with a feeling of virtue. Daily he wrote to Alice—he was certain he loved her. He drank far too much whisky, stayed up far too late and spilled millions of words.

One musky sub-tropical evening with the chief reporter from one of the city's dailies and two girls they had picked up in a lounge at the bottom end of George Street, he was sufficiently drunk and exhilarated to be unfaithful to Alice in the back of a car. Remorse next morning was unbearable and rendered more hideous by the heart-stopping appearance of Marie Schell who had been dragged north in the compulsive way of love by an intensity of feeling that reason told her was misplaced.

The knife had barely touched the steak when her hand touched his shoulder to accustomed guilt. Anger was the first impulse. Flattery came a bad second.

"Surprised?" she asked.

"You mean astonished," he corrected acidly. "This is very stupid of you, Marie. I'm astounded that a woman of your intelligence could act like this. Do you want to cause me trouble?"

Marie bit her thin lip. Cause him trouble. Him, him, him, him, him. There was no thought in his piddle-puddling fornicating mind for anything but him and she knew it and hated herself for this insanity that drove her in spite of herself towards this suddenly prim-pursed forty-year-old face withdrawn into a chilly indignation.

"One thing about you, Brewster," she said, unable to stop herself, "you're so anxious to avoid trouble you don't give a tiny hoot about anyone's feelings."

"If you're going to argue . . ." he said, placing his knife and fork together. The threat, the action begun. She remembered he often said that he and his wife never had a cross word. Now she knew how. . . . She added quickly, "Oh, don't be silly and stuffy. You've got a bloody great hangover. Drink your coffee and try to be nice to me."

131

She sat down and put her narrow elbows on the table.

"When did you get here?" he asked with an effort, waiting while a waitress took her order.

Her unpainted face looked him over.

"Last night."

"What on, for heaven's sake?"

"I wangled a lift on a plane with a press pass. The pilot is in love with an old boyfriend of mine. I brought pressure to bear!"

George had to laugh.

"That's better," she said. "Now say you're glad to see me."

"I'm not. Not really. Things are complicated enough without your turning up."

"What now?" The waitress put her breakfast in front of her, the boarding-house still-life.

George eyed her as she pushed through the swinging doors.

"Pretty girl."

Marie blinked rapidly. "What has complicated your life, dear Brewster? Women?"

He gave her his Candid Look. "That's just it."

Her thin heart in her thin body beat thinly and fast.

"Well?" she asked. Her lower teeth clinked against her cup. She watched the level of the liquid tip towards her in an enormous tar lake.

"I've been unfaithful to Lissie," he confessed, still with that same staged seriousness that was not really staged but appeared too sincere to be true. Marie laughed violently.

"You should worry!" she exclaimed. "When?"

"Last night."

"Young?"

"Yes."

"How young?"

"Nineteen."

132

"Pretty?"

"Delicious."

"I don't want to hear any more," she said. "Brewster, the man who can't even be faithful to his mistress." And on the last word rose and walked out, away from the breakfast congealing on its plate. A lift carried her agony two floors up. Her room took her in to a privacy where she could chew at and worry and tear her hurt over and over until it became as flavourless as gum. Her discardment was worse than losing every garment she had on and she sought over and over a means for his humiliation until she was almost crazed with frustration. "Even God would be flat out," she reflected wryly.

Yet when he came down to dinner she was there before him and through the prismatic colours of mingled liquor and tears he concocted a visionary's image of her green silk trapped behind striations of flowers moving in the fan-draught.

"Hello, nize Marie," he said.

She had made her decisions. "I am not going to ask you what you did all day. You ask me."

"What did you do with yourself?" he asked obediently. He had a trick of immediately responding to commands from women that melted their resolutions and private theories about him.

"I offered myself as a camp follower and got knocked back."

"That's the wittiest thing you've said all day," George said beaming.

Towards the end of the meal, however, reminded perhaps of his indiscretion by the vision of a pink *bombe* fantastic with meringue ampersands that had been set before him, he raised his eyes from this kitchen harlot and said, almost weeping,

"Shall I tell Liss?"

"Tell Liss what?"

"You know," he said, pleading for pity.

133

She stared so long at him he began eating clumsily and dropped a spoonful on the leg of his trousers.

"No," she said deliberately, "No. Why should you?"

"It's more honest."

"Then what about us?"

"That's different."

"How?"

"Well, Lissie knows you. She has met you. You have been to our home. It would be terribly damaging to her self-respect if she knew about you. That's what makes it different."

"Oh, nonsense, George. Think of her. Think of someone for God's sake. All you're interested in is heaving the burden off your conscience. You really don't give a tuppenny damn about how she will feel, do you?"

He was outraged.

"Not care about my Lissie! How can you suggest that? How dare you! I care about her more than anything else in the world, including you, my dear Marie."

"If you do, *if* you do, then don't tell her," Marie repeated firmly. "Oh, don't let's squabble, George. I've got to go back the day after tomorrow. I took three days' sick leave."

"Have you?" He brightened. But she tried not to see the light on his face.

After he had gone to bed that night, she opened his door and went in, treading softly on the carpet to where she could see his big humped figure coiled. As her hand moved across his face he jerked awake and sat up, blinking his fright back until he realized her whispered assurances were fact. He was tired; his guilt sang all over his breathing body.

"How did you get in?" he whispered.

"I swapped your key, baby, with mine. You were too tight to notice all that jiggerypook at the door when I left you."

"Clever bitch," he hissed. "But do go away, there's a good girl. We can't here. It might cause trouble."

"Nonsense." She laughed. "There's nothing more impersonal than the big expensive pub. They're made for this sort of thing." But when he repeated his words with such urgency and pleading, she hesitated and sat on the edge of his bed, unsure what to do next. Here she made a mistake. She began to argue.

"You're joking!"

"No, I'm not. Do go, Marie. Please."

"You can't mean this," she insisted. His face, cheese pale in the dark, sulked and scowled. She put a finger on his bushy eyebrows and rubbed them the wrong way. "Oh, George, I've come to Brisbane specially to be with you. Surely you don't mean it."

"I'll be brutal with you, Marie. You make me brutal. I've come to be away from you, can't you see? I cannot take this constant tugging at my conscience. It's driving me mad. I think we ought to end it all."

His face hardened behind his protest. Along the corridor a door clicked, a cistern flushed, a lift ground down towards the gladioli, the servicemen and the night clerk.

"Please," he said to her martyred face. "I don't want to get cross. But you must go. Let's make an end of it now. There's nothing to prevent our being the good pals we've always been. But let's discuss it in the morning. This is far too dangerous. Do be careful leaving, there's a good girl. It would be terrible if you were seen."

Caution flew out of the cote and she began to shout. They were fearful harsh sounds from one who hardly ever raised her voice. Using his hands like silencers he gripped and squeezed the flimsy brachial muscle of her upper arm, halted her long enough for her to hear him say,

"Shut up and get out, Marie, or I'll ring and have you put out if you don't stop making this bloody scene."

Her eye captured the movement of his hand, fat, pawing, hateful hand, to the phone and she saw him begin to claw it

135

from its cradle. The heart's canker slipped sideways, the scuttling crab motion took it burrowing until it was hidden. Without a word she left the room and did not see him again before she returned to Sydney.

His soul forced the words through his lips when he returned home. He loomed over her charmingly submissive figure—seen forever, reader, in blue cotton garments of small girl simplicity—tucked up on a tapestry chair. His hand held a glass of Scotch to steady him. Hers darned a sock. He spared himself nothing but told her the tale of his defection from start to finish while she cried and cried.

"I feel better now," he said. "I had to tell you, Lissie. I couldn't have gone round not telling you."

But she still wept. Nothing could calm those small heaving wings, not even the fullest, the deepest protestations of love. Nothing, she told him, would ever be quite the same. He assured her that it would, that if anything his love for her was greater than ever. But her simplicity could only measure love in the conventional terms of restraint and denial. What astounded her husband more than anything was not the intensity of the pain his wife endured which, he was sure, would fade in time, but the sudden sharp admonishment of the priest to whom he confessed.

"Can't you see," said the unknown but irritable voice behind the netting partition, "that telling her was an even worse thing —a complete lack of charity? You administered an absolutely unnecessary hurt."

George bowed his head in the missal-velvet wax-scented air. Leaving the confessional, he went to kneel in front of the side altar of the Virgin where he prayed a long time. Never before had it been suggested to him that he was selfish. Candle flicker duplicated and reduplicated on brass candelabra; genuflections burrowed the heavy air; the warm, the homely, the wonderfully homely red glow from sacristy lamp formed his resolution of sinlessness. The fleshy shutters of his eyes prickled with sorrow. Behind him the brown cathedral dusk vanished in gothic silences and suggestions of heaven or hell where the human cough exploded uncannily by the eastern door letting in for five garnish seconds the circus sounds of traffic.

Benediction began. The tumbling Latin broke its sounding tides in every secret place in his heart. Although for years he had attempted to convince himself that his religion was an intellectual argument and his acceptance thus based, this romantic simply revered intellectualism with the swash-buckling allegiance of a buccaneer. Incense and stained glass coupled with logical progressions of Gregorian chant can be irresistible. Resolutions formed in this climate may still fulfil their purpose.

Unfortunately with George elation of heart that came with new-found purity of impulse, that wild lovely thing that took him home on the ferry across the wet dark harbour, did not survive. It was impossible for him to avoid Marie. He saw her constantly on the *Voice*, was trapped in lifts of idiot hoity-toity silence, in cold exchanges at Father O'Neil's presbytery. Eventually the immaturity of this reduced Marie one day to crazy laughter, rocking backwards and forwards on her chair like senile gammer—and from then on their relationship renewed itself with a toffee-twist queerness.

Marie's thin hungry body grazed all over private pastures of revenge where Brewster, maudlin and disgustingly suppliant, was rejected in a radio serial climax. The picture caused her laughter but its idea persisted and evolved as an unconscious indifference in her attitude to him that was a spur to his desire. There should have been more fuss, he puzzled. She should have begged, chased, harried, laid traps. Was his charm failing? He had to admit she had taught him a lot. He had begun reading in history and *belles lettres*, discovering he had, after all, a flair for criticism he had not suspected. Since Morgan had left he had often done special reviews and was hoping that he would soon be in charge of the books page entirely. Her wit had glacial attraction that was glitteringly distant; her intelligence still dazzled him. Gradually he wanted her back.

Marie was determined to have him, too, but out of hate, not love, and it was only a matter of time before the patchy affair was resumed.

Once—only once?—he offended her unpardonably.

He was dictating a feature for the Saturday magazine and observing, as he dictated, the meagre, almost white, straight hair falling forward over her pale bony cheeks. Her delicate freckled blonde wrists flipped backwards and forwards across the typer.

"You're not at all the sort of woman to have an affair with," he said thoughtfully during a pause while she caught up with him. "Not at all."

"Oh." Her colourless lashes flickered slightly but remained lowered as she completed the sentence. "Why is that?"

"Oh, you know," George said, laughing awkwardly. "Other women always have mascara and gorgeous clothes and—oh, the works!" He was utterly naïve.

Slowly Miss Schell rose from her chair and came over to him, her eyes gleaming into his blood-shot blue woman-chasing ones.

"Have they?" she said softly. And before he could anticipate it, had slapped his face so hard her hand rang.

Yet even after this he was not cured. All his life he had a convenient blind-spot about the hurts he dealt out and even when the victim harped on it and dragged the wounded part under his good eye, he would refuse to admit it. "You're trying to hurt me by doing this," he would say pettishly. "I simply will not fight. I hate fighting." In time this gentleness, which he proclaimed *ex cathedra*, became an article of faith in his

138

mind, so a thousand slaps would have failed to ram the truth home on that thick skin. Marie's only joy now was to have him hankering after her special brand of comfort. Once, to punish him, she left down his back a long deep scratch she made with her toenail which she had sharpened to a point. It festered and was a dreadful embarrassment at home. He should have known by this that she at least had been cured.

Passion spaced can become "crystallized," as Stendhal suggests; yet it can also lose zest. He kept telling himself that it was she who used him; he came to believe this. There he would have a whipping-post for the final separation. The girl was getting bored, too. She was twenty-five now and the aimlessness of the relationship shone its torch on desert patches in conversation, on routine in their love-making. Hatred is more tiring than love. She was tired of his stories, tired of his egotism, tired of his ladies' man unctuousness and tired of his stinginess. Not that she was grasping, but she was female enough to wish for an occasional application of love in a formal sense—a flower, a scarf, a handkerchief. The gesture betraying personal concern. He had the habit of passing shop windows with her, goggling at the pretties and saying:

"You know I wish I could be buying that for you." And to her instant protest he would persist with, "You do believe that, don't you?"

At first she had been deeply touched and allowed her confusion to reply, "Please. You mustn't talk like that, George." But when he insisted upon unpacking on the office desk at Christmas or Easter fripperies he had bought for his wife and daughter and had said, "You know, Marie, all the time I was buying them I wished I were getting them for you," she became so angry at a stinginess which he tried to conceal by a sanctimonious subscribing to appearances, that she pulled him up with a curt,

"Well, bud, what's stopping you?"

139

His outraged face had swung a slow arc of disgust and prudishness upon her, the nasty little gold-digger. His finest sensibilities were outraged and he rewrapped his family gifts prissily with his mouth tucked in at the corners. When they parted finally he often tried to tell himself she really had been rather grasping—but he knew it wasn't true. Still, he had given her a couple of books (two, said his accurate angel), and if they had been review copies, well, Marie had never known! In fact, no one had ever been less demanding than she in the normal way of women with men, although perhaps emotionally she had worried too close to the bone.

Sometime in the beginning of 1940 she met a virile greaser called Larry Dickinson, who gnawed his way through night school with the persistence of a mouse through cheese and managed to chew himself a niche as a trade union organizer. Some antithesis was the attraction. He used to wait for her in the vestibule of the *Voice* or on the steps outside. One evening as Marie came down with George she stopped for a few words with her companion before she noticed him standing beside the picture case in the front of the building. Rowers and beach girls and anglers and week-end brides all smirked back triumphantly at his gaunt young features. Slouching, he burrowed his hands into his pockets. The open neck of his shirt framed tanned skin sprouting masses of black hair. He was coatless. She glanced at the double-breasted paragon beside her, hanky peeking ever so perkily from left-hand breast pocket, paunch swelling robustly under a hand-woven tweed. Their eyes will prove each other quickly thus, she thought. And was right in only one instance, however for Dickinson did not aim at personal beauty in himself and his own especial bitterness of feature with its intelligent ironic mouth should have driven a first truth home ineradicably. But George perceived only those external attributes—the down-bitten nails, the roughly combed hair, anger and insolence and pride—all things that could be

140

loutishness. His own urbanity spread like wall-to-wall carpet on which Larry Dickinson wanted most urgently to stamp with mud-caked boots. But he restrained his feelings and presently was struggling with smalltalk and then listening to the other man in full anecdote while Marie stared between them at the unending five o'clock surf of civil servants and office girls and private enterprise boys, sharp cards with a dame in each glinting orb.

Next day George plucked her sleeve as she went past him in the corridor on her way to the features room.

"New boyfriend?"

"Yes, Mister Brewster, sir."

"Oh." His lips held the vowel bubble and then blew it away. It made no impact. "Serious?"

"Now, that is an interesting word." Marie inspected him with her narrow fair head on one insolent side. "Do you mean cornily—'marriage'? Or do you mean 'sincerity'? When you talk about our being serious, I mean."

"I'm very corny. I'm stuck all through with barbs like that," he replied abjectly, sulking for a minute like a child. "But yes, I suppose I did mean marriage. You know I would never question your sincerity for a minute, Marie."

"Marriage is intended. How about that, Mister Brewster?"

He was jolted horribly. He fiddled with his chin, grunting about for words like truffles. Finally,

"Does he know about me?" his ego asked hopefully.

Marie abstracted this particular picture of him, frizzy-haired, plonk-handsome, self-involved forty-year-old, already bagging heavily below the eyes, and pressed it with sardonic tenderness into a mental folder.

"Now, why?" she asked. "Why should he?"

"No reason really," George said, "except it seems more open."

"We've had this before, haven't we?"

141

He shrugged. "I suppose so."

She wouldn't let it go. "There goes that masochist in you longing to inflict pain on yourself and muck up others in the process. You remind me of an old aunt of mine who used to insist on doing her Christian duty no matter who got hurt."

"Oh, that's good!" He repeated the phrase "no matter who got hurt" after her in an absent-minded manner and walked off equally abstractedly. The chief sub poked his narrow face around a door and called him, but George in his preserving armour of introspection practically brushed him as he went down the corridor to his room. Remembering the priest's words before the *absolvo te . . .* and now this. Did charity couple with dishonesty? He did not think so. But concealment with no reason for revelation—or repression of unnecessary facts, rather—that was it! Mr Brewster, master of the well-turned phrase, held on to it: repression of unnecessary facts.

Turning ponderously in the corridor he went back again to the feature-writers' room and found her sitting on Hilbery's table roaring with laughter. But he walked straight up to them and with the sincerity he knew to be so dramatic, said, looking her full in the eye,

"Thank you, thank you. You were quite right."

MAKING WHOOPEE, the party opened up its yellow screaming throat on the night.

It was unexpectedly raucous in the dumb dark where Brewster and Hilbery, staggering a little along the Darling Point Road, came on the hilarity and then the light carved into shapes as the bodies crossed and recrossed the jazz. They hesitated in the doorway of the flat waiting for the drunken cries of recognition, and there was the rush of familiar, unfamiliar, interested, uninterested faces turning towards, away, using the better profile, the lost islands of phrase and story. George, alone, as Hilbery, seized by a screeching blonde bonhomie, was rushed to the drink table, searched with sweet expectation about the room. That bright magnetic eye! Gantry, drunk and victorious with publication flush, was explaining to a circle of six the full measure of his talent and the worth of his new novel. Envious George saw behind him Marie Schell waving to catch his attention, but he deliberately looked away and she remarked softly to her companion,

"He doesn't know me with my clothes on!"

At the end of the room, disposed with artistic foresight against a curtain of scarlet, there leaned a beautiful shingled creature who swirled the gin in the bottom of her glass dedicatedly. An ice sliver whisper-thin rocked in the storm. Waves of gin crashed in the glass and in her mind, obliterated sense as she heard the first idiotic cliché and looked up. Anticipatorily his tongue was licking his lips.

143

"Hello, honey!" he said. "Where have you been all my life?"

Her luscious mouth attempted a smile but liquor twisted it awry and her head shook pityingly at herself.

"Waiting for you, honey!" she said.

He was tone deaf to mundanity. Ravished.

"Allow me." He took her glass with assurance of gesture that would have made refusal discourteous. "I'll get you another drink."

"Uh-huh."

"Gin again?"

But she did not answer. Her smile was a rich and drunken affirmative. When he returned, two men had moved in, ogling her with their officers' pips, leaning above her dark and beautiful head with a familiarity that George recognized immediately and resented. Waiter-straight, he held his two glasses. Between khaki her carmine smile reached out to stroke him lasciviously and draw him closer.

"Thank you, darling," she said.

Flamboyancy of their conjunction sent a crescendo rush of excitement through his senses so that he regarded her with an open lust that would have moved an onlooker to pity. Across the room, sifting salted peanuts onto a newly engaged palm, Marie Schell watched him amusedly.

"Look!" she whispered to Larry Dickinson. "Wet flong!"

The glittering unconcealed desire, the recognition, strip one down to the soul. That argument was metaphysically spurious yet attractive enough to present itself instantly to George, leaning through the flirtatious webs of years as the other men drifted away. The unambiguous design they were about to create was perceived with shocking immediacy that should have taken each by the throat yet affected only the one who bent closer and inquired of her affirming eyelids,

"But isn't this marvellous? Isn't this absolutely and unutterably marvellous?"

144

"Are you married?" she asked starkly. Only the huskiness of her voice pardoned such a *gaffe*. He was angry and examined the possibilities of a lie.

"Yes," he admitted after a tiny hesitation. "But don't let's talk about it. Are you?"

She nodded giddily at a group behind him.

"That one, honey. That nice, tall, skinny one. That's Pete. Darling Pete. Hi, Pete!" Giggling, she flapped the air with a spare hand. "What d'ya know?" she complained. "He won't look."

His sick intelligent face leaned back on the length of Gantry's voice, resisting the pull. He was hollow chested, his ears were prominent. At a glance, what in God's name did she see in him?

"He's gentle and unaggressive," the rich voice explained defensively.

"But I didn't . . ."

"That's all right." When she smiled, the curve of her mouth broke his heart. "I thought I'd get in first."

Mr Brewster laughed at the perceptive darling. His false teeth dropped and he hoped she hadn't noticed. He ran his thick tongue over the front of the upper set, pursing his lips, and longed to tell her all about himself.

"I'm George Brewster," he said in his deepest voice. "Am I allowed to know your name, or will it spoil the magic?" The ponderous flirt!

"It could." She examined her drink. "But we'll make more magic, won't we?"

"Oh, lots more. This is only the beginning."

"Well, it's Nancy Reardon, but call me Pat. Everyone calls me Pat."

"Pat," grumbled father bear, to please her and himself. "But Nancy is infinitely better. Shall I tell you why?"

"Tell."

145

"You're the girl I've been writing about for a year. The girl of my book. Sophie, actually. But it's the best possible magic, the extra astral most libanophorous magic of all time." He wet his lips with Scotch and looked hard at her, demanding approval.

Smile lit smile. It was unbearable, really, but reticence does not usually breed love. Desire and need are two such different episodes and here was only a surprise monolith of lust flung up amongst the banal weekly titillating verbal encounters he allowed himself with lady columnists, junior stenographers and copy girls, the sexual prerogative that was, he and his drinking buddies assured themselves, a distinction—the affirming tick beside the manhood.

"You write?"

"This is in my free time. I'm a journalist. But this novel has become part of my life. The characters are as real—more real now—as you are standing there so charmingly. You see,"—he bent till his hair petals mingled with her sleek locks—"that is what is so supremely magical and marvellous. You *are* Sophie, the central character. You even look the same. Beautiful."

"You pretty man," she said.

They sipped, their eyes glued to each other.

"I'm not very good at parties," the full lips pronounced after a while. "I don't know any of the arty flap."

"Don't you?" But he was charmed. "Let me educate you." His reactions could always be guessed at two platitudes away. "But seriously—Nancy—seriously, why haven't we met before if you know all these people?"

"I don't really know them, darling. Pete knows them. But we've been in Melbourne, and his firm transferred him back last month. Just before Pearl Harbour. He's gonna fight them single-handed."

She swayed gloriously close and he placed an instantly alert hand under her elbow.

146

"Would you like to sit outside for a little?" asked solicitous George, letting his cheek catch the reply from her smiling mouth.

"Darling!" Behind him Marie's voice etched the word with delicate acidulousness. "Darling, you remember Larry. Larry, you've met George Brewster, haven't you? George is my ex—er—ex-lover."

Indignation wound him up like a toy, but when he looked about they were all laughing at him and although this was something he could not tolerate, he forced a mask of genial endurance onto his features. Marie, blonder and plainer than ever and more dangerous because of that, was wearing a dress and a smile, neither of which quite fitted.

"You dreadful girl!" George exclaimed doggishly. "Taking away my honour."

Marie's eyes narrowed behind their curtains of near-white lashes, and, tucking her arm through Dickinson's, she leant heavily, awkwardly, against him.

"Darling, that's unfair," she whispered. "I never rob the poor."

Dickinson laughed so loudly he choked and had to be banged vigorously between his padded shoulders as he coughed and spluttered into his drink.

"You're well up to form, Marie," George hissed back maliciously during the racket. But the young woman merely looked sideways at him and lifted one thin shoulder. Mrs Reardon nodded absently.

"You two, don't you like each other?"

"Of course," George protested quickly, hoping to forestall Marie's spite. "She's a brilliant woman. Mind like a man."

"God!" Marie murmured to the room at large with her white face set in an ironical agony. "That's a compliment if ever there were one."

But it was lost, a wrinkle of discontent under the sweep of

147

introduction that included in its wavering perimeter, Hilbery, returned with a thirty-year-old blonde called Hope who was gay gay gay in a permanently hysterical way, and who flung herself first on Dickinson, and then on George, kissing them with the precision and emotion of a woodpecker.

"*The* most marvellous abstractionist and all in muted reds."

"Who?"

"—never another colour. Remarkable really. What vigour! What interpretation and—" a brief impression of mouth to mouth—("John darling! Really!")—

"*Who?*"

"—what moving sensibility." She gave the open mouthed laugh of the society hostess, the professional warmth that is nothing but coldness.

"Lancaster, of course."

"Lancaster!" Their wonder all echoed the syllables.

She confirmed her statement by repeating the name and blowing a featherdown kiss into the air.

"The marvel has won a scholarship to Italy. That's what I adore about his work—all that *personal* evidence of the class struggle—the tensions, the conflict in his design."

George nodded wisely. He knew as little about art as he knew about music, but he was aware of how to handle a conversation that threatened to move beyond his interests. Adroitly he cornered a word with aplomb and tossed it like a pancake. It came down as a long and doughy anecdote.

"Mother of god," murmured Marie to Mr Dickinson, and yawned openly into George's tubby face.

"You know, Brewster," she remarked, "Shaw's comment on women fits you to a tee. If they're beautiful you can look at them all night. If they're witty you can listen to them all night, but if they're dull, there's only one thing to do."

Hope screamed with laughter. She adored malice.

"He doesn't, does he? You don't, do you, George? Ooooh,

148

the agony of it for you! You'd have to go to confession. Imagine!"

"You've misquoted, Marie," George said, ignoring Hope who had placed a tentacle around his waist. "The word was 'ugly' not 'dull.' Now why on earth would you change it, I wonder?" he asked viciously. "*Some*times I listened to you."

Yet he was not enjoying his victory; for, although he was a selfish man, he was not an absolutely cruel one, and the sight of Marie wincing had a back-lash flick to it. Mrs Reardon's beautiful face was still turned to his, her lips parted in amusement that charged him with social vigour. He gave the buck-toothed smile that pandered to the maternal glands.

"The trouble is, we all need another drink. Give me your glass, Marie!" The man of charity. "What would you like?"

She shook her head at him and could not speak.

"We're leaving soon," Larry Dickinson said, coming to her rescue. "It's nearly one."

"It can't be!"

"It was a mere eleven hours when John and I reached this delectable spot."

"Wrong, old boy," Hilbery said coming up. He belched and bowed. "Terribly wrong. We didn't leave the club till eleven. This'll be the last of the good times for a long long while."

"This isn't so good," said bitter Dickinson.

"Wait till the Yanks get here. The grog will vanish entirely. You won't even get any of this black market stuff, George, and your dear pal, Mr Wine and Spirit Merchant, will be making a packet. Still, it won't be a bad thing for you, Brewster laddie. It'll keep that gut of yours down."

They toasted the vanishing glass.

Peter Reardon, exhausted and sagging, sloped over to them. His eyebrows interrogated his wife.

"Had enough?" asked his twisted mouth.

"No," said the gay thing, "but we'll go. Oh, Pete, before we do I want you to meet this nice grumbly man called Brewster."

"How do you do?" George, unaware of idiocy, gave his man-to-man handshake. The frozen distances between words lengthened into tundra as the men acknowledged each other, a prophetic sourness on Reardon's part.

"Can we give you a lift?" This bird wobbled towards its doom.

"I live at the Hill," George explained. "I'm going to be skinned as it is, so I may as well take a cab from here."

Mrs Reardon placed a rounded brown hand on his. "Stay with us. We're just down on the water here, and there's plenty of room. Ring your wife and explain. That will make everything—" she paused—"sweet and reasonable."

"Sweet," George repeated with emphasis, stressing his glance too greatly, "and, as you say, reasonable. Brilliant argument has won me over."

"You could come back with me." Hilbery grinned. "You know I'm your watch-pup and Alice depends on me."

"What! And sleep on the floor as I did last time! Not on your life."

"We'll take you too, then," Mrs Reardon offered obligingly. "I'm fond of dogs. You can come and guard him for all you're worth."

Her husband bit his lip, then turned away. "The car's out the front," he said. "It's a blue Chev. Hop in. I'll be out in a minute. I want to say goodbye to Hope."

In a maze of kisses and extravagance they moved away from the dirty glasses, the mutilated lobsters, the cigarette butts, the endless *a b c d e f g h I got a guy in KAL-a-ma-zoo* that a queer in yellow strides had been playing over and over on the fuzzy pick-up. In the street, parked cars hung about like hobos and spivs and, as their buddies came up, the girl swung about, running unsteadily back to the house where her green dress glowed for a minute in the light. A thick male body in uniform swung her giggle off its feet.

"Damn' pretty girl," Hilbery croaked to George's rage. "Don't start getting ideas."

George laughed guiltily. "I'm too old," he said, hopefully awaiting denial which didn't come. Hilbery had crawled into the car and was sprawled in the corner already half asleep. His face, a drunken glimmer in the yellow seepings of veranda and hall-light improperly blacked-out, recovered an adventitious innocence in parted goldfish lips, fallen hair and foolish vulnerable nuzzling of one alcoholic cheek into an open palm.

Three of them came out the gate. To George's swooning delight Mrs Reardon without preamble swung herself into the back seat shadow and seated herself on his lap. Quite involuntarily he hugged her to him.

"Comfortable back there?" Reardon's mildly satiric voice enquired.

He eased himself behind the wheel while Colin Gantry, speechless for once with drink, tumbled in the other side.

Hackneyed hand-pressings sufficient to send thrills across his middle-aged skin tip-toed along the brink of rapture. Her breathy voice spoke directly into his ear, "I like you."

"Oh, God," George moaned. "Oh, don't say that." He giggled nervously. "I mean, you mustn't." Their whisperings must be throbbing all over the car, he thought fearfully, creating a Bayeux tapestry of secret lusts. Cautiously he held her off, in a suspended agony that observed every quiver of the back of her husband's neck.

Birds and bells chimed in Hilbery's brain, sounds that were integrated in dream and continued puzzlingly for half a minute after his waking. Trellis and veranda and crab-apple-tree. White flaked paint. Across the waking garden, beyond red

151

brick elm-netted, sudden harbour blue. Rooms away a woman sang *Voi Che Sapete* and there was contrapuntally with song dish-clatter and the sound of running water. Deliciousness of such unreal quality craves continuance. He closed his eyes, his lids attempting to clutch and enclose the outer landscape and stamp it like a transfer on his soul. Cautiously he removed the wet paper of sleep, opened his eyes and discovered the components present but the deliciousness somehow fled. Across the veranda he could hear Brewster grunting the day in.

Shovelling his blankets to the veranda floor he saw on a stretcher fifteen feet away the profile of his friend upturned to heaven. Curious, mused Hilbery, that a man so world-possessed should give the impression of being drunk with religion. Romantics seek adventure anywhere—God or girls. He supposed it made no difference, except God would certainly not be hoodwinked by that fake sincerity—that big-hearted intellectual tenderness—that was passed off as genuine coin. Sceptically he watched as George with heavings, pawings and snortings pulled aside dream ribbons still cluttering the day's light. White legs ridiculous in underpants paddled the air. The frizzy head, groping back towards consciousness, swung forward and Brewster, obese in singlet, sat up spinning in sunshafts, with desert mouth, volcanic eyes and a prescience of rapture.

The smile—to himself. The sucking of teeth. Private speculation of success under the crab-apple that poked and thrust above the railing. He stepped across the splintered boards to Hilbery who plunged immediately into artificial slumber.

"John," he whispered, bending down and shaking the words over him, "John, did I ring Liss? For God's sake, did I?"

Through false surprise, Hilbery proceeded to wreck the other's morning, and George dragged on trousers, stuffed in his shirt, and wandered the track of his own anxiety to the bathroom where Gantry, curdled white, was seeking revival under the shower.

"Where's everyone?" George shouted above the roar of the gas-heater.

Gantry shrugged hundreds of contemptuous droplets onto George who walked out again, following the clue of the singing voice and tap, and found her, sleeves above elbow, stirring the dimpling porridge. From the doorway where he halted for the pronounced effect of distance, he caught her turning eyes, gauging like a crack rifle shot the exact moment to move in as her lip fluttered from such probing of her modesty.

Everything has not that simplicity which places the white object on the black, that causes knife to seek fork, sees the matured fruit drop from the summer tree. There were the complications of husband and scuttling dog, an enormous red setter which prodded its quivering nose between George's amorous knees, of guests groaning for razors, of burning toast and coffee boiling dry. During breakfast, too, Hilbery, made malicious by the maudlin sentimentality of Brewster mono-logue, kept needling him about several articles he had been preparing and which were now a week late. Gantry's soft pink mouth curved about baroque pronouncements during lulls. Bouts of nausea were still bending him forward in his chair where he sat sipping coffee and watching others push porridge across their bowls.

Mrs Reardon's beauty remained, even without the protective flattery of artificial light. The boyishness in daylight was charming and correct. The open smiling mouth offered no subtlety, only a candid sensuality that drank in compliments, exchanged a swift gasping kiss in a snatched privacy as the other three walked to the garden, and made only two remarks that were not downright silly.

A clock said ten, five minutes ahead of Hilbery's watch. Having adjusted the hands with a passion for seconds, he

153

surveyed the breakfast group, observing a relationship to the history book plan of Agincourt or Malplaquet, or any primitive debate. Here the French. There the English. Colin Gantry, despite indisposition, with quiverfuls of slender barbs to fling; while all Brewster had lined up was a group of blunt and battered cudgels of awe-inspiring antiquity. Uncontrollably giggling, he was forced to excuse himself and, having gone down to the harbour end of the garden, brooded in the hot sun over a pair of chrysalids knocking emptily and brownly from an oleander tree. Auguries? He plucked them from their twig between fastidious forefinger and thumb and spun them away into the sun dazzle and the blue below the garden.

His watch hands crept forward fifteen minutes. Achingly his legs carried him back past the house where words were bounding with increasing loudness over the grass, and turning then he saw the four of them strolling along the gravel.

Brutally Hilbery shattered a cobweb aerial of silver with a switch he made from a duranta bush, and whacked and whacked at the upper garden fence angrily until Gantry and finally Brewster caught up with him. Shrub-framed, their hosts waved all sorts of farewells.

They were silent in the tram through illness or love or anger, which are much the same thing, perhaps. They stood near the entrance to Museum station where the Sunday-smelling air of the subway, mingled with the isolated giggles of a sailor and his girl, came crazily up to them, the giggles expanding like a trumpet bell as they waited before the khaki park. Soldiery sprawled on grass alongside girls, on seats with knees spread, by stone margin of fountain, so vigorously the park seemed overgrown.

George played three sad notes on his tie.

Gantry's illness communicated itself to him as he wondered what explanation would appease Alice. He left the others and walked slowly to the Quay, finding solution—he would be too

154

ill to be questioned. All those tender wells of sympathy that made her love him so dotingly would instantly repress wifely prerogative! George must not be worried. Not! Not!

He rang her the next day. And the next. And, when he could no longer contain his bursting agony, he went out there one steamy Thursday afternoon with three bottles of beer. The mile walk along Darling Point Road in the heat failed to bring him to his senses which, upon her opening the door to him, staggered entirely.

Not being a man for preambles he took her straightway into his arms.

"I had to come," he said. He only knew the well-worn phrases. But they thrilled her as he knew they would, for she was just as silly as he, and it was some moments before they remembered the beer which he had put down on the veranda table.

"How did you manage it?" she asked.

"I'm always free on Thursdays. Afternoons anyway. Don't send me away."

They both knew she had no intention of dismissing him, but it pleased them to pretend, and him particularly, because his emotions, not being more than nerve-deep, needed constant whipping to retain ardency. They drank beer, they made love— with discretion. The dog worried them a good deal until finally she had to tie him up in the garage at the back of the house from which his laments boomed for the rest of the afternoon. They confessed to love. Really George should have said, "I love me," seeing his blue slightly wary eyes reflected in hers. They imposed limitations to their passion that were refinements of torture.

At four o'clock the practical man in George asked, "When's hubby due?"

Even Nancy shuddered at the term. He was a man who,

despite the glossy appearance of education, lapsed into vulgarities barbaric in their simplicity. Detected or reproved, he would pass them off as pieces of deliberate preciosity—and get away with it.

"Not until six," she replied from the muffling recesses of his arms.

He looked fondly at her dark, straight hair, really believing that he loved her.

"What sweet pain," he groaned. "Oh, God! Why do I have to meet you now?"

She shook her dumb brunette head.

"Do you know," he continued, "you're the girl of my book?"

"You told me."

"Did I?" He was put out. "When?"

"The other night."

"Well, you are, you know. You're it exactly. Beautiful, untamed tomboy. Oh, everything! And now to meet you! It's too much! Oh, Nancy!" He began to cry, just a little. "It's too much."

She kissed each glistening eye in turn. "But why do you love me?"

"There doesn't have to be a reason. One simply knows."

"But Alice. What about her?"

"I love her, too."

"Can you?"

"Of course." Testiness crept into his voice. "That's something quite different."

"Is it?"

"Yes, of course. Don't ask me about it, Nancy. It upsets me. Don't spoil a beautiful day. I can't bear to be upset. Let's do nothing to mar this, shall we?"

"Nothing," she agreed doubtfully. "Nothing."

He went the long way home by bus for a change and sat

through four suburbs festooned with his guilt, vowing that he would be especially nice to Lissie, especially, especially, especially. . . . Her calm face turned to his, when he came through the back veranda door, a faith that shook him a little.

"Wonderful Liss!" he murmured into her thick curly hair. "I got caught up with extra cables. Everything's bloody well crazy with Yanks."

"You should have rung!"—the closest thing to a scolding.

"I know. Forgive me, darling. I was so busy I forgot. Hilbery has been off sick and there was no time to turn round with the stuff that piled up."

She turned, perennial saint, to her jam making, while George went out to shower where he found the water a shriving force.

By the tortuous devices he alone knew how to handle—a maze pacer by inclination!—he contrived that the four of them should assist at the grave absurdities to which married couples subscribe—the *missa solemnis* of the suburbs—Sunday dinner. Once facial familiarity was established, the difficulty of keeping her name unuttered no longer pressed thorns into him hourly. Accordingly it blossomed from him constantly, flowering in sentence after sentence, planted in ground where it had no right to flourish at all, until it began to assume some of the luscious and dubious attributes of the artificial.

Passion concealed itself in a tender joke. "The Red Setters are coming to tea," George would say. "Get them some lovely bones, Lissie!" Even Alice took it up unsuspectingly. "I saw your Mrs Red Setter in town," she would tell George—and his heart would stand still in love's panic and joy. Outsiders remarked on his obsession, but not his family who had a wearied familiarity with his emotional investments and merely waited for its termination with unvarying patience.

But termination did not appear to be at hand.

Once a pattern of exchanged house visitings had been established, there came a flirtation with the arts that required

157

evenings at the theatre, at lectures, at concerts to which George did not listen. The advantage of culture lay in the fact that Alice could not always accompany them, for there was no one to mind Jeannie, so at week-ends he would generously compensate Alice for this by taking his daughter with him for long healthy hikes with Mrs Reardon and the Red Setter through Rushcutters Bay Park and down to Parsley Bay. They would amble through the torn summer trees of the parkland, find some sheltered seat and simply "be together" as his daughter used to describe it in later years, pealing her wild giggles of laughter.

Jeannie, who was eleven, would perch on the grass near them and watch every move they made with total absorption, refusing to budge even when George tried to send her away on spurious errands. In her beastlier moments she would bring a book and lie beside them sucking her prominent front teeth noisily as if they were toffees, whistling up the dog so that it bounded all over them in flurries of sand and saliva and salt water, huh-huhing above their prone bodies.

From the beginning there was a natural hopelessness about the whole affair that made their infatuation more pardonable—or so George tried to believe for he was constantly reassuring his rearing conscience. One Thursday he brought with him as well as the beer, a soft brown paper parcel which he tossed onto her lap.

"What do you think of that?" he asked.

She pulled the wrappings off, thrilled, as the black evening blouse sprawled its prettiness across her skirt. There were patterns of pearl and gilt around the neck. A small cry of pleasure escaped her and she looked up, smiling, to thank him.

"I bought that for Lissie today. It's nice (sorry), isn't it?"

Nancy shrank back in embarrassment. "Oh, yes," she agreed. "Yes, it is. Lovely." Thanking God she hadn't spoken and hating him underneath the love that still flowed on in the face of his insensitivity.

"Put it on, Nancy," he said. "Go on. Put it on. Every time I see Lissie in it I want to remember you."

Her hands drew away from the black jersey. Outrage silenced her.

"Go on," he urged. "What's the matter?"

"No," she said. "I couldn't."

"Why?"

"Lissie. Lissie thinking you bought it for her in affection and you—"

She searched for her answer in the dark lost places of his face.

"Yes," he agreed, almost smiling. "Yes. It would be the worst thing we've done, I suppose." He shook his head and looked from her black hair to the black garment. "Go on," he whispered and flicked at it on her knees. "Put it on, I want to remember you in it."

"No." She stood up and it fell between them to the veranda floor. Eye glutted on eye; there was the terrible gravity of silence loud with flesh close to flesh. His angel of despair could not meet her face and fastened eyes on the brown feet in their toppling sandals.

"Go on," he pleaded, committed to insanity. "Put it on."

But she turned from him abruptly and went to the kitchen, so George picked up this nimbus cloud, re-wrapped it clumsily, and simply could not see where he had offended.

She forgave him, of course, because he always made sure that his hurt cried more loudly than her own.

Six weeks of variegated rapture went by. Sitting on her windy veranda that looked down to the harbour had become ritual. Seasonal dust, its granulations sifted thick on leaf and blade, stirred and settled, stirred and settled. For long moments George gazed into her face. Her eyes were as unquestioning and receptive as a child's.

159

"What are we going to do?" his anguish demanded of her. "*What* are we going to do, Mrs Red Setter? Tell me that. I don't suppose you'd leave Peter, would you?"

She had thought of it, but only in an academic fashion that shivered away from the reality of final decisions.

"I mean," he pursued, "with you there is only Peter. But with me it's different. There's Jeannie as well. A man'd be a pretty sort of bastard to leave his own child, wouldn't he?"

She appeared to muse on this for a while.

"I don't know," she said reflectively. "I've had a child."

"You?" The harbour rocked.

"Yes. Years ago. Ten years ago next November. The father was married. She—I had her adopted."

George knew his heart to hesitate with its rose-red freight. Even his love paused. Jealousy demands a dozen different answers to the one unbearable question. Fighting back the silly urge to ask and ask and ask uselessly, he said,

"Yes, well, what else was there for you to do? I don't know whether I could, though. But it's not the same position at all. Besides, it would be a question of uprooting and going elsewhere. I don't know whether I could stay on at the *Voice* under those circumstances, and one has to live. Adultery is only popular when you're committing it yourself."

Even in his stress he was foolishly proud of that last remark until he remembered Marie saying it to him years—how many? —before.

"I hate Pete. I hate Alice," she stated in such a flat tone the words carried shocking force. Then they proceeded to annihilate them with love, proceeding through the symbols of lust without reaching a conclusion. Poor battered combatants!

"We'll have to do something," they assured each other stupidly. But what? There was nothing to do.

Oppression sat on his chest.

When he returned home, however, it lifted ironically as he

passed between the hedges of passion-vine and tecoma to find his Alice sitting on the lawn below the lemon-tree, her head bent slightly as if to watch the progress of an inner pain.

He switched on ebullience like a light.

"Hello, darl!" (They were gay rumbling tumbrils.) "Had a good day?"

She did not answer at once but picked a grassblade and another and another. Presenting guilt to its owner is always a reason for hesitancy.

"I feel sad," she said finally. "I've heard about Nancy."

The tweed legs walked three or four paces across the grass. He heard his voice say,

"What do you mean? You've known Nancy as long as I have. Well, practically as long. Darling, what is this nonsense?"

The tweed-clad arms interpreted marital love around her small shoulders which stiffened at once and pulled back. He experienced thereupon an illogical sense of injury synchronized with a heaving fear, as he lowered himself, white-faced, to the grass beside her. His lips set in the firm line they did when he was discovered at fault.

"Go on," he said bravely. "Tell me."

She had been coming home in the ferry with Hope Reader. Closing her eyes now she could still see the harbour crinkling blue, crinkling white, and the foreshores by Drummoyne hot in the sun. What had Hope been doing over this way? Oh, visiting, she expected. She hadn't bothered to ask. She could still see the harbour from the rise of the back lawn; it was still brimming with blue tides.

"Isn't Nancy Reardon beautiful?" Hope had asked, for no reason it seemed now, except to spill venom.

"Yes," Alice had agreed, surprised. "Yes. I suppose she is."

"And isn't George jealous of her?" the other pursued, beating her vulture wings. The harbour had still sparkled most gloriously its lupin blue and silver. The ferry had rumbled like

161

a comfortable lion and Greenwich bumped into them clouded in trees.

"I don't know what you mean," she ventured at last.

Hope had laughed prettily and viciously. Her rather ordinary face was radiant.

"Oh, don't tell me you didn't know about the big affair George is having with her? You're the only one in Sydney who doesn't."

The laughter whirled its spirals while the blue and white harbour slipped away. In the bus going up the Point Road, Alice thought she would vomit but contained her heart until she had reached shelter.

Across the slope, above the other terracotta and slate roofs now she could still see laughter scattered impersonally all over the water but was too stunned to weep.

"It's true," he said at last. "And I'm glad you know. It has been a burden to carry inside me."

"Poor George!" Alice said bitterly, ironic for the only time in their marriage as she recalled his previous confession.

For once he was stung.

"Do you love her?"

"I don't know."

"Oh, but you must know, surely."

"I'm infatuated, I suppose. That isn't the same thing quite, is it? I mean, I just want to be with her and look at her and tell her she's beautiful."

"And you do, of course?"

"That's all she seems to want to hear."

His wife did not speak for so long, and for so long continued to watch the blue water between the red roofs and the grey, that George wriggled uncomfortably as he searched for a suitable way of continuing the discussion, for if there were one thing he could not bear it was for problems concerning him to peter out in silence.

"Does her husband know?" Alice asked, carefully keeping her head turned away.

"I don't know. I don't think so. He's a fine fellow. I'd hate to hurt him."

"Of course."

"Do you think I should talk to him, man to man?" George asked eagerly.

"What good would that serve?" Alice asked a little testily.

"None, I suppose," he replied miserably. "Oh, Alice—" he flung himself at her mercy—"what am I going to do? What *will* I do?"

"Don't do anything silly," she said. Her calm baffled even her.

He could have handled an emotional scene. It would have given him a sense of injury and self-justification. He pondered crying and then decided against it.

"I won't," he said.

His work suffered the inroads of his loving distraction. Cooped in his battery on the third floor, he swivelled restlessly, deluged by news-sheets waiting to be sorted, importuned by letters aching to be written. He had just put a sheet of paper into his typer and written "Sweet madness, you are destroying . . ." when Hilbery bounced in, all chirrup and peppermint. Whipping the sheet out, he crumpled it into his waste basket, fumbling like a schoolboy.

Hilbery regarded him coolly, extracted a lifesaver from a roll and perched it on the end of his fleshy tongue.

"Go away," George said.

Hilbery indicated the piled-up work with a hands out gesture and shrugged his crooked shoulders. His narrow face caught at pity and held it for a second or two.

"What's up, old boy?" he asked.

"Oh, God!" George groaned, holding his head in his pudgy

163

hands. "I'm in a bloody awful mess. Liss has found out. I don't know what to do."

"Not as lucky as last time, eh?" the other commented thoughtfully. He rolled the sweet around his mouth, then suddenly crunched it. "I can never wait. Simply have to bite them. The man who can suck a rainbow monster, George, through every changing colour is a man of iron will indeed."

"Oh, don't ride me! Just go away, will you, if you can't help."

"Look, you'll have to clean this stuff up," Hilbery said. "The first edition is half an hour late as it is. Penbrook says he wants all this down by two. Shove it across and I'll give you a hand, then we'll go and have a drink somewhere."

"You're a good scout, Johnnie," George said. "Here. Give me the top half and I'll flog myself along. All this damn war news. I've had a gutful."

At the end of an hour riddled with peppermint, Penbrook's secretary came down, so prettily enquiring that George cheered up as he handed her a trayful ready for setting up.

"You're a dear girl," he said.

"Marvellous!" Hilbery cooed, watching him over the tops of his glasses. "Simply marvellous! What recovery!"

But George's deafness to criticism of a certain kind was now a long-established and pleasant-to-have defect.

"Make sure," he was saying into pink mouth, liquid eyes, hair shimmer, "that the one on top gets an extended two-inch cross-head, will you? Tell Mackie. I've written it down but it might get overlooked. I don't want any of the subs to change that one. There's a picture with a fifty-word title to come. I'm still waiting for Chivers to send up a print."

Hilbery speculated, as Brewster tapped away with high-speed brilliance, on the functional baritone and emotional shallowness—a kind of Harpo Marx, he thought—yet could not really dislike him. Probably because I'm not a woman, he told himself. Any intelligent sort of female must find him an excruciating bore. He had his good points, true. He was never malicious. He was perennially genial. Hilbery sketched a profile on the blotter and scribbled wire-wool hair all over the pate, smudging in half of the ginger moustache the other had grown during the month. He emphasised an enormous polka-dot bow-tie like an obscene joke, then tossed it over to George who twinkled with delight, and rang through for a copy boy.

At four o'clock they came out of the building and walked to Pitt Street, these two benevolent gentlemen of the Press, thrusting past the screeching lout with first editions on the corner, down towards a pub near the Quay. Hilbery was braced for repetitive agonizings but mentally lip-licking in hope of salacious detail: he slung one long leg after the other as George fussed along on his small feet. Although he was less selfish and more genuinely tender than Brewster, they were at heart both good-time boys, jollying along on a wealth of liquor, anecdote, belly-laughs and a baked enamel sophistication which resulted from inside knowledge on public events. Liquor at first confers urbanity. Nods are exchanged; citizens toss hand familiarities across bars; bookmakers, lawyers, accountants, commercial artists, librarians taste in that first sip (whatever the day has been like) the assurance of self. *Bibo ergo sum*— to be inscribed in ornamental gothic above the saloon bar.

"And what are you going to do about disentangling all this mess, old boy?" Hilbery enquired after he had listened to a prolix account of the affair.

"But that's what I'm asking you."

"Whom do you want most?"

"Her. Oh, I don't know. I can't leave Liss. I love her, too."

"Spoilt bastard! Then give up the fancy nancy."

"But how will I do it?"

"Tell her."

"I couldn't, Johnnie. I couldn't do that. She'd cry."

165

"Does she really love you all that much?"

"I think so. She says she does. Look, I'll be honest with you. You know I always try to be honest, don't you?"

Hilbery grunted. He never deliberately hurt his friends if he could avoid it. George, delivered from sublety by three whiskies, was not listening for replies.

"She's dotty about me," he said with a simplicity of self-conviction that was moving.

"Well, write to her. That's fair enough. Write her a nice long letter explaining how much you love her etcetera but that duty etcetera and you feel sure she will understand etcetera. All that crap."

George's eyes gleamed in temper.

"This isn't the time for joking. This is serious. Oh, why does no one ever take my problems seriously?"

"I was serious. Write."

"But what will I say?"

"I've just told you."

They stared at each other.

"Same again," George said to the girl. Remembering suddenly to give her his smile. Smiled.

"I don't know," he said finally. "I don't know whether I could bring myself to do it."

Hilbery paid for the drinks with some impatience.

"In that case, old boy, there's a third possibility—if you don't give a damn about her feelings, that is."

"What's that?" George asked, innocently eager as a baby. Chubby hands reached up to grasp the bottle. There were anticipatory whimpers.

"Do nothing. Don't write. Don't see her. Pretty gutless, but it will spare your sensitivities."

"But it would be terribly cruel, wouldn't it? Or would it be terribly brave?"

Hilbery looked at him a long, long time over the rim of

his glass which became in that moment a wall or a world of separation.

"Bloody cruel," he said. And tossed the last of his drink down his throat.

And that was what George did.

The simplest and easiest thing responds to the first cry of the flesh for comfort.

Not that he didn't suffer from his renunciation—but it was the deprivation, rather than any self-analysis or concern about what she might be enduring, that caused him pain. To put a seal on his decision he vowed on his rosary beads that he would have no further truck with her—a vow which gave him a marvellous moral excuse for offering no explanation and no apology for his behaviour. Instead he swelled with the consciousness of self-sacrifice bolstered by opportunist religiosity that guaranteed him defence against the fleeting scruples that visited him. Wrapped in a sanctimonious self-justification, he wept—but not for her.

When he failed to arrive at two, then three, then four, Mrs Reardon dared telephone the *Voice*, to be informed that Mr Brewster was not on duty. Delicately she put down the receiver as if it were some unlucky talisman and went to change her dress. He will ring, she assured herself, succulently apologetic.

But he did not—although she waited in for the rest of the day, lusting over the black instrument, willing it to shrill. Nor did he ring the second day and when once more she telephoned his office, a snap-frozen secretarial voice said he was in conference. (Mystical refuge of trapped executives!) He was in conference all that week, it appeared.

Nor did he write.

Between the terrifying bouts of tears that shook her and convinced her of love, she would repeat for comfort various statements of his adoration, re-read his profanely physical letters, and grapple the words to her like a credo. But blind faith wavers in the absence of divine gesture, however tiny. That assured flow of verbal concern—had it been too assured? Her frantic gaping wounds of pride and self-esteem were pinching their harsh edges by the fortnight's end, but not sufficiently to prevent trickles of anguish escaping from time to time, for she had genuinely loved him.

During a risotto of veal and pork mince one evening, observing the grey crab-apple limbs fumbling against the railing towards her vulnerable heart, she lowered her head unexpectedly and sobbed aloud. Her husband pretended at first and extremely foolishly that she was not crying at all, until his silence raised a tumult all about them, and he was obliged to place his fork to one side, his long morose face uncomfortable on her behalf.

"In another fortnight it won't be nearly as bad," he said.

She gaped at him a wild startlement of distended mouth and rosy eye.

"What?" she gasped. "What?"

"I know all about it," he said, absolving her gently. "It's all right, my silly Nancy. I only regret I didn't warn you at the start."

Preliminaries flew away in a cloud of gnats.

She said, "But he used to say he loved me! How can you love someone and treat them like this?"

Reardon shrugged. "Eat your dinner. Try to eat something and I'll tell you," he said. "Brewster loves no one but himself. He doesn't know that. He wouldn't believe it if you shouted it at him, but it is nevertheless true. He's not capable of selfless love. Can't you see? Enormous egos like his with little real talent to support them must seek an emotional support. He *uses* people."

168

"But he did say he loved me. He sounded sincere."

"He puts love—or the words for it—in, so that he can take love out. And perhaps he did mean it for the moment. But it doesn't go deep. My poor dear," he said, reaching across to touch her hand in tenderness. The disease he was cherishing within his fragile flesh and which was to carry him off in another year made him cough drily.

"He's by nature a bough-flitter. You must see it. Haven't you watched him at parties, even when you are there, and all his obsession should be directed at you? Perhaps he wants to believe in the grinding racking emotion for himself, but the truth is he's simply incapable of it. No one's fault. Not even his. And he's an utterly selfish man."

Wanting to accept, to assuage hurt, temporarily accepting but incapable of sustaining buoyancy for long. For long. At night, in communion with the weather-beaten stars, her husband stretched his frail body beside hers and, sensing her noiseless sobbing gently shaking the bed, hated Brewster in an explosion of passion.

But everything dwindles to the merciful vanishing point of perspective that in its alchemy causes the fact to become insubstantial. Remaining. Vanishing. Both at once.

For a time, from sheer dumb animal reticence, she avoided the parties he would be likely to attend, only to hear through the complicated Christian devices of friendship that he was drinking and talking as unendingly as ever, whirring with his formidable propellers of compliments. This nagged and nagged. Weeks and weeks flowered and withered and one day, shatteringly unexpected, they strap-hung on a tram going to the Cross. Her thunderous heart embarrassed her. George could see the pulse in her throat racing beneath the silk of brown skin. At intervals their lurching bodies claimed a specious intimacy, shattered by the conductor to whom Nancy paid her own fare. Her face, travelled over by patterns of grief, still reached out

to him its creams and browns and scarlet. He had to cling
rigorously to his vow.

"Why didn't you ring?" she asked pitifully.

He felt like crying.

"I couldn't," he said. "I just couldn't. That's all. Please try
to understand. Alice knew, and I could not bear the pain on
her face."

"It's hard to understand unkindness."

He said nothing.

She repeated her words. "You were unkind."

"But what was the point of it all?" George asked, ignoring
her. "Where would it have got us? It was so futile, can't you
see, Nancy? There was no future in it for either of us. You
have Peter and I have Alice. It was impossible from the
start."

"Then why start it?"

"Oh, there's no point in arguing about it now," he said
impatiently. The inclination to tears was gone. Decisions froze
like rock.

The tram became angry, too, and shook them together so
that she touched him for the last time with her beautiful tanned
hand. William Street's plate-glass cliffs reflected them, and
their twins leant forward, touched, parted across bland car
salesrooms and breakfast bars.

"Won't you come out?" whispered her desperation. "Won't
you come out again on a Thursday and bring some beer the
way you used to?"

"No," George said firmly. Oh, so firmly. He was confirmed
in strength and morality. "No."

He had to get off at the Cross and, because the tram was
reeling around the corner opposite the hotel, there was no
time for them to say any more. But he gave her one of his
Long Level Looks as he raised his hat—for he was rigidly
adherent to the little courtesies—and after crossing through

traffic to the corner where the underwear and the tarts both hung about, he did not turn. He did not dare.

Yet she travelled on, cushioned against further jolting by a type of supernal pain that was so close to bliss and so blinded her with tears, she was carried four stops past the one she wanted and was forced to walk back the best part of a mile.

# [VII]

NOT MUCH of a vintage.

What he had snapped off in a second's time took two years to heal in fact; and even then there was a kind of spiritual convalescence that dragged prolongedly with queasy malaise past places where once they had met at parties, where eyes copulated across rooms and slid away. His wife never mentioned Nancy again unless she had to, so that George, who was primarily interested only in his own emotions and rarely gave a thought to what those about him were feeling, was convinced she had got over it long before he had.

Her resilience irritated. But he stuck resolutely to the vow he had made and never again deliberately sought Mrs Reardon out. He communicated; and if, during his post-Communion prayers, inevitably his mind would seek her image, he examined his conscience as he had been taught. Grave matter? Certainly. Full knowledge? Yes. Full consent? Indeed no. Satisfied, he would savour streams of glitter along candlesticks, ripple of vestment, that special waxy stuffiness of church. After all, the sin, if there had been real sin, was confessed. There was nothing further he could do to appease God except perhaps display the fullest and richest devotion to Lissie, who laid her own feelings so generously at his feet.

"But if there were no adultery," the nameless confessor had said on the other side of the partition, "I cannot understand your continued concern. You have made a good confession.

You are sorry for what you have done. Surely you were given especial grace to resist this terrible temptation."

Maybe, George thought, leaning his devout face against his hands, it would have been better if I *had* committed adultery and got it right out of my mind, This was an attractive speculation and he meandered with it some distance until the shuffling of the congregation rising for the last Gospel roused him.

Yet he was still gluttonous for gossip about her—("My dear, at least half a contingent," Hope had whispered maliciously at a party recently)—and when he did see her modestly avoiding him at a gathering he would send her one of his starving glances. But that was as far as it went, so that in time, by this very affectation of light-heartedness, the affair gradually lost its sombre coloration and George knew he was cured. It was safer to be cured. Jeannie, now a buck-toothed adolescent with short tight black curls, would drop her soft head to one side and stare at George from under her lashes with such skilled and gentle insolence he was afraid to put a foot out of line. Sensing this, she would laugh her silvery laugh and tuck her arm through his. "Pretend *I'm* your girlfriend, Daddy," the precocious wretch would say. Two octaves at least of wild laughter!

She had no education at all in a formal sense.

"We cannot make her learn, Mr Brewster," querulous nuns had complained. The square cheesy face of the Reverend Mother took on an impassive granite quality when she spoke in the bees-waxed ikon-cluttered parlour. "It is not that your daughter cannot learn, you understand. It is that she will not. One after another of her teachers complains of work not done, of careless assignments, and a complete absence of shame when reproached with this. She has, too, if I may say so, a less than serious attitude to her Faith." She paused and breathed deeply. "A flippancy, Mr Brewster, that is not only unbecoming but that verges on the blasphemous."

173

"Oh, indeed, this is shocking to hear." George shook his head in a horror conditioned by twenty-five years' Protestantism.

With a mannerism too worldy for her habit, the Reverend Mother rotated a broad blessed band of gold that wedded her to Christ; and, in graceful gesture that blessed the multitudes, proceeded with cold eyes to outline Jeannie's misdemeanours. ". . . in the Chapel. Not only on one seat, Mr Brewster, but on two."

"Surely not! Surely not!" George goggled at the enormity of it.

"It is so. Exactly as I have described. Were it not for the esteem in which you are held by the dear Bishop and particularly by Father Beckett"—she allowed herself a rudimentary smile of reminiscence—"I'm afraid, Mr Brewster, we would have had to ask you to remove your daughter some time ago. However, now that you tell us she herself wishes to leave, both of us are spared a painful decision."

The beeswax was overpowering. Combined with the clangour of scented flowers and the sterility of perfect peace, it made George feel sick and faint.

"She has some talent," he ventured to protest. "Her ballet work is extraordinary for her age."

The black coif conceded this. "But it is outside our curriculum."

"I know. Yet I hoped"—hopeless George was wistful even to Mothers Superior—"for a rounded education. After all genius in one direction isn't sufficient in this mechanized age, is it?"

"Genius, Mr Brewster?"

"No. No. Perhaps not. Merely a phrase. But the child is so talented she took three senior examinations at the one time. Quite an achievement, they tell me."

She had been prepared to be more clement under the persuasion of George's pleading tongue and eye, but egotism was intolerable to her professional humility. In an irruption of bad temper she clasped her beads and lowered her voice to that frequency which caused postulants to shiver apprehensively. Coolly impassive saints watched from behind protecting glass the entire routing of a man who even achieved the mildest and most spiritual of flirtations with amused nuns. She rose before he was prepared for it and the shock of this initiative made him knock his chair clumsily as he sprang to his feet. Reverend Mother smiled. Imperfections suited this unctuous man with the ponderous voice, she reflected. But she would give no inch. Graciously she accompanied him to the head of the drive, a gesture she accorded only a few; and, with the wind carving her veil into several delightful attitudes, offered Mr Brewster a well-kept hand.

"God bless you," she said. "And Jeannie, too."

He could not bear her indifference.

"I'm sure He will respect your wishes," he murmured indistinctly and so charmingly she was deceived for the few moments it took for him to walk across the gravel; but then, as if catching the impertinence and its exactness, she stiffened among the cubist shapes of conifer in an annoyance that revisited her at intervals throughout the afternoon and later than that during the examen of conscience, whereupon she extended the twenty minutes' meditation period to a knee-breaking forty.

Yet Jeannie survived this displeasure. With the energy of the liberated she practised her *battements*, her *pas de bourree*, assiduously, and developed at the *barre* magnificent calf and thigh muscles, a sophisticate's veneer that could cope with inverts of both sexes, talk glibly about books that everyone else was talking about and call her parents by their first names. This sudden adulthood intrigued her father. Proud of her false-eyelashed precocity he delighted to have coffee with her in city cellars, simply revelling in the gay numbers of sleek-haired dancers, all looking rather alike, who postured and exclaimed at his deadpan stories. Alice, sanctified, full of grace, let them invade the house, smiled patiently as they burned cigarette holes in the sculptured off-white carpet and endured like a saint her husband's enthusiasms for this dancer and then that.

"But have you noticed her legs, Lissie?" he would ask with lovable innocence. "They're all hairy."

"Are they, darling?" Alice would say placidly as she cut his lunch in the kitchenette

"Didn't you notice?"

"No. I can't say I did."

"Amazing. What do you suppose she does? Do you think she shaves them?"

"I really couldn't say, dear." Expertly she stacked sandwiches packing them away in grease-proof paper. The impregnable calm on her face was vanquished by nothing, certainly not by the hairs on a twenty-two-year-old leg. She felt sorry for George. He was forty-four now and it didn't seem as if he would ever grow up. A great gush of love flooded her heart and she packed two extra cookies in his lunch tin.

Cookies were not the only nourishment of the news editor of the *Voice* but despite the expertise he might have brought to the indulgence of a taste for good food and liquor, the staffing position during the war had almost doubled his work and in the early months after peace was declared he found the pressure so tremendous he was forced to cram a coffee and sandwich down while he went on working with the help of the cables editor, a pole of a fellow with light ginger hair and a sandy temper. A bias of pigmentation! He had been with the *Voice* for only a few months but had become a substitute drinking companion in place of Hilbery who had been gone for a long time as war correspondent in Greece. This tongue-fondling of

176

fermented barley with such a sour expert was not his idea of pally pen-boys, but the sourness spilled out one late night as a grinding shrew of a wife with a jealous temper and puritan possessiveness that made his life unbearable.

"I'd as soon work back for nix," Jockel confessed. "If I'm properly late it seems to worry her less than ten minutes unaccounted for. Christ!" he said with feeling. "There's times I could put the whole paper to press single-handed rather than go home to Sadie." Full baby lips kissed liquor; narrow blue eyes stared out across King Street at the trams.

"Sadie?" George stirred a marmalade of memory.

"Yes. Used to knock around the *Voice* years ago. Sadie Klein. A Fleet Street complex in full flower. I met her doing social reporting in Melbourne. I mean *she* was. God! That was a time. What made me do it? I wonder. Never thought she really wanted me—just a husband so she could say she graduated *M rs*. You know how it is with some women? And after they've got it, never satisfied. Still hankering after romance and all the sentimental crap that goes with it." He drank with a quiet acrimony and dribbled a bit on his sloping chin and his tie but refused to notice. "Think she used to be stuck on some character round the *Voice* when she was there and she never got over it. Wish I could meet the bastard now. He's welcome to her."

George pop-eyed his miserable companion curled untidily above the bar, one elbow paddling in a beer ring without a care in the world. Two lank tapes of jaundiced hair crept over the white and freckled forehead corrugated by lines almost to the hair-line.

"Jesus!" its lips said feelingly and to itself. In a compassion born of guilt George leaned forward, aware of the staleness of the other's breath, and Jockel bent down to scratch a skinny shin. Each sock sported lilac clocks; the delicate note of mourning was repeated in a diagonal lavender stripe on the flopping tie.

"Did you know her?" Jockel turned his head up with an unintended archness as he scratched. Sharp eyes bored suddenly into George.

"Sadie Klein?" asked careful George, playing for time. "Let's see now. Was she a fair girl? Fair with the sort of figure that makes men yowl?"

"You're joking," Jockel said mournfully. "Same again, Marie. No. Dark and curly and the most enormous eyelashes I've ever seen on anything. That includes Guernseys."

"And you complain?"

"That was seventeen years ago. Seventeen longlashed years."

"Oh, come. It can't be that bad."

Jockel raised his shoulders and let them drop. "Maybe it's me. Maybe she's still the sweet little sexed-up bit I married, but I tell you I wouldn't know it." A drunken palsy hand teetered across to clutch Brewster's genuine tweed. "And another thing." He stopped and took a huge gulp from his glass and his bloodshot eyes fastened on his companion's. "Another thing, sir, now that we're getting matey." Oh, God, pleaded George. Oh, God. Oh, God. "I told you a whopping great bloody lie then. I knew you knew her. First thing I get this job, what do you think she says, eh?"

"I can't imagine."

"Come off it," the cables editor said crudely. "Don't be so modest. She said"—he paused with the flair of the drunk— " 'See if there's a George Brewster still on the staff.' So I see. Every detail she wanted to know. Every piddling little detail. How you looked, what you wore, what you said, how many kids, did you have a girlfriend. I could run up a dossier on you, Brewster, that would rock you, man. Yes. I know the lot. And do you know it?—you're still in her skin like an itch."

The bar rocked. A protesting trochee whimpered from George's mouth; but, unheeding, Jockel's triangular pale face loomed.

178

"Don't think I give a bugger. Lucky for you."

George's lips opened and closed around a plum-sized nothing.

"Tell me," persisted white lips, "how far did it go?"

"Nowhere," George said, able to speak a confident truth. "It never did. To tell the truth it nearly killed me. But I wouldn't."

Enlightenment suffused Jockel's nagging brain. "So that's it! That's why she's got you still on her mind!" Each coated word! "God! You wouldn't come at it and she's had it nagging the tripe out of her ever since."

Some freakish deviation caused Don Juan Brewster a pride-shimmer in his powers both of attraction and prescience but his private gloatings and false compassion were not for long. Jockel might give him winks with a secondary meaning; they laughed more readily over their drinks. Preliminaries of friendship. They were cut off by an editorial summons in the second week in May. Editor Gowanloch had been replaced five years back by a university man interested in "tone" as well as news. Rapes and homicide no longer affronted the eye of the front page reader. Editorials were conservative and vague. Columnists went for whimsy instead of malice. A weekly column called "This Australia" duplicated the intellectual titterings of "This England." Cheesecake photography was banished. Brewster, who had the non-degreed man's reverence for affixes, was always slightly fawning, laughed just a shade too loudly at Wyatt's jokes. Wyatt noted this casually, and wrote it down against him as deterrent to promotion. Brewster was no psychologist. He took the editorial smiles at their surface worth ("He's not a well man," he would explain unctuously) and his costiveness as an essential in a busy superior. He bore no grudges. Usually he failed, through the localized insensitiveness of the extremely thin-skinned, to see why he should. Yet Wyatt was a just man. The aridity of

179

this virtue caused him to see Brewster's good points dispassionately, and when he recommended him as a representative for
an international press conference in London he was according
the man no more than he deserved after twenty years of efficient service in a senior position.

After the interview at which he had been again a shade too
grateful, elation transfigured his middle-aged face. Bouncing
downstairs, a ball of success. Back slapping. Telephoning.
Drinks at the Phillip Street pub. He went home on an early
ferry so that he could bask in Lissie's pride in him. With the
vision of a briefly returned youthfulness he observed the lie
of a rope or apprehended the certain timbre of the ferry bell
and the intimate grating of hull against wharf, between which
busking things harbour water whipped itself green and white.
All the western shores were homely and friendly and well-loved.
Smoke stacks at Cockatoo offered George Brewster's personal
sacrifice of thanks to the Lord. I'm getting away from it.
Getting away, he shouted in his mind. I can afford to love it.
In the ferry shed opposite the park where he waited for the
bus, leaves crepitated in the wind; a dandelion ball, silver-
spiked, trapped itself against a leaf and shuddered. Grotesque
with glory an unseen traveller's shadow teetered on asphalt,
a massive-shouldered giant of a man that proved itself in the
ticket queue to be a public service weed from two streets
along. Thirty heads in front of him sat in caged submission.
Hatted. Hatless. Crocus. Cerulean. Swart. Ivory. O Driver,
trolled George's inward singer, we worship and we bless.

After the staff party, after the private parties, after the hang-
overs and the swinish mornings, he sailed with twelve others on
a small cargo ship that was travelling through Panama.

"Bring me back tourist trash, Daddy," Jeannie cracked
brightly. Balletomane, she stood poised for a *grand jeté* along
a wharf crowded with journalists and friends. Associate

editor Penbrook had come down with Fred Chivers, a staff photographer.

"Smile prettily, boys," someone said as they bundled up along the gangplank. Barkly from Newcastle drunkenly removed his false teeth and held them out provocatively. Whinnying with laughter, Chivers rolled up to George.

"Caught you nicely, Brewster. Full profile. Lots of gesticulation." George's mind did a crazy somersault and saw Chivers pawing his books, amiable ignoramus.

"Complete Shakespeare, eh? Got that outer the *Herald*, didn't you?"

"What do you mean?" (Reprint? Plagiarized? For God's sake!)

"One of those coupon books. I got one ten years back."

"I really don't know. It was my father's."

Not listening, Chivers had said "Only remember one thing from that. Rape of Lucria—Lucrezia—something like that. Light and lust are enemies. Wow!" (Misquoting? George couldn't remember, either, but the silly grin on Chivers's face made him look twice at the boyishness of jug ears, bulbous freckle nose and chin dimple.) Light and lust. In the clear afternoon sun, fruit-yellow, George turned towards the calm face of his wife and threaded his arm into hers.

"Be good!" he cautioned cornily. "Jeannie will keep an eye on you."

"Oh, George!" Alice, the realist, laughed. "It's you who should be good. And who will keep an eye on you for me!"

"I will, my dear," staid Vincent Mackie said over her shoulder.

"Yes, yes!" George became enthusiastic even at the vaguest hint of naughtiness. "And we won't be in Paris long."

"Ooooh, those French Girls!" Chivers sighed. "Lots of ooh la la!"

"Not much of that nonsense in France." Penbrook said.

181

"There's a damn' side more to be recovered for the poor devils than the nightclubs."

"He's going to work, aren't you George?" Alice played an affectionate arpeggio on his arm and he took her fingers in his. "Two columns a week will keep him out of mischief."

"More than keep me out of mischief." He looked fondly at Penbrook. "A funny and a serious, eh? Light and lust—I mean shade. Oops!" No one minded.

"Enjoy the trip," Penbrook said. "You might send us a spot from the boat. Post-war travel conditions. Scenic. Hardships. You know the line."

"I know."

"Not too funny. You know the old man."

"Do I not?" He was full of good humour.

Everyone shoved up the gangplank and into the cabin he was to share with Mackie. Someone whipped out a bottle of Scotch with a blue bow-tie around its neck (howls of laughter) and handed it to George (cheers). Another appeared. They toasted separation and fine writing. The lady feature-writer put an orchid between George's teeth and when he bit it obligingly, rolling his eyes like an *Esquire* sketch, a bitter flavour prickled his taste buds. But he kept it there and went on clowning and rolling his eyes in a way that made Jeannie tinkle with mirth and Alice smile sadly. Babble of talk rose like air beads in liquor. Buck-sprightly, George squeezed back and forth in the narrow stinking cabin wearing the smoothly pressed suit of his self-importance with great style—its only modesty being that it covered a spiritual nakedness that shivered sometimes under the social trappings.

"Look up old Eddie Lumsden who went to the *Express*. He retired last year and is living in Tunbridge. I've got his address somewhere." Chivers mulled over an address book. "And there's another one here that might interest you. Not press feller. Wapping Old Stairs. It says 'up back steps behind

182

tobacconist's between nine and nine thirty." There were gales of laughter. (But George didn't forget *that* one and jotted it down in his diary later on when the ship was rocking between the Heads. Getting Friendly with the Natives.)

Fatuities dropped everywhere. "Say hello to Trafalgar Square for me." "Give my love to Piccadilly." "Bring me back some French wine and postcards, darling."

In one corner of the cabin Jeannie was being squeezed against a bunkhead by Barkly who had wandered in from a party in an adjoining cabin. And liking it.

"All hands on deck!" the lady feature-writer carolled gaily, as she observed this; and the laughter crashed against the crushing walls.

Stranger faces kept appearing and disappearing. George was swept off for ten minutes to a drink-happy finale three doors down. During that moment Alice suffered the tiniest pang that he was so willing to be parted from her during these last moments together for half a year. Saintly, she repressed the thought and in answer he reappeared wearing a paper cap and a lipstick smear on one cheek. But it all had to end. Kisses and more kisses. Barkly almost forgot himself in the absence of his wife and had a vast picnic on feminine faces. George clung to Alice, publicly sentimental but sensing his heart tear. This was different from the fashionable "darling" and the clinging superimposition of scarlet mouth from the feature-writer who had always had her eye on him. Alice's eyes were calm as dawn and gazed their benediction.

"Goodbye, old boy," she whispered, barricaded by the blare of voices. "Come back safely."

"Don't worry," George whispered back into her greying hair. "You'll hardly know I've gone before I'm with you again."

Jeannie was too young to feel sad. Tipsily friends and relations crowded back to the wharf and mouthed farewells and jokes across the airy wall. Everyone held streamers, made signs, pulled faces. Barkly was wearing a celluloid Semitic nose and glasses visible even when the boat was forty feet away. After a while they all grew tired of waving; the sun burnt red holes on every port; the ship swung about and turned down the harbour. There was no more to be seen.

A white scarf that Alice had been flinging across the sky was tucked back into the scented neckline of her coat. She caught hold of her daughter's hand, trying to pin on her some of the glumness she alone seemed to be enduring. Jeannie pulled away with a jangle of bracelet and ill temper.

"Don't *fuss*!" she said impatiently. "You fuss over both of us too much."

"Do I?" Alice's mouth tightened. "Well, darling, I'll try not to do it any more."

Alone in the big sagging bed that night in the hollow created by George's heavy body she thought of him plunging up and down the green valleys off the coast and fretted dreadfully. She was only a shape, an outline of efficiency in their lives— and she knew it. She had become the neatly ironed shirt, the well cooked dinner, the absent-mindedly taken marital comfort. And she had failed him. She had forgotten to pack his tyroid tablets.

After he had returned home London became the lump in his throat.

A place lost has more loveliness than the place achieved. But then he explored this ancient city in detail and with joy. Theatres and churches, buildings and monuments, squares, lanes, waterfronts, all recognized in part from a boyhood curiosity in books, acquired the tender cognition of friends. He felt more observed than observing. He rambled about bomb sites, went to Mass at the Oratory although he was closer to St George's, joined queues to talk to old ladies, (human story, Vince).

184

If you had asked him twenty years away what he had brought back from that overseas trip it would not have been the image of a packed conference room full of pressmen; no instant recollection of the hours and hours of political talk on the train going south through France; nothing much at all except an adumbration of meetings with Royalty or statesmen or refugees. Instead, an incense-heavy Benediction in an East End church, carpet smells and sunlight in a country house, a few cheap kisses, a priest who sucked cough lollies. It was always the emotions that bothered to explore him which he remembered clearest and longest.

There was not much time in this confusion of people and talks and interviews for even genial peccadilloes. Most evenings Brewster and Mackie, the exact model of journalistic virtue, would be up till midnight working on the notes they had taken that day, sorting them into presentable form and tapping out their stories in time for the deadline Sydney had set them. There was a temptation to exploit the reading public's pity and Sentimentalist Brewster had constantly to check and re-check and then cut his own writing cruelly. It was easier to be funny. Alice devotedly kept a scrapbook of all the articles he wrote during that time, and during the evenings when she found the house gloomier and larger than it should have been, she would curl up in his favourite armchair by the drink cupboard and search pitifully through each story, hoping inanely for some *double entendre*, a code message of love in their little language. No beacon flared. She wrote urging him to look up a couple called Learmont who had lived close to them at the Hill. He wrote back when this meeting had been achieved, sentimentally enlarging on the delightfulness of old faces in new places and the sheer warm lovely heart-rending unselfish thoughtfulness of his Lissie who always managed to suggest exactly the right thing. It was with enormous relief that he left Mackie and his stale jokes in the brassy care of his

185

London landlady and travelled down to Sussex to spend a week-end at the Learmonts' home.

Everything was a picture-book tangle of folksy thatch, roses and low ceilings. Sally was all golden and giggly. Her husband, a lumbering hog of a man, all air-force and moustached. Catriona, their only child, was an elfin creature whose chief talent lay in being able to say the Ten Commandments backwards faster than most people could repeat them forwards. Someone had taught her the national anthem backwards too but this was the *pièce de résistance* for their ginny parties; while at other times she played it only softly with one finger in case of misinterpretation!

"How could you misinterpret it?" George wondered. It sounded like nothing on God's earth.

When George went down again to Uckfield the husband was away at an air-force base in the north so that George and Sally, absolved by a ten years' friendship in another country, consoled themselves with lots of drinks and cuddles and conversations so *risqué* that each of them, glamourised by the twelve thousand .miles of sea separating this place from their former suburban ordinariness, became stimulated and love-curious.

Austerity-pressed villagers would glare disapprovingly at this racy blonde in egg-yellow slacks who would roar up to the local pub on Saturday night, stride in, straddle a stool and proceed to match her companion drink for drink. Her aggressive lack of respect for local gods culminated one mild spring evening in a vicious exchange of insult with an elderly quavering fellow who was driving a horse and brake down the narrow lane. The horse ambled from hawthorn hedge to hedge, undisturbed by Sally Learmont's resting one sharp angry elbow on the horn of her car.

She leaned across George, her narrow face white with temper.

"Get your damned horse over, can't you? Do you think you own the road?"

He shouted something back they couldn't hear and suddenly, deliberately she edged the car forward so close to the brake they could hear the bump of wheel against the mudguard. Without turning she kept the car moving until they had passed and, glancing in the driving mirror, she saw the old man standing up in his brake, waving his whip at them.

"Who's that old geezer," Sally demanded of the pub-keeper as they sat over their gins, "the old boy who drives a brake and takes up all the road? I had a fair go at him this afternoon."

"What did you say?" the pub-keeper asked interestedly. He wiped down the bar and winked fatly at George.

"I asked him if he owned the whole damned road," Sally said indignantly.

"He does."

"He what?"

"He does. What a lark! That old boy is Sir Thomas Wyse. At least half a dozen of the lanes here are private and run through his properties for the convenience of tenants." The man began to laugh. "I bet that's the first time in years he hasn't had a forelock pulled." He grinned admiringly at Sally. "The next is on me, Miss. You've earned it."

"What makes you so carefree and happy?" George asked her later as they washed the tea things in her kitchen.

The dishmop in her hand slopped soapily to a stop. Her pale green eyes regarded him unsmilingly.

"Care-free? Happy?" Still holding his eyes with hers, she removed her hands from the sink, wiped them sketchily against the velvet of her trousers and with a deft movement that took George entirely by surprise dragged her shirt away from her left breast. It was purple with bruising. A dark red mark underscored it. George stared in horror.

"Who did that?"

"Bert."

187

"Good God, why?"

She shrugged and buttoned her shirt again. "We had a bit of a row and he lost control. That's nothing, really. Just the latest in a long line."

"It's a matter for the police," bubbled protesting George. "No woman has to take that. He must hate you."

"I don't think so."

"You don't think so?"

"No. And in a queer sort of way, I don't mind him. But just don't get the idea that everything is all roses and violets in this neck of the woods."

George was sobered for the rest of the evening; but in bed, try as he would, he could not put the memory of that poor bruised and still lovely breast from his mind. True, almost three months of abstinence had wrung from him the letters of a schoolboy lover, letters that he posted home to Alice at least three times a week. She read them with a mature amusement.

"My dear," she had written back, "if it is too terrible for you, and I know it must be terrible for you, and if you found some nice girl who was clean and willing, I would not mind."

His exaggerated reaction was to kiss the generous note, cable back "I love you"; and then, because of the inner cunning of Alice's liberating him, became instantly incapable of taking advantage of her kindness. Perhaps she knew this. In many ways she was more of a sophisticate than he.

Therefore it was with a confusion of spirit, an almost complete unenthusiasm, that he regarded Sally Learmont as he lay bulging with cake and tea on her floor the next afternoon and observed her raise her skirt above her knees and pull it back to her thighs.

"No," he said. Dispassionately, her legs were far too thin.

"Oh, come on!" she said. "What's wrong with it? You've got permission."

188

"No."

"But what's the harm?"

He shook his head awkwardly, rolling it from side to side on the carpet; and when she put her foot on his most vulnerable place, he writhed with a disgusting pleasure even though he said "Stop it." Drowning in ecstasy he was hardly prepared for her removing the foot abruptly and rubbing it violently over his face. He lay there, detumescent, his eyes closed. Under the tense fingers of his right hand he could feel the pile of the flower-tatooed carpet. Visions of brown roses and orange tendrils. In the orchard below the kitchen garden Catriona's sexless treble voice raised its candle flicker of song among spring boughs and trembled into nothing. A swing door closed. A tap chattered into a sink. His outraged face could scarcely bear to confront the room but he opened his eyes and saw he was alone and sat up in his squalor. He could never forget, if he tried, the chumminess of the two easy chairs, the untidy book-cases, the tray of used tea things on the sideboard, the rust lengths of withered curtain or the contempt that had been stamped on his face.

They drove to the pub later and became gently drunk and did not refer to the incident that pressed itself like some corrupt flower between their pages; and by the next morning with sleep between fact and fact, both regained poise and kept humility out of sight.

After lunch they walked in the orchard under a sky cross-stitched by tiny buds and leaves. Silver Catriona patted a ball all over the acre of garden, racing with young litheness among the fruit-trees.

"Do you grow apricots?" George asked impulsively. He could forget the present in the past.

"We have a couple of trees. They didn't bear well last year. Over here." Sally's bangled wrist rattled out a direction. The light metal lay askew on the slender bone. George was ploughing through nostalgic grasses knee-nigh to pick a spray of bloom.

With heavy sentiment he said, "This has all sorts of associations."

But there was no one to hear and turning round he glimpsed their bright blue dresses criss-crossed by tree-limb at the far corner. He started to walk towards them, a fat middle-aged ball of self-assurance, holding with over niceness the delicate sprig of white blossom in his hand. Birds of joy sang faintly in his fairy forest yet audibly still at forty-four and he pursed his lips to whistle in his own toneless and unmusical fashion a scrap of song popular when he was a boy.

"Tee tumti—she's-my-ladylove." His note pattern followed rise and fall but was not exact and the melody became a shadow of the original. Catriona danced across the grass on windy feet. He felt absurdly happy. Yesterday was almost erased from his mind. Catriona danced closer and he held out his short plump arms laughingly to catch her and swing her up, up, up. But she swerved a little as she pranced forward and the next minute struck him a stinging blow across the face with a little switch of privet she was carrying.

George squealed aloud, clasping his face with his hands. In front of him the child hesitated, her eyes fixed in a round stare in her pale face.

"What did you do that for?" George demanded angrily when the pain had receded and he could speak without shaking.

"Mummy told me to."

Catriona was a wisp of fear. She dropped her gaze from the red weal she had created on his fat white cheeks. The angry blue jelly of his eyes sparked beneath shaggy brows.

"She *told* you to?"

"Yes."

As he stood glancing through the orchard lights and darks he could see Sally watching them both, pillar-still beside an apple-tree. The creaking of this aged, this turning head. The

190

revolution of some ill-hewn idea. Ruffling Catriona's thin hair. Patting her cheek. And saying "It's all right. Never mind." Then striding through the grass to the young woman who spun shadow all about her but said nothing to his fury, merely inspecting the red weal with a placid interest.

"Why did you tell the child to do that?"

Mrs Learmont smiled past him. She was quite certain that he would not believe her next words.

"I wouldn't have done it if I hadn't liked you."

George was staggered. "*Liked?*"

"Yes." Her expectation proved, she was sullen now. Good-bye giggles and tossed curls.

"Was it because of yesterday?'

"Perhaps."

"Don't you know?"

"No. Oh, I don't know. I did it because I like you."

George turned away from this fragile monster, puzzling it out, shocked by the possibility of a perversion stronger than his taste. That bruised and lovely breast. And she hadn't appeared to mind. He walked back to the house ahead of her with his busy important step and went straight to the bathroom to dab calamine across the raised bar of scarlet.

They parted that evening and the six thirty-five took him away for ever from that boyish figure in slacks. When he heard three months later of her death in a car smash in Scotland, he wept with a guilty release and temporary but genuine affection. Apple-boughs, apricot-trees, a curved length of privet, long grasses and a child's puzzled face. Somewhere, tucked back, a vivid pastiche. He wrote a delightful little feature on spring in Sussex which his paper featured with a picture cut from *Country Life*. Alice read it with her Sunday toast. There had been no letter from George that week and she had prayed so strongly and terribly for him during early Mass, she was sure this must be a sign. Perhaps it was, for George brought home

191

little else. A rosary beads purchased in the doorway of Notre Dame, beads whose Parisian background made the sin for which penance was said on them seem venial; a memory of the weather in Normandy; and, more strongly than the agonies of the hundreds of thousands of homeless Europeans, was scribbled into his mind the attempt at reparation he made on his visit to the *Poulette Rose*, Paris nightclub and brothel. There were six Sydney pressmen with him but George in a stubborn determination towards purity was the only one who didn't go upstairs. Later he told everyone about this and only the unkindest said old George had always been impotent.

He came home through Suez and somewhere near Aden smashed a mirror in his cabin. Although it was one of those freakish accidents caused by florid gesture and good humour, George thought ruefully that there would be seven years' bad luck ahead. And to a certain extent he was right, for ill fortune began with boils that endured for at least five years afterwards; and on keeping score he found the tally to be nearly two hundred. Carbuncles insist on a gravity of mind; pitifully enough, of an artificial kind, but it was during these five throbbing years that George wrote the bitter and provocative leaders on post-war reconstruction that won him recognition not only from Wyatt but from editors of many other dailies as well.

"You're in line for the next associate editorship, old boy," Hilbery said to him. Since he had returned from Greece his ebullience, his expectations had all diminished. He drank less. Someone said he had "got" religion.

"Do you think so?" George rumbled in his magnificently black way. He craved promotion. He seemed to have become static in the position he held—senior enough—but not sufficiently important. There was a world of difference. London had made him restless. The dandyisms he had assumed as part compensation became permanent. There were specially made bow-ties, specially crafted suits, a slightly pointed shoe.

"You dog!" Hilbery would comment, testing fabric texture between a knowing forefinger and thumb.

"Like me?" One hand on a pudgy hip, Brewster would execute a slow *fouetté* that Jeannie had taught him. ("Oh, Daddy, you look a regular queer!")

Hilbery's hint settled in his mind, the most dangerous of seeds. He was not a greedy man but the thought of outside confirmation of what he really believed himself to be worth elated him. Foolishly he commenced hunting for definition from Wyatt, holding him in private talk after the daily conference, button-holing him with a charm that was to be his undoing. By a vicious turn of fate Wyatt had met some months before, while George was in England, a King's Cross boulevardier who took him half-drunk to a bed-sitter party. There he met Mrs Reardon, still lush, still cropped, still available. The mistakes she had made in her franchised years had softened—not hardened—her, to a state of generous toleration, of a humility that expected little. This did not mean she had become a woman easily dismissed. On the contrary the lack of that brassiness gave a false impression of intelligence and reasonableness. Within a week Wyatt and she were lovers. Within a fortnight he was in love with her.

A few days before Easter Wyatt was drinking with four or five others at the Journalists' Club. Nancy Reardon, pliably lovely, Grishkin-like, clutched at a gin and every word he uttered. George, too early for Hilbery, nodded as he went past their table and Wyatt, relenting, gestured to him to join them. Mrs Reardon was too guileless to practise a Gioconda face and gave instead the full-lipped luscious smile on which he had foundered three years before. Wyatt raised his heavy brows when they greeted each other.

"Old friends?" he asked.

"The oldest," George said with heavy whimsy. "If I may venture a little anecdote . . ." It was too easy, he thought. And it was. This facility for taking over a group like an invaded country was getting away from him. He was in the middle of his third and longest story when Mrs Reardon excused herself and went to the powder-room to correct any loss of self-assurance. After she had gone Wyatt interrupted George's story without apology.

"I didn't know you two knew each other?"

"Knew is the understatement of the year," said Don Juan Brewster unable to resist the hint of conquest. He winked at Judge Urquhart on his left.

"What does that mean precisely, Brewster?"

"Well, it's a long, long story. And I never like to talk about a lady."

Wyatt narrowed his eyes as he stared hard at George across his glass. He sipped.

"No. That's something a gentleman doesn't do, I believe. Is there anything to stop you really?"

George missed that one again. He was thinking of something else.

"Did you know," he said, turning to Judge Urquhart, "that Newman defines a gentleman as one who never inflicts pain? What would you say to that definition, Judge?" He savoured the title as if it were a fat olive.

The judge shrugged. "Fair enough, I suppose, but rather negative."

"Refraining can be positive, you know." George was enjoying himself. "The actual abstention from delivering pain might take tremendous reserves of moral strength. Not to be vicious. Not to be malicious. Not to detract, calumniate. All evidence of triumphant overcoming of the commonest temptation."

Wyatt shifted restlessly and angrily. "You're protesting too much."

194

"I?" George was all wondering innocence of big blue eye. It was maddening to see.

"Implication can be as unpleasant as factual statement, I would suggest, Brewster," Wyatt said. "You are a careful fellow, I've noticed. Implication but never outright statement." Wyatt was losing his poise. He had been drinking half the afternoon. He could see Mrs Reardon swing out through the wash-room door and suddenly regretted his impulse to add Brewster to the group. "Were you meeting anyone?" he asked quite rudely.

"Johnny Hilbery," George said. He drained his glass, unaware of tension. "Hello, loveliness!" he said to a renovated Nancy. "You look as good as ever!"

"Do I?"

"*Do* you!" George smiled to himself. It was that inward smile unendurable to the onlooker that caused Wyatt to rise abruptly.

"Come along," he said to the woman. "We'll be late as it is. Sorry, you others. We have a dinner engagement."

Here there was the shifting uncertainty of a scrambled picture: the screen wobbled, shook out voices, facts, apologies, lies and half-truths from wavering patterns of lips, noses, eyes. Disjointed furniture, lift-attendants, waiters, confused areas of light and dark trembled and cohered. Hilbery, focusing unexpectedly in a larger-than-life close-up, stepped across the room and dug George in the ribs.

"See that!" he said, jabbing a thumb after the pair as they went to the lift. "That's the latest Big Thing in Tiger's life."

"Oh, God, Johnny! That's not true."

"True it is."

George stared solemnly into his glass. "Why weren't you here? I've made the *gaffe* of a lifetime." The overhead lighting was sombre. Drink-waiters scooted around him. He didn't see or care. "The *gaffe* of a lifetime." He brightened as a thought hit him. "At least it's nice to know I was way ahead in the queue."

Incurably sanguine, George cramponed his way along the slope of the next two weeks, taking cheer-swigs from his oxygen flask with all the cheek in the world. Penbrook was leaving at the beginning of May. Yet, when Jockel was appointed over George, it nearly killed him.

Tricksy self-analysis insidiously began to replace the former bumptiousness. He refused to seize the simplest explanation. Where had he gone wrong? Surely a sexual triumph could hardly affect the judgment of a skilled editor. Triumph! What wry irony! He cursed the impulse that had made him hint at a victory he had never achieved. He had cried "Wolf" (wolf!) once too often—and been believed. Yet surely Nancy would admit the innocence of the whole affair to Wyatt. Surely. It did not occur to him that Wyatt might not be bothered probing the jealous nerve-centres of his being to worry and worry at something lost for ever. So, in a series of mental evocations he revised his literary *faux pas*. The time of the waterside strike— could that be it? He had slipped in a sympathy pill in his editorial counter to the paper's policy. Or was it that series of election articles when he had argued and won his point over the use of biased domestic photographs? Or—? But it was useless to speculate and though Hilbery insisted he had ruined his own chances, he always had a suspicion that his work might not be up to standard. The morning scowl he now delivered at his shaving mirror was gradually becoming the fruit of clear vision. He was nearly fifty, with more chins than he liked, a bagging under the eyes and a paunch that promised magnificence. O God, he groaned. But God gave no indication that He heard; and for two years the gay *flâneur* was lost in the fleshy folds of a man who walked to the ferry to regain fitness, ate cut lunches in his office, took vitamins of frightening commercialized potency and began in a fussy incipient way to worry about his health. Jeannie would recount with her soft amusement how one evening after Alice had prepared an elaborate dinner, washed and wiped up alone and was wearily cutting his next day's sandwiches, she sneezed so audibly from the kitchen that George had interrupted himself in full anecdote to say, "I hope that wasn't in my lunch, Lissie."

Sobersides Brewster!

All at once everything appeared to be deserting him. Even his religion failed to give security. The affectionate trust that had bolstered him through setbacks of all kinds gave way to genuine doubt in the efficacy of prayer. Once, he had been able to confide his guilt and remorse to an unknown and eternal judge who, he was confident, would dispense a remote and impersonal justice. George could afford to wait. Less frequently did he take out the horn beads from Paris. Less frequently did he kneel after Communion vibrating with grace. He took out his *Apologia* and re-read it. It seemed sterile and when it reached the point where it took one man from Littlemore to Rome he could not be satisfied. After all, the primal postulate had always been solidly fixed in Newman's mind. But what if you didn't have that? He felt Catholicism a rational and unavoidable conclusion for any student of Christianity who believed the basic axioms. But that was the point. Could he believe those? He read a series of popular conversions. At that stage in the religious development of each subject where he felt the greatest need for intellectual proof was called for, it all tailed off into emotionalism. "It's true," thought George, not daring to say so to Lissie, "Kierkegaard was right. Christianity demands the crucifixion of the intellect." But he was a softie. He knew it. Something inside him wanted that crucifixion and the very fact that something else denied and fought against this made him an unhappy man.

That summer Jeannie went south in the *corps de ballet* and with the stimulation of all her demotic teen-age jargon gone, suddenly George felt unexpectedly old as well, went to fewer parties and could be found most evenings in slippers and dressing-gown, lovably sloppy, lovably abstracted, reading until one and two in the morning. Fat. Solemn. Dedicated to good prose and still with the fantastic memory that enabled him to quote lavishly from scores of writers. He and Jeannie exchanged long amusing letters, pulsating with gossip. There began to be, he reflected, real value in fatherhood, and with a desperation for distraction he attached himself stickily to her problems and gripped hard with all tentacles. It was pardonable. It was sad. But for the first time in his life George was thinking fully and sympathetically beyond himself.

## [VIII]

TIME, MR BREWSTER, SIR, a voice had begun to call across saloon
bars of thirty years' reasonable drinking. Time, time, time,
time, time. Would shave each morning the stubble of fifty
years from his chin and say to himself, "I'm not really old.
The trouble is at heart I always feel twenty-five."

Which had always been his trouble.

The parties at first caused certain queer clashes. There was
the remarkable disparity in age to start—daughter's friends
and father's friends. Ultimately daughter's friends won.

They were far more exciting to George. They looked better,
they spoke dazzlingly if idiotically, wore the sort of clothes he
longed to wear and drank with hyperbole of snobbery cheap
bulk tar-coloured wine. Some of them were ballet dancers,
some beat out bronze cuff-links and ear-rings, some painted,
acted, played pianos or were writing novels—but none of them
worked. The rigours of nine to five they understood meant
pee em to eh em. It was all gay febrility and rather dated.

Insouciant Jeannie, now twenty-one, knew dozens of effete
young men and amazonian women. She was normal apart
from this. She was seen at many places but in unvarying
attitudes—the open-mouthed laughter, the slightly malicious
glance, the hand gentle with love around the glass. People
full-length upon divan or floor or crouched over gramophones
would see her undulate from group to group with a sideways
movement. "A balletic crab," Hope, ten years older but still
going strong, used to say in an aside not quite soft enough,

squinting beneath her own carapace; and, "Darling! But you look marvellous, marvellous!" A spurious and thin vein of culture coursed through the group. Old copies of the *New Statesman* would be found in their lavatories. They wrapped scraps in the *T.L.S.* They had talked through more Bach than even he would have dreamed possible.

George, despite warnings of a physical kind that came privately and intermittently, would stick it out until the deathly four o'clock end. Watching Jeannie made him proud. "Even if she's not the Queen," he would say, the wicked old witty thing, "then she's certainly the princess!" It was as good as having a rejuvenation course to live it up with all those bright kids. Since he had missed out on the associate editorship, half the impulse had left his work. True, he was efficient. True, he could still write amusingly and well. But the dedication left him and he knew in his heart that he was over-looked old Brewster who ran the magazine section, wrote a feature or two and the tinselly editorials.

Alice was completely grey, although her spirit retained spring tints. Parties bored her now; she stayed at home more often, developing a surprising taste for Maurois and Gide, who perhaps caressed old sores. She would gaze fondly at the old dog togged up to kill or be killed in his polka-dot bow-tie that he began to affect soon after the war, and all her outlines would melt or crumble with affection. Their daughter, now a fully-fledged roc, astounded them both, although George would never admit it, not even in his most secret prayers at side altars.

A young man with sand-papered face and hair *en brosse* was to be Jeannie's Austerlitz. Cascades of laughter from her coral mouth had held him fascinated for half an evening, after which he approached her and asked with the uninflected directness that only a lover might miscall charm if he could see her home.

Jeannie turned on him a slightly drunken but brilliant smile.

"Of course, darling. So long as I don't know you one teeny scrap. I always let everyone see me home, especially strangers."

There was another waterfall of mirth.

"Someone's flushing Jeannie out again," Hope buzzed to a curly bard.

Crewcut smiled tightly. He was not as hard as the stones he made a study of in his profession, but would have delighted in being thought so, having lived for a long time in rented houses. Jeannie, *nuancière*, noticed his face shift into top gear.

"Oh, darling," she cried repentantly, "I was only joking and being double bitch. Of course you may. Truly. I would love it." She widened her green eyes in a way she knew to be effective and peered under her lashes at him with a coy lust.

He thanked her in his arid voice of which the vowels were perfectly rounded like pebbles and the consonants were flints that decorated the unchanging desert of his speech. Jeannie was temporarily lost for words although not for ideas. When in doubt she laughed. She laughed then and observed him smile. The smile lavished toleration.

"Well," he asked in his cool uncaring way, "shall we go?"

That staggered her.

"But it's so early!"

"That gives us more necking time."

Her tongue was sliced out. She pressed glass to wet lip carefully for a moment or two, taking every little bit of him in.

"It's twelve thirty," he added, half turning.

"Darling, you're crazy!" exclaimed Jeannie, bobbling her tight curls. "That's madly early. Madly, madly."

"Well, I'm going. You won't get an opportunity like this again." He carefully underlined his irony.

"I won't say goodbye to anyone, then," she compromised, "and if you're a washout, I can come back!"

Blinking their way out to Missenden Road where taxis

201

cruised like sharks, these minnows were gobbled up and in the instant dark of the back seat he began to cuddle her.

When they were standing on the footpath below her house and the taxi had shot back along the Point Road towards Gladesville, Jeannie giggled softly and said,

"You know you'll never get back from here at this hour."

"I know."

She widened her eyes. "What are you going to do?"

"What are *you* going to do?" he replied or challenged.

She flapped at the air with her painted nails.

"Mummy will have to make you up a bed, I suppose."

Alice was in bed but awake, and George, who had been prevented from attending the party by what he coyly called summer sickness (let us draw a little veil!), was reading in the livingroom, owl-like in his glasses. He did a wonderful pater-familias. Even Jeannie was proud. She kissed his gross cheek and George smiled like a happy lion, a happy baby lion. He had been piqued at not being able to go to the party, but now a small element of it had come to him, he was childishly joyous.

Donald Eastoe had never met people like them before. He visited them frequently and took them or their daughter for long motor rides in a secondhand Riley he bought through a friend of a friend. When he drove it was a concerto for car and driver with lots of brilliant cadenza work at high speed on the Gosford curves. Until it became apparent that his anti-Catholicism and his interest in Jeannie were going to cause dislocated relationships, he was always received with whisky and smiles. Both these, however, appeared less and less frequently.

"Doesn't the old boy like me?" Donald asked idly one Saturday as they lay on the sand of Parsley Bay.

"He thinks you're godless, darling," Jeannie giggled. "Godless and immoral."

"That's strange," Donald said. "He seems an intelligent

202

man, one who appreciates the viewpoints of others. I didn't think he'd be a narrow-minded old bastard."

Jeannie's face, a duplicate of Dad's, grew taut despite its plump outlines.

"You mustn't, darling," she reproved gently, "simply simply mustn't talk that way about George. I adore him."

"You're a stupid bitch, sometimes," Donald said, icily appraising.

Jeannie instantly gathered her towel and beach-bag together but as she sat up and dragged on her sandals the boy grabbed her fat arm and pulled her back beside him.

"Shut up," he said, "whatever you're going to say. Listen, I wrote a poem for you last night. I write exquisite love lyrics." He closed his eyes against the excruciating core of afternoon sun.

> Your bird hand, small curved wing
> Keeps circling my sky,
> Trembling against remote wishes
> That I would rather hide
> Or beating frantic
> On spiked iron tracery
> Of vine-wild lust.
> Rather let it hover,
> Then rest here on my body where
> The living bird of my heart
> Threatens to break through
> This shell of breast.

They captured a rhythm of affection in the silence that followed his words when, turning to examine the map of her face, he discovered a shy possibility of tears.

"Oh, that was beautiful," she breathed through her lip-struck mouth where sand-sugar sweetened the words.

"Yes. It is rather beautiful." Donald spoke with deep satisfaction. "Jeannie, I think we should get married."

When she told George and Alice that evening between the potato salad and the fruit flan, there was a hubbub of objections. She was too young. He was too young. (George, although he kept this close to himself, could not bear the thought of being a grandfather too soon.) There was the matter of religion. In addition, how on earth could the lad support her? He was barely through university.

Jeannie kept dipping a finger into her calm to test it.

She had no real wish to marry at all, but opposition piqued her contrariness and accordingly she withdrew to her room where she drew sulky curtains, turned her two holy plaques to the wall and began to think bravely about Donald. After some time she convinced herself that she was being spitefully frustrated by repressive older people who, having gobbled their cake down to the last crumb, were concerned that she should never even acquire nibbles at the stalest of buns. She even managed to giggle at the image and sometimes afterwards would call Donald "Bun" and gape open with hysterical laughter. So for a week, aloof as a gooseberry, she moved about the house with swollen red lids and pinkly shining nose.

From then on she stopped taking George to the same parties and although she and Donald continued to meet without approval, by necessary discipline the pair of them would scuttle away earlier so that she could see herself home on the last ferry. Love gnawed endlessly and one Saturday night, having missed the last boat to the Hill, Donald drove her home through Gladesville towards two o'clock and a darkened house. They removed their shoes and padded up the side to the washing-hung veranda.

Jeannie began to sob in his arms.

"They like me to be unhappy," she sniffled. "They like it."

Donald rubbed against her like a young bull.

"Come through to your room," he whispered. "My back aches holding you like this."

204

Yet he did not comfort her for long.

Pontifex Maximus in shot-silk smoking-jacket of indigo loomed enormous in the doorway and confronted them with the blasphemy of a light.

"I must ask you to leave this house," he ordered, making heavy weather of it. "At once. You are outraging all my hospitality."

Donald levered himself off the bed and made minor adjustments to his clothes.

"She needed comforting, and I was only seeking to do that," he explained in his rather high dry voice.

Brewster's lower lip dropped as he looked over the tops of his horn-rims.

"If you don't leave at once, I will ring for the police." And meant it.

"Oh, for God's sake, Mr Brewster!"

Donald was ignored with third-rate groundling's drama as the other man, touching the circumference of all outrage, flapped ponderously to the chair by the telephone and, stubbornly turning the pages, licking a deliberate finger, began searching through the directory. Donald's heart exclaimed in pandemonium, and Jeannie, emerging from the bedroom, followed the young man and tucked her arm through his to form the prettiest of family groups. George did not raise his heavy wrinkled lids but carefully began to dial.

"Oh, go!" Jeannie said. "Go, Donald! With George it's either drama or trauma."

George's blue bulb eyes speculated quietly on them for a moment while his finger hovered over the next number. He had found his power (his supreme dominion over them, his religion-trained mind qualified) of a definable pleasure and he did not replace the receiver until the front door shuddered from the impact with which Donald shut it.

He was repaid nevertheless.

That week they married between lunch-time and afternoon tea at the city registry office, and when at four that same day they called at the offices of the *Voice* to tell him, he was so enraged and then so disgustingly tearful they were appalled.

It was six months before George or Alice spoke to either of them and then the reconciliation was only achieved because Jeannie became pregnant.

The refusal to age spiritually despite the flagging energies of the body can be pitiful or miraculous. In George it was pitiful. The sweating unctuous geniality was repellent to his contemporaries who had grown beyond the need to impress; but on the other hand the young men and women who gathered at his daughter's parties were privately amused by the sight of old George living it up.

The pattern of these gatherings had not altered an inch and he could always count on forming a small cell of acolytes in one corner of a drawing-room where kids might cluster about for some minutes, drawn by his fruity voice rolling fulsomely over a criticism of this or that writer. But an occasional impatience lurked in their eyes and shifting impolite feet. He withstood it. Or rather did not know of it. He grew fatter and lazier in love. Pretty girls were still targets for verbal insanities but that is all they were. The heaving loadings of flattery implied a sad impotence. He should have been plunging or soaring in search of God, but instead went weekly to Mass, drugged rather than stimulated by ritual, confessed rationally, communicated unemotionally, and listened uncritically to sermons that took him no further away from himself. Father O'Neil was now a bishop whose office gave George vicarious satisfaction. When they met, George could never make up his mind whether to patronize him because he was celibate or admire him for it. It was very difficult.

He understood and wanted only the simplest God, the God

of reward and punishment; and when, by fluke, he commenced not long after Alice's reception into the Church a completely entrancing correspondence with a lady journalist in another country, he rationalized his mental infidelity as a rewarding and privileged friendship. In the way of these things, it quickly became emotional.

"Darling Rachel," he wrote, "it seems long ago now since you captivated me, made me your prisoner in mind and heart, and the wonderful spell still holds. It is all indescribably wonderful. Why was it my rich fortune to meet one so understanding and responsive? And like you I haven't the faintest notion how all this befell. Am I really enchanted, you ask, always the ever-woman. But, whatever I reply, again you know already. Enchanted, captivated, enslaved—the whole related sequence. And in the most devastating way, for one with a mind like mine. It gives me no respite. I can scarcely concentrate on anything. God forgive me, it is you all the time! Sometimes I suffer a feeling of being crushed under an immense weight. At others I have a richly compensating sense of high elation. My whole spirit is uplifted with an unwonted buoyancy. I feel twenty-five again. I sing. I whoop. Mad, eh? Mad goings on. Then I realize that it is an old old story. Quite simply and primitively, I am in love."

She replied with a spontaneity that was astonishing and emotion that was formidable. Each was convinced of sincerity. He sent her a flattering photograph taken some years before.

"This is what my friends call a speaking likeness," he lovably confessed. "I'm much what I look. Basically a facetious fellow, I suspect. I can always make the morning conference laugh even when they sit looking like a bunch of constipated owls. But I'm almost fearfully conscientious. Now, this will make you laugh, I hope. I have a pot, a tum. I can't hide it. I'm a bit curious looking as the photograph reveals. No husky Balmain Forward. Pale. Yes. I have hateful white skin

207

that won't brown no matter how I try. It freckles. You know. Turkey egg arms. I hate that about myself, but what's to do? I have pudgy hands, but *not* dirty ones. Not dirty nails. Nize clean boy no fleas. But too 'comfy' to be elegant. Some people think (flattering) I look like Churchill. Others G. K. Chesterton. Get the general impression? And the booming voice, of course. Usually have too much to say but can (and do) listen attentively, especially to bores. Make a thing of listening to bores, just to teach myself not to be a bore. Happily there are those who think me entertaining. Happily, too, I do know (without being conceited) that my friends *do* love me. I'm being awfully frank, darling. To WHOkM (it's this w rteched downstairs typewriter which I use on Saturdays) else could I say all that. I suspect I am just a bit pompous, but I don't mind being laughed at. I am quiet, mostly, and just a bit humble. Not pushing. Dogs can't smell any other dog on me, and so don't bother much, but they don't cringe when I happen to pat them. Cats I don't much care for, but they seem to like me and even spring up in my lap. Our own weird cat ignores me. Children think I am utterly crazy, tell me not to be mad and seem to regard me much as a big kid. All the young office cadets, male and female, use me as a sort of confessor. Some people have said I would have made a good priest. One man (a very piggy-doggy type) once said I was nothing but an old woman. Maybe true. Against that, I once had a surgical 'op' with only a local anaesthetic. It took forty minutes and the eminent surgeon gave me a 'ball by ball' running commentary. I missed both wars, so have not roughed it among men. But when young I was a keen peace-time soldier, rose to be sergeant-major and sat my examinations for commissioned rank before journalism made it impossible to continue further. I did years of night work and my 'copy,' I'm proud to say, is regarded as some of the best in the office. (Oh, what skite, you make me sick, George!)

208

"My life tends to be dull. I'm not perpetually in quest of entertainment. But I enjoy the theatre. I get on well with the clergy. I can rub shoulders in a bar and barmen always give me big grins and their favours. Nowadays I scarcely enter a bar. I do what little drinking I permit myself at home. I love pouring drinks for other people.

"What emerges? I'm not really so wonderful, Rachel; but there's a slice of me. My daughter finds lots of faults, yet says she is proud of me. She drags me round to longhaired parties so she can't be ashamed of me. I work hard at my job. Always have.

"Oh, but you might find me in the flesh tedious and terrible! You might laugh at yourself as well as at me and say, George, you are unspeakably tedious. Out of my sight! Go at once!!"

It was her turn to be enchanted and she sent in reply a photograph taken when she was twenty-four. Some fashion detail in the dress she was wearing warned him of duplicity.

"That is a charming photograph," he wrote, "but could you send me something a little more recent?"

"How astute of you," came the reply. "Here is one I have had taken specially. It is just for you." It showed her in ski pants and ski helmet, her happy rotund face and her complement of chins upheld by the strap of her head-gear.

George's male pride was knocked but he bore it bravely—he was fourteen stone and fifty-two after all—and the letters crossed the Indian Ocean thrice weekly burdened by proxy love.

She was his emotional blotter—to be discarded when too scrawled upon.

"I think (in fact I know, to be frank) that it was Thomas Carlyle who said that the uttered part of a man's life bears to the unuttered, unconscious part a small unknown proportion, and that he himself never knows it, much less others. And, as I remembered this, early this morning, I began a meditation in

209

a dreamy sort of way on all that has befallen us. So strange it all is, and so very nearly incredible. Did Carlyle mean the imagery of the mind, not wholly of the spirit, but with the flesh as partner, and all unlimited by the laws of probability, possibility, or any other 'ity'? Of what subtleties is the mind capable? What ecstasies! I think it is because of all this, that this, our strange love, burgeons so, separated though we are by long leaping leagues of sea and God knows what viewless horizons of space. But what is space, distance, when we are so close? See how we leap to each other, mind to mind!"

There was something mildly disgusting about this, George could see, but he was such a complete romantic he closed his soul to any tawdriness. And after some months it did assume many of the aspects of real friendship, for letterless days depleted him. He sulked in his editorial room and snapped at copy boys. Days of tenderness solved themselves in a euphoric idiocy. He whistled like a gormless office boy, he attempted stairs two at a time. Athletic Brewster!

"Is there?" he would enquire in the "little" language he had developed with his secretary; and she would smile knowingly and hand him the air-mail envelope.

"Hooroo, hooray!" Frabjous George beamed moronically. "I don't care what you think."

A certain polished glibness in his letters drew from Rachel Marks a cautious question. Had he often been involved this way before with other women? George smoked two cigarettes thoughtfully on reading that, burnt her letter neatly into his metal basket and tapped out a reply between bites of a meat patty sandwich.

"You *must* know, I suppose. I will give you a short, immediate answer. It is *No*. Never this way. Never anything one tenth as magical. But I should be telling you a most horrible untruth were I to tell you that I never had a love affair! Oh Rachel! I fell in love when I was eleven. And I remained in love with that one until I was twenty-four, when she abruptly married another. After an interval, as I couldn't have the bride, I married her charming bridesmaid! How's that for devotion. There were some minor sweetie-pies in between, of course. But I don't think you mean anything of that. You mean, I am pretty sure, has there been anything 'after'. Frankly, yes. Once. Difficult to describe and define. She meant a lot to me. In the beginning she was one of a group. You know how it is. So I saw her frequently. All our group were friends. But with this woman I was particularly friendly, for a long time. She had a mind like a man. Great executive capacity. She was self-reliant. A great battler. She had split with her husband early in life, and he contributed nothing. She battled for herself and her children, and gave them a splendid education. Her hospitality was generous to a fault. For a long time we were just friends. Very, very good friends. Then the war. Almost imperceptibly we became something more, though always in terms of physical restraint And that is true. She seemed to turn to me for comfort. Once we had a wonderful night of petting. There, I've told you. But it was only petting, at which, I discovered in that hour, she was a past mistress. Why 'nothing happened' I still don't know. Is it fair to say 'Perhaps I didn't try'? I don't know. But I didn't. She just seemed to be unbearably hungry for some physical loving—and there I was. It was as simple as that. Quite honestly, I often yearned for some further experiences of the same sort. But the occasion was not repeated. She went to England soon after and married again, is very happy and remarkably successful in a social sense. She was a strange woman, who would have been remarkable in any city in the world. She could cope with any situation—or almost any. Mostly I remember her as a great and lovable friend who enriched my life. In fact, that is my main recollection of her—that she did enrich my life—a phrase I have used conversationally quite often. Two or three occasions aside, when she was catty, she was always kind and helpful, with a lovely sense of humour and gay as a bird. But please, don't suspect that there was ever, at any stage, even the beginnings of any relationship as you and I enjoy. There was nothing faintly comparable."

It was odd that this epistolary romance remained as secret as it did in the office, but his secretary was a woman of much humanity and dignity. She never discussed Mr Brewster. He was childish, she thought, but rather sweet. At home Alice smiled with saintly indulgence, listened as he read aloud to her the folksier bits or the newsy tinsel about London. Alice's love for George was a kind of insanity, unreasonable in its toleration, for in a way that very toleration ruined him.

"I don't know why Alice puts up with the old bastard," Jeannie would complain to Donald.

"She adores him!" Donald replied in his high cold voice. "She wouldn't want to destroy her own idol. She's a deeply religious woman."

"A saint of God!" Jeannie giggled, quoting her father. Donald patted her bulging stomach.

"I bet junior is the image of him. Curls, anecdotes and all."

After six months the imagery was rubbing thin, but they flogged themselves along genially. Miss Marks knitted a terrible shapeless garment for the baby. George wrote over to his enricher, Mrs Timbrell-West, and suggested she meet Miss Marks. His motives were not pure. Mrs Timbrell-West wrote back that Miss Marks was fun, but forty-seven if she were a day, and boredom in Brewster found here its reason. Still, he decided to wait until the book she was having published that spring came out. For years he had game-fished through his reviews, throwing out lines to lady novelists in the hope that, having taken the bait, they would begin passionate correspondence of the proportions of Hugo's Juliette. (Those letters! Seventeen thousand!) When he received through the post his complimentary copy of *I Was a Prostitute in Paris*, his disgust was not with the title but the fact that it was only a paperback. Flicking through its functionally sized pages he saw at a glance that the writing was only mediocre and the content unpolished pornography. After reading two chapters on flagellation and one on white slavery, he picked it up between regretful thumb and forefinger and dropped it into his wastepaper basket.

"Thank you darling," he wrote, "but I feel the book doesn't do justice to your very real powers, to the ability I know you to possess. There is realism here, but realism is not enough, if you will permit me humbly to say . . ."

There was more like that. He prided himself on being able to spin nothing into three pages of something. Then he concluded with a perfunctory endearment and hinted that he would be busy for a few days—the "exigencies of the job!" he explained with adorable exclamation-point. He did not write again. It was brutal—but an incident of the previous Sunday had diverted his emotional direction.

"We need strawberries," Alice had suggested that afternoon in the after-lunch torpor of sprawling that went on in hammock or on straw mat across grass. They did not need with any desperation, but the word stuck with George. He dived bravely after the silver elusive flash of the thing and groped among the weeds until he caught it.

"Strawberries," he said, inspecting the fish for size and determined not to fling this one back in the water. "Strawberries . . . strawberries. . . . Doesn't Mrs Red Setter have a strawberry farm out Windsor way? Yes, of course, Lissie. Remember when we drove over there just after she married again and they were undecided what to do with the place?"

The name lassoed his wife who jerked to a halt, one over-ringed hand on the tea-tray. Her heart complained bitterly but silently.

"There won't be any shops open, Lissie, and you can have them freshly picked."

"I won't drive you. I mean—" She was shocked by the sound of protest she had not intended to make. "Someone has to look after the baby."

"I'll drive you, George," Donald said, "if Alice will trust me with the car."

"Oh, of course." An unnatural pink topped-off her cheekbones and she laughed lightly. "All right, darling, I suppose the outing will do you good. Take Jeannie, too."

"Oh, Jeannie wouldn't want to come," George said quickly. "She never liked the Red Setter."

"I hardly imagine buying strawberries would be an occasion for showing likes or dislikes."

"Oh, Lissie!" George sulked and then smiled as engagingly as he could, which was less now than ten years before, but still persuaded his wife.

"Go on, darling, then. You make me feel like your mother." Which was what he loved.

The countryside breathed Sunday as if it were the surd of Saturday. Grass lay mute. Cumulus shadows on the multiplying hills created illusions of more and more trees. And the shadow of love created in George's spongy heart illusions of more love, shivering nuance of the lost and unattainable in his present correspondence with Rachel Marks, inexplicably ramming into his flesh a barb like an unsolved problem, all the more irritating because of that.

"Next on your right," George advised. "And then follow the high road for a couple of miles. I'll tell you at the turn-off."

Oh, these enchanting distances, he thought. Then recollected that as you fling yourself forward to rapture upon green faraway places they become to the critical close-up orb, coarse browned hair, twigs, ants, split branches, tattered leaves, crumbling earth; but farther away again irregularities merge softly.

214

Chasing beauty in the Australian landscape was like trying to tread on one's shadow. Would she be pleased, surprised, outraged? It was so long since he had seen her—five years and then several times before he had gone to Europe. And before that—before that the desert of his anguish obsessed him and he could not bear to think.

⸮ "This very charming woman I am taking you to see, Donald, is a very very old friend of mine." When Eastoe made no comment, not rushing his bull, he added, "a very dear friend, also, if I may be allowed the use of such a phrase."

"Yes, George," Donald agreed dutifully, temporizing.

"She used to be very lovely. Of course when I first knew her she was quite breath-taking."

"And did she take yours?"

"I don't know what you—oh yes!" George played musical teeth. "Well, she did, you know, but that's an old story. I feel I can talk to you, man to man. Lissie was so hurt about it. So terribly hurt. But I suppose Jeannie told you." He rather hoped she had. He relished being thought a dog by Donald.

"She told me something of it." Donald cut neatly in beyond two dawdling cars with bravura.

George nodded. Locking his fingers across belly-mound, he slopped back into reminiscence, faintly regretful that he should appear so gross. But it was dragonfly regret, for he still envisaged himself as perpetual twenty-five, the soft-mouthed, jocose fellow who had laid them in the aisles.

Humming happily and grittily he watched the Nepean.

"Next turning," he advised.

"How do you know, George?" Donald asked. "Have you been out often?"

"I told you," George offered patiently. "Only the once. Lissie came with me to see the property just after they bought it."

She was working in the fields when they first saw her.

Donald, walking lone-wolfishly apart, saw their marionette

215

figures against the transparent afternoon: Brewster, fat, self-conscious, elderly, trotting with a touching anticipation over brisk turf to the lean athletic woman in slacks. Her hair was cropped short as a boy's at the nape of her neck, and she rested from her digging as they approached, with sun-polished arms leaning on the handle of the fork.

"Hello, Nancy," George said, grasping her arm.

Rapturous idiocy hooked their eyes together, noted observant Donald.

"Why, George!" she exclaimed in her lovely voice. During the introduction the greedy old thing simply gluttoned on the admiration in Donald's face.

But her first vision fading, Mrs Red Setter, moving sensuous palms on the work-smoothed wood in her fingers, smooth and round as the tears he had once caused her to shed, reached out silently towards the core he referred to as his heart and found it wood-hard still. At the funeral ten years before her soul had gushed out those shadowed lids of hers and she had not cared whether he should measure her grief or not; but later again at parties, torturing herself by covert glances, she had examined every corollary possible for her illicit and inexplicable longing and in an impatient satiety had flung the textbook aside to prove her congruence with an American lieutenant. She was unlucky in love, and when this affair ended with a bullet in the islands somewhere near Borneo, she took lover after lover. It was a simple addiction. Sedative upon sedative. And none really worked.

Returning to the *Voice* after drinks at the Journalists' Club, George would glimpse her sometimes, her full wide mouth crammed with laughter as she dragged on a khaki arm; or hurrying for trams in King Street, or even unexplainably at the Quay, profile down-bent beside duplicate down-bent male features, staring in a romantic fuzzle at the harbour waters, glamourized by blackout, catching light in unexpected places

216

on the lips of wavelets, the paper fleets luminous, the rafts of fruit-skins and peelings lost in the caverns around the piles. Yet although she thought him hard and selfish and although he often said of her that she had the soul of a whore, his stupid blood lurched in response to her brown boy head and she would laugh more gaily than ever, aware of this, and drink up quickly, quickly.

Looking at her now he wondered idly "How many Yanks?" but it was only a mathematical interest that could have tolerated, he felt sure, any numbers, relying on the fact that quantity would prove either a harlotry of spirit or an emotional indifference in her, either conclusion being equally emollient

"Will you come up to the house?" she invited. "Ross is working."

George gave her arm an almost imperceptibly intimate squeeze; and vulgarly, so Donald thought, their eyes laid claim to a world of familiarities neither had forgotten.

Behind mounds of typescript, her husband, a short blond weary fellow, idled at a table on the eastern veranda where a honeysuckle trellis trembled and tumbled in the wind that bit suddenly at the crest of the hill.

"Oh, hello, Brewster!" he said. "What in God's name are you doing out this far? The fresh air will kill you. Have you brought a smog tank?"

"My dear Ross," George fawned, "we really are in search of the strawberry."

"Well, that sounds bloody specious." Harrington laughed and stared hard at Donald.

"This is my son-in-law, Donald Eastoe," George said. "The father of my first grandchild." (A tucket sounds at left!)

"We heard Jeannie had married," Harrington said. He shuffled papers and books into some sort of heap and slammed the lid onto his typer. "Well, it won't be your last, either, Brewster, I suppose."

"Most certainly not!"

Donald's thin lips smiled with difficulty, it appeared.

"What is this, George?" he asked. "Feudal rights?"

They drank beer. Nancy brought up three deep punnets of bright red fruit and set them on the table.

"What's your book?" George inquired.

Harrington ruffled about for matches and lit his pipe.

"Nothing world-shattering. Pacifist stuff. Don't think you'd go much on it. Bits of wartime background. Not very original, I'm afraid. A few potted biographies of reluctant generals. You know how it goes."

"I say," George bubbled eagerly, helping himself to the nearest fruit, "have you heard that one about General Freyberg? Oh you must put it in, Ross. If I may have two minutes of your time . . ."

Donald writhed, but giggled all the same at the punch-line and George smirked with pleasure. Gug gug, Donald reflected. Sublimity for him consisted in the admiring attentiveness of a handsome woman—no matter how brainless—and the ears of the rest of the party. She must have been quite a doll! And he inspected her handsome features, the red mouth parted over the big white teeth. Thirty-two? Thirty-four?

Mrs Red Setter leaned across the arm of her cane chair. "You look young to be a father. How old are you?"

"I'm dreadfully old," Donald said in that clipped way that often sounded very funny.

"And are you literary as well?"

"I write brilliant little lyrics."

"He does, too!" lied George who could never understand a word of them. ("A line meets a line on a flat plane," he had once parodied to someone who asked him what sort of poetry Donald wrote.) "I don't claim always to understand them of course."

"I don't think sense matters nearly as much in poetry as in

218

prose," Harrington said. "A sequence of sound should be sufficient to stir the emotions. Or rather words whose meanings have become as evocative as sound without necessarily opening up new philosophical ground."

"Oh, I'm very much that," Donald said. "Little Magazine. Minuscule and chopped-up lines and thick white paper."

"Don't run yourself down, boy," George protested. He wanted to show someone off. "He's really a very clever lad, Nancy. Alice thinks the world of him."

Harrington's grey eyes held patterns of river-flats on their light shining surfaces.

"How's the job, Brewster? Is Fred Rush still on the art staff?"

"Still there."

"Is he still the same old bombastic Fred full of sexy innuendo?"

George raised his chin and swallowed the beginnings of joy.

"He's a dear fellow. I'm very fond of Fred. I can always talk to him, man to man. Often go down to have a little yarn with him. It does me good to hear someone like Fred who is so down to earth."

"But he isn't particularly talented, is he?" Harrington persisted. "The stuff I've seen around the women's magazines looks pretty patchy to me. Lot of rehash."

"I don't really know," George admitted. "But his work seems to be highly regarded on the paper, you know. And he has such enormous popularity with our crowd, they close their eyes to any free-lancing he does on the side—and believe me, he does plenty. Why don't you come in some time and have a drink? I'll tell him you were asking."

"Do that. Nancy and I usually go in to Sydney on a Friday. We'll give you a ring."

Oh, that's good!" George said. "I'll look forward to that."

"Same old George!" Nancy commented with a hint of querulousness. After all, his anticipatory enthusiasms had always been his most blatant frailty, the speculative eye prancing about a safely packed salon in search of diversion.

He was hurt, of course, and protested, asking could he never give tongue to simple pleasure without misinterpretation. Everyone reassured him. It was like patting a dog. Harrington opened another bottle of beer and they looked down towards the river drained of colour in the late afternoon. Now and again George explored Nancy's face, twelve years older, but still full, still tangibly handsome. After a decade it was difficult to pin-point the exact rapture of kisses, although he knew that re-enactment would again seek it out.

Would it?

Anxiety jabbed him with the fact that the same decade had aged him more, produced a ponderously padding walk, a great gut, the beginnings of jowls. Maculae on the stretched skin on the backs of his hands were large as coins.

"Oh, God!" he said involuntarily.

"What's up?" Donald thought the old boy was looking a bit queer.

"Nothing. Nothing." George said, recovering himself with a smile. He put his half-full glass of beer down. He never liked the stuff. "I think we'll have to go, Nancy. Alice will be wondering where we've got to."

As the four of them strolled down the hill between the lemon-and orange-trees to the dirt road where the car was parked, George contrived to loiter and take Nancy's hand for a sentimental fraction of a moment.

"You're still lovely," he whispered. "Are you happy?"

"Very."

"Do you ever—remember?"

She hesitated. To lie and say she did would please him—but would breed its own cruelty for she had grown beyond him in

220

wisdom and was perceptive enough to realize he could only draw unhappiness from wells of re-opened nostalgia.

"Not often," she said.

"Oh!" His hand released hers. Everything went flat. Their feet stumbled over tussocks, out of step.

"But you don't regret it?" Perhaps he was seeking to prolong his suffering.

"No, of course not."

"Ah, that's good then." He expelled his waiting breath and placated, took her hand again which he shook up and down in a movement friendly rather than erotic.

"You still look young," he said.

"Do I?"

"Oh, yes. But I don't." She would not deny it. "I've got terribly fat."

"How's Alice?"

"Oh, much the same, you know. Grey now, of course. But sweet as ever. Sweet and good as ever. But do you think I've changed all that much?"

"Not that much, I suppose."

"Oh, that *is* good. I thought perhaps you might not even recognize me."

"Never! You still *sound* the same, anyway."

"I suppose so." He felt every month of his fifty-two years all of a sudden, and suddenly terribly, wanted to be home with Lissie fussing about him.

"Here we are!" he said.

His small feet tottered to the car where Donald stood with one young, young, young,—he could scarcely think beyond that fact—arm on the bonnet.

"Goodbye!" cried the four voices.

And in the receding countryside George found the image of Rachel Marks receding too in the dazzle of reflected sunsets. He would never write to her again. The pointlessness

221

of it hit him savagely and she touched him not at all. Somewhere there was a regret for those letters of wildly physical passion he had sent her *poste restante* and he hoped vaguely she had had the good sense to burn them. But he would not burden himself with this and could not bring himself to answer Donald's smalltalk, so knotted was he with this confrontation of a vanished affair that outlined his tiredness, his age and a certain quiet despair that remained with him for a long time after that.

But she wrote.

At first her letters pleaded for reply. Then they became angry demands, instead, for the return or payment of articles his paper had requested. "She's mad!" exploded George in his irritation. "Utterly mad!" And was indignant, even as he carefully made sure a cheque was sent off. The end was a sad little note a few weeks later still.

"Dear George," said her typewriter, "you appear to have stopped writing. Let me congratulate you on your unbelievably vivid imagination.—Yours sincerely, Rachel Marks."

Bliss is lonely. It rarely shares itself.

In the marriage of Donald and Jeannie the ecstasy of each reared its pinnacle on an island. Sometimes their shadows might touch across the water, but it was never more than that, and soon, because the intensity of the lonely joy engenders madness or falls into disuse, so here each began forgetting shortly the true reason for awareness, for their excesses of sensibility, for tender reunions with God which neither would acknowledge.

Into the abeyances of loving, other faces, mnemonics of yet other faces, sidled; and as one must necessarily be at home to attend to the child, so they came to take pleasure separately. They used Alice often enough for baby-sitting, and she was as much the willing martyr as two selfish youngsters could wish.

Small storms constantly burst the former heaven of their skies. Baby Lisa squawled. The kestral-eyed visionary in Donald which is, one supposes, the alternative description of the businessman, suggested to father-in-law Brewster that he purchase a home for the young marrieds near his own so that some semblance of family life might be shared by all of them. After all, everyone agreed, there was no more impossible suburb in which to live in Sydney than Hunter's Hill. It was like an outpost of Empire. If they didn't all live near by, indeed they might never meet. George's money glands began to secrete. He popped the proposition in his mouth and rolled it all over his tongue. In the interim, hinted daring Donald, might they not all share the Brewsterian *ménage* at Vernon Street?

Unwisely, George agreed, subjecting himself to the never-ending torture of watching Donald stamp untidily all over his new wall-to-wall. Communal family life, instead of lessening quarrels, seemed to stimulate discord. Radio and record-player, damp napkins, wailings, boiled over milk, visitors, food-grinders, periods of silence and sound—all, all clashed. "They must go, Lissie," George said one evening when the happy couple were at one of their claret parties. He laid down the evening paper, removed his spectacles for special effect and repeated the fact. "We cannot have the Eastoes here. Life is becoming intolerable."

That other angel which smiles every second week discovered for him a double-storeyed timber house in Slow Avenue. The estate agent and George sang nauseating duets of speculation as they mulled over the possibility of converting the place into flats.

"I am not a two-house man, you understand," George stated with an air that was a very contradiction of the utterance. He sipped his scotch with every assumption of luxury. "However, I think I can possible manage this. I'm doing it for the sake of darling Lisa, you understand, Donald, who means as much to me as my own child. Even more."

223

When Donald made no reply but swung his sybaritic legs higher onto the settee, George annoyedly said,

"I said your daughter means more to me than Jeannie."

"She does to me, too," Donald said unruffled.

So it was accomplished.

The twining vines of mortgage were capable of disentanglement only by George's lawyer who assured him there was no real risk at all.

In a month the two families lived but one hundred yards from each other and Lisa, the kernel of their delight, learned to eat sieved foods with her very own pusher and to say "no."

Dozens came begging during this period of housing shortage to rent the downstairs flat, but finally George let it to one of the telephonists on the *Voice*, a cheap London sparrow with a heart-shaped face that was her only acquaintance with that particular organ, a peroxide brain and a quick-deal Jewish husband. She had only been on the paper for a couple of months but already her shapely legs and flat Cockney accent had become a warmth in some remote room in George's mind. (The fire. The drinks on the side table. And let's slip into something comfy, shall we?) Spare-time fantasies involving "Baby" Isaacs made a sumptuous change from the arid country of mere letter-writing where the concretion of ideas depended on symbols and was generally unsatisfying. George could do a lot with a typewriter but never quite that. . . . With delicious Victorian hangover, too, he refrained from a first name relationship, and thus retained a piquancy for his mental venalities. She was glittering efficiency. At the office, awe of his position kept her respectful although pert; yet at home, when he ambled over in his baggy old velveteens on Saturday mornings, with ineffectual plans to help dig the Isaacs's vegetable patch (he always called them "vegies"), familiarity was batted back and forth. Benny, her coarse, handsome, slick, go-getting husband, would stick around pinching her bottom or patting her suggestively and driving George into a turmoil. As he stood gossiping with her one day beside the lettuce rows, he was conscious of someone watching; and, swinging about in confusion, found his daughter to be giggling from an upstairs window. She gave him no peace after that.

"Oh, you old bastard, daddy!" she would cry joyously. "Alice, he's on with Baby Isaacs."

And Alice would smile her long-enduring bright smile underneath which dwelt the griefs of twenty-five years, and would say,

"Don't talk like that about Dadda! It's not nice."

"Not nice! But it's he that's not nice."

"Oh, Jeannie, don't be ridiculous!" And wonder in bed at night alongside his time-ravaged baby face if it were ridiculous —and worry without ever speaking of it.

"Oh, God!" Baby used to sibilate into hubby's hairy ear. "The silly old codger! Do I have him on a string!"

"That's my Baby," Benny would say, well pleased. (He hated owning things no one else wanted.) "Come on!" ordered one possessive amorous paw. "How's about it!"

George really got a zest from entering the *rentier* class. He brooded over the flats as if they were eggs, salving his own gregarious itch in part by dropping in on Jeannie and Donald, lending books, or going down some evenings to play poker with the Isaacs. The husband's full, oily-faced animality fascinated him and the coarse grain of his stories rubbed tantalizingly against the nerves of his mind.

"Is that so, Benny?" he would ask simply. "I can't say I ever saw anything of that when I was in London. Though mark you. . . ." And off he would go, while Baby kicked Benny under the table. Once Baby kicked Jeannie by mistake, who went back upstairs to Donald, furious to the point of tears.

"They make fun of the old boy! Oh, I hate them!"

"You're odd, Jeannie," Donald would say consideringly.

225

"You don't care what you say about your family but you'll never be dispassionate enough to allow outsiders to make the smallest criticism, no matter how justified."

"That's not being odd. That's loyalty."

"Oh, crap! The lot of you—you all have a peculiar inbred quality. The whole house revolves around patriarch George. It doesn't matter who suffers so long as he doesn't. Not one of you has any damned sense of proportion where he's concerned. Alice is lunatic on the matter, and you're practically as bad."

Jeannie propped her curls on one hand.

"I know he's got all sorts of faults, that he's irritating and a bore, but he's lovable and well-meaning—and utterly harmless. If he likes to roll his eyes at Baby Isaacs's exposed thighs, let him. It's not doing anyone any harm. But I simply cannot bear to see the twit-brains making fun."

But he did not, did not become aware.

He was getting older, was asleep sometimes in the early evening, his book still open and his glasses dropping off the end of his nose; declined sometimes invitations to parties, did not hear the jazz or the dirty stories or the queers giggling. A syncopated energy flung him between office and home, but it was at office he was happiest, vested permanently in a kind of Lenten purple, a shrouded figure of editorial untouchability to small fry but with still enough sparkle to make the junior reporters laugh.

His leaders lost *gravitas* and flirted shockingly with whimsy and sentiment; there was a wistfulness not always suitable to essays on the budget, trade expansion or the desirability of government subsidies in the primary industries. A lot of "bite" was gone and, instead, a cajoling note crept into his work. Once or twice he got out his enormous and unpublished novel and glanced over it in secret wondering if he could ever do anything but burn it. After reading a chapter or two ("Lissie,

226

remember when I wrote this? Remember when I described you in the bath?") he would pack it away in its box like the first tooth pulled that one preserves for years.

"Daddy's starting to grow old," Jeannie said to Donald one night. "He hates me making improper remarks."

"Pity he can't hear the bunch downstairs." Donald was making a wonderful ragout and slicing mushrooms and aubergines.

"Outsiders is fun. Daughters is wrong."

"True."

Below the Eastoes night was frequently rent by volcanic rows that ruined their sleep and woke Lisa. Words like radio blast could be savoured, of course, as they lay awake giggling, but eventually the sport lost flavour and they became richly irritated.

"You'll have to ask them to leave." Jeannie stood behind the rampart of her indignation, in the parental livingroom.

George crossed his feet neatly at the ankles and leant back.

"I can't. They've got a lease. Anyway, they can't be so bad, surely."

"It's not me," Jeannie explained slowly and insolently, as if she were speaking to a baby. "I *know* what all those four-letter words mean. It's Lisa. I'm becoming so suburban. I don't want her saying them to the children down the road. Anyway, more important than that, they wake her up. I just can't put up with it any longer."

"You'll have to put up with it until the lease expires next April."

"Well, then, we'll have to go."

"Oh, don't be so silly. *Where* will you go? You can't come here. The house is far too small. We've been through all that."

Familial rudeness appeared sanctioned. Jeannie flounced away and that night while she was attending a party escorted

227

by her father (Donald's turn to baby-sit!) she vanished from the crowded room with an Italian of volatile manners, leaving unaware George sipping his whisky and waiting lugubriously for her to reappear. He waited until one and then went home without her.

At two he was awakened by a shout below the bedroom window; and, rocking across the room on his corns, gazed unfocusedly down into the pale oval of Donald's face.

"Where is she?"

"Where's who?"

"Where's Jeannie? Did she come home with you?"

George blinked himself awake. "Don't take that tone to me!" he said peremptorily. "I've no idea where the girl is. You two have been making your own lives for a long time now."

"But she was with you."

"Lower your voice. You'll have the whole street up."

"What happened? I insist on knowing."

George looked down compassionately into the shrubby garden, pock-marked with shadow.

"She went off with some moustachioed Latin round about twelve. I waited an hour and when she didn't return I just came home."

"Who was he?"

"I've no idea."

"But, God Almighty, why did you let her go?"

George closed the window and shut his rage into the bedroom where, in the twilight, he could see Alice leaning on one elbow, her nightgown slipping from her shoulders.

"Damned rude pup!" George growled, easing his cold feet back under the sheets, and resting them on his wife's warm legs.

But Donald crashed jealously into the panels of the front door until he forced George out of bed again.

228

"Look," George explained. "I can't control the girl. I never have been able to. She does as she pleases."

"May I take the car?" Donald's mouth stretched thin and sullen. "Can I go and look for her?"

"No," George replied firmly, modulating his anger into a different key. "I can't let you have the car. It took me three years of privation to acquire one, and I'm not going to lend it to you in the mood you're in. You'd probably smash it up. You should have looked after your own."

"I'll be careful."

George saw his face become suddenly and sickeningly white.

"No. No, definitely not. Go home and try to calm down. She'll turn up soon. You know she will. There's a good boy."

That night's precision separated them.

Donald moved, from the clarity of her behaviour, to a flat on the other side of the city, and promptly retaliated with lusty frequency that only wrung from Jeannie her chromatic laugh until a lull in her own affair prodded latent resentment. These erotic holidays pinned George's age to him like a badge. Alice prayed and prayed that the situation would culminate in reunion. Below Jeannie, the Isaacs made love and crashed furniture unremittingly. Summer was turmoil.

"Dadda?" Lisa asked unceasingly for the first week.

"I'm Dadda," George would explain as he jogged her on his knee. Little warm freckled starfish, she clung to him, peering with her speckled eyes through the fringe of ragged hair.

"No!" she insisted. "No, no, no, no! Where is Dadda?"

"Poor little wee one," crooned sentimental George.

He roughed out a heart-rending series of articles on divorce, the children of broken homes, the calamity of early marriage.

When the *Voice* featured them, Donald almost choked, but later, after he had regained his temper, wrote an acid letter in reply, signing himself "Mother of Five" and saying that since her old man had gone she had never been so happy. The letters contained embroidery of scurrilous detail he knew would delight George enormously. Taken, the dear old thing rushed across to No. 24 where Jeannie was downstairs drinking an armistice with Benny and Baby.

"Oh, oh, oh!" George exulted, his tongue busy around his gum margins for some rich and secret deposits of a baked dinner. This organ lingered over the intimacy of discovery. "If I may be pardoned the barbarism"—he waved the letter at them—"cop this!"

He began to read Donald's letter, exaggeratedly groping through the forests of crabbedly disguised writing.

". . . almost as soon as we got married. Now, you'd hardly expect anyone to put up with that sort of thing. And it wasn't only women. He was drunk half the time, too. I've enjoyed life a deal more since we parted, I can tell you, and I aim to keep it that way. Single blessedness for me from now on. You ought to give it a try yourself.—Yours, Mother of Five. (Emmie Brinker.)"

"Well, why don't you, darling?" Jeannie asked unkindly. "Give Alice a break."

"You're joking, of course," George said.

"I think Baby and I should separate for a while."

The light polished the greasy curls, nose, eyeballs and wet lower lip of Benny Isaacs. "Until I get this company floated. I've too much on my hands to keep her happy."

"Ooooh, *leebling*!" she protested, waggling her little rump.

"No, Baby. Women are all right in their place. But when a man has things to do, they are just a distraction. Isn't that so, George?"

"A gorgeous distraction."

"Ooooh, Mr Brewster!" (Baby.)

"Oh, God!" (Jeannie.)

Benny stretched his enormous chunk of a body along the faded upholstery of the divan. "They should come when you

230

whistle and cringe when you scold. Like well-trained bitches."
He twinkled to conceal conviction of the truth in his own
words. But no one was deceived. "Up, Baby!" he commanded.
And she sprang with a shrill giggle to straddle his chest and
dug her spike heels deliberately into his ribs. Instantly he
swung her over and smacked with open palm the revelation of
a plump bottom in expensive underwear.

"The man's a pervert!" George whispered to Jeannie in a
tone he tried to make disapproving but which could not muffle
a throb of excitement.

But the scuffle reorganized itself around a poker game,
around the staid and dreary recounting of dirty stories, around
coffee at eleven. Jeannie walked around the front in the dry
night afterwards with George and gave him an unexpected
peck on the cheek.

"You're not a bad old boy," she said, squeezing his arm, and
causing him in this unusual display of affection to feel so
tenderly towards her he could have wept.

"That's the nicest thing anybody's said to me for a long
time," he said. "The very nicest." And ambled away up the
road.

Upstairs Jeannie lay listening to the Isaacs wash up, brush
their teeth, use the lavatory and flop into bed.

"Come on, baby. Aw, c'mon, Toffee!" Benny's nasal
cockney drifted up in the insomniac darkness.

"Aw, leave me alone, *leebling*!"

Jeannie ground her teeth together and plunged her face into
kapok depths. "I can't stand it," she said aloud, hoping thus
to drown the sounds coming from below. "I can't, I can't, I
can't, I can't, I can't."

Jungfrau, *liebling*, pressed palms against eyelids to tear
impressionist patterns from the darkness; and six feet away
Lisa began to whimper through the passages of a shapeless
dream whose very formlessness held terrors that choked her

small throat. She took the child, warm and urine-damp, into bed with her; and, bodies pressed together in a knot of unhappiness, they fell asleep.

A hundred yards along the road, George also slept, diverted from Baby's metallic charms temporarily by Mother-of-Five to whom in his dream from force of habit he was already composing an answer breathing ready and irresistible charm.

"Dear Emmie Brinker," he typed at an enormous dream machine shaped rather like a juke-box whose stops, pressed in requisite pattern, would emit the typed equivalents of romantic musical saccharinity that the real machine provided. "Your letter moved me strangely. It is a long time indeed since anything has had the power . . ." Oh, even in his smiling sleep he was conscious that it was too easy!

Alice, wakened by his mumbling, looked down on his lumpy features and with a rush of tenderness, patted one fat cheek. "Emmie," he murmured gratefully in a merciful blur of sound; and Alice, not hearing, smiled brilliantly and pressed her face against his cheek.

"You silly old thing," she said softly.

THE TWENTY-FIVE-YEAR-OLD HEART discovers in the glass the fifty-seven-year-old face with all the mutilations and barbaric developments of five decades. The mottled hand trembles some mornings as it draws razor along a pleasingly clean path of skin through the lather. Hairs tuft from ears and on the end of nose, and, captured in the morning sun's cruelty, grey ones shock the dark. The white sagging face is sick, is elderly, is cheerfully insolent about it all, purses its lips and whistles corn.

Through the bathroom window there is a moment of the Lane Cove River widening out near Riverview, a flash of gulls and some shifting craft on the incoming tide. Happy, happy birthday, George! chant the family, the wife, the daughter, the grandchild. The window fights for its view through loose tentacles of passion-vine. The blue sky is clotted with its green stars. Happy, happy, happy. Nicks his chin and dragging up lower lip renders the bottom part of his face shapeless while inspecting and dabbing a tuft of cottonwool on the cut. Removes teeth and cleans with face suddenly dropped in and someone else's shamelessly watching in the mirror. Replaces the miracle muscle-plumping plastic beauties and smiles again. Tie. Melon-chin once more, raised. Brushes the curls. Pear-shape potters plumply out, hello-ing the girls and then basking succulently in the white sauce of presents and embraces. Tumtiddy.

"How is it this morning, darling?" Alice's tenderness lost

233

none of its genuineness by repetition. Her sympathy had its conditioned reflex, however.

"Not so good," he said, putting on his sick face. "Don't really feel like making it there today. Those damned ferries. When you're wobbly they are the ultimate torture."

"Well, don't go if you don't feel up to it. After all, it is your birthday!"

George speculated and then grunted. "No. I must go, Lissie. There's too much to be done and it's silly to complain over teeny things."

"Your health isn't teeny, darling."

"I know." He paused and filled the silence with his brave despair. "You're so good, Alice. A saint. What's for brekkie, darl.? I must eat, I suppose, if I'm to get in."

He managed his steak competently, drank his coffee and complained to her to come and sit down. Alice's long grey hair was caught back in a loose and charming tail that made her look like a twelve-year-old. He told her so.

"A pretty old little girl," she said, laughing ruefully. "More?"

"Thank you, Lissie. Oh, I do love you so."

"And I love you, too, darling. Have you had your tablet?"

"Not yet." He fished vaguely in the pockets of his dressing-gown, but Alice found it for him where he had left it next to his cigarettes and she popped it onto his tongue and kissed his forehead. Through the window the bright clipped spears of the lawn already dried of dew stretched out to the corner where the fire-bin stood. Mr Next Door was burning-off on his side and smoke tailed away between turpentine-trees to a meaningless blur on the November sky. Prickling warnings of tears came behind her lids and stung her nose. Poor old boy, indeed, this birthday morning, that caught him exposed in summer light, mouth pleated with age and pinched more tightly than

234

ever by the pains that gripped and squeezed the foolish little valve of his heart.

Some journeys catch at memory. The particular grouping of ferry travellers or a newspaper flapping, caught against wire at the quay; a turnstile jams or a stranger with a strawberry birthmark needs directing; the harbour, an especial verdancy, is seen for the first, first, first time. And, everywhere, people appear cruelly young.

Even the office building seemed to be more youthful that day than he who, had crossed its parquetry for thirty years now. During the previous spring it had received an architectural facial, was a smirking successful monument of grey marble, checkered floors and panelyte. Lady writers, perkier, bustier, and brasher than ever, tittupped about and hardly noticed him except when he went out of his way to be charming—and even then they always seemed to be in a hurry. So he was charming less frequently, for a tail-end of laughter had lingered once in the eyes of the editorial stenographer, and he could not suffer being laughed at.

"Greetings, greetings," unctuous de Frissac said to him near the lavatories. "How is the master mind?"

De Frissac had risen like a shooting star from the ranks of reporters to become George's assistant for the Sunday magazine. They loathed each other. He was a centre-forward type physically, with pansy mannerisms that had begun as a joke but remained as habit.

"No bloody good." George scowled. This morning the maddening prefix reared a unicorn's ivory tusk in George's susceptibilities.

"Piles, pyorrhoea, gonorrhoea, heart-burn, constipation, scabies, rabies or enuresis?"

"Can you spell 'em?"

"Every one. Every single one."

George shoved past him and went into the wash-room. De

235

Frissac's soap bubbles, disgustingly grey, coated the institution soap. A crumpled damp ball of paper hand-towel had been pelted into the left-hand corner, missing the bin. But the voice did not miss its target and curled in after him.

"Also boils, hernia, paraplegia and pox. Not got the pox, old man?"

George stared at him through the mirror with a yellowed eye.

"Yes. That's it."

"The pox? Oh, delicious! And may one be so bold as to ask where?"

"In the usual place."

"Oh, no. I mean"—de Frissac laughed like a set of castanets —"from whom?"

"I really couldn't say."

"Oh, a Titan!"

"Shut up, will you!" George patted a damp hanky against his eyes. "I can't talk bloody nonsense all day." Someone swayed.

At first it might have been the other man who rippled in the disjointed fashion of a figure seen under water; but then he knew it was himself and he walked fear-larded to his little office at the back of the building where he had been for so many years. Before him the sick brilliant harbour. Behind, patiently holding a half-completed article, his typewriter. Half a dozen books awaited review in their causeway stacks. Amphibrachs of wisdom.

A knock on the door. Jockel's head poked round, his ginger eyebrows raised, but George shook his head and jerked a thumb at the work on his table.

"I'm a bit off today," he explained. "But rest assured you'll have the stuff by ten."

Jockel made noncommittal sympathy noises. He had no time to commiserate. If Sadie could see the great man now, he thought unkindly, she might wonder what it was used to bite so hard.

"Do your best," he said. "I want to get all that stuff set up today. There's going to be a special Christmas number this year and I'll need you on it all next week."

The ease with which George flung words into phrases and phrases into sentences had long ceased to be a delight; a tennis professional similarly ceases to be aware of the curving planetary beauty of his stroke. It is nothing but a clever trick.

Each key of his machine with its black symbol overlaid in light shattered some especial privacy within him, having learnt how to make use of him by his own need of them. Hunched over the table he patted out the remainder of the article.

Finished, the bell brought his secretary, a heel-high tight-skirted shorty not nearly as foolish as her goffered hair might make her. She would stand (consciously) in one of two postures—bright eager office girl or bright hard cover girl. The tender little palm of each mottled hand was often damp with sweat. The toes sobbed in their pointed machines.

"Miss Rankin," he barely managed, "take this bundle of stuff down to Mr Jockel, please. And bring me back a powder or a couple of aspirin from the canteen, there's a good girl."

The jujube of softness that was really Miss Rankin became moistly concerned. Brittle surfaces cracked.

"What's the matter, Mr Brewster?"

"I'm just no good today."

"Would you like me to ring Mrs Brewster and ask her to come in with the car?"

"There's a kind girl." He honestly did feel terrible. He spoke to both Misses Rankin with the kindest of smiles. "I don't know whether cossetting these frailties helps. Perhaps after I've had the powder I'll feel better."

The three choccy faces of his secretary crumbled in pity.

"I won't be a minute," they said.

George could hear himself mumbling away into the two hands he was unaware of putting to his face, into fleshy bowls of nicotine smells and an unpleasant sickliness he could not recognize. I am afraid, he told himself rationally and quietly, in order to curb the helter-skelter heart mocking his sagging frame. His mind prayed a Hail Mary in an intensity of appeal he had never infused into the words before, for he was frightened of gasping it out to a terrifying and lonely finale on an office desk. When he put a hand towards the phone, pain snarled at him to be still, so he sat, poor soggy heap, while tender efficiency bearing a glass of water and two small white tablets on her pretty palm blotted out the terror of sitting by himself.

Fuzzy inaudibility of his wife's voice speaking into the delicate secretarial ear. Genteel suggestions this end.

He closed his eyes upon her pursed pondering lips solving his problem and her two mature brown eyes which estimated Mr Brewster improved sufficiently to make his own way to the lobby.

He was in bed for a fortnight, built up on tonics and vitamin preparations, breath-taking in their claims, and was returned not quite as good as new to office routine two weeks after that. All the time he was home the Christmas cards began to come in. Not so many now. They were propped up on the bookcase in the corner and he used to wander out and examine the scrawled messages. There was one from the Harringtons this year, he noted, first time for ages. And Lippman had scribbled something jocularly rude under a blowsy Santa. And there was one whose envelope had made his heart stand still with its resemblance to the unformed scribble of lost Nita—but it was only a get-well card from the greengrocer up near the Figtree turnoff. The Bishop wrote two saintly sentences on the back of a holy picture and Marie and Larry sent a Chevallier Penguin. To fill in the last days of his sick-leave he wrote a long amusing letter addressed to them both, but aimed at Marie. They didn't reply. No one ever replied.

Depression so swaddled George when he went back to work that the baubles of Christmas failed to animate him. Fred Rush of the art department greeted him with blasphemous cheer, nailing him to the door with the bullets of three dirty stories, while his grey eyes, opened innocently as flowers, sought in George's own the reflection of raped purity. A man who would manipulate the curved soft bud at the end of the fern and snap its tenderness. But George's fern was sere and in his recognition of this he went two nights later to a party of mixed tricksters at the Rushs', expecting thereby some spiritual rejuvenation.

The Rushs had done the fashionable thing that year for artists and had redecorated a terrace house in Paddington.

Goodwill towards men was blazing away fiendishly. There were hack writers and black and white boys, yoga experts and flap merchants who yapped through Beethoven with the same expressions on their faces as when they yapped through Bartok. One would have sought dissimilarity in pain—but no, there was that same deaf gaze. There were broadcasting personalities whose empty skulls made wonderfully resonant sound-boxes for their fruity voices, a gaggle of models and their *couturière*, a rasped-voiced tow-head called Sugar whose rectilineal figure was a perennial source of warning to the girls. Booming documentarians were well under way, holding out to each other trays of stale ideas and munching loudly.

". . . just written the finest short story this country has ever seen," a tall parrot profile was explaining to Rush. The Brewsters went past respectfully and a trifle uncomfortably, searching for known faces. A model tucked under the parrot's wing gazed up adoringly. Freddie was nodding and nodding. ". . . boyhood," croaked the parrot, "the magic time when grass is greener than it is now."

"Look, darling," whispered Lissie, not always saintly, "there's Jockel over there with some woman. Would that be his wife, the one you used to know?"

"A silly girl," George replied. "And now she's a dried-out shrew. Please don't wave." He steered her towards the sideboard and the drinks, where in a cosy corner behind the hall door, a lecherous old Scot with a fern-frond moustache was poking salaciously at a teenager.

"Go won!" he urged. "Go won! Tell us." It giggled madly. "Go won! Go won!"

Freddie's wife, Fantasia, who was going through her Regency period, kissed each of them in the Continental manner ("George, my dear! Alice, my dear!") and moved graciously to the piano and posed there with her long bosom splendidly revealed above grey silk; one hand, a dove at peace, on a pile of ragged volumes of *lieder* and French art songs. The oval of her face lengthened as oval vowels purled from that church portal.

". . . a little thing we would like to do for you."

Her accompanist, whose oiled black hair and Spanish profile struck a pleasant minor chord with Fantasia's abundant gentility, smiled above her jangling chunks of jewellery. *Simpatico*, the reflection in the walnut piano gleamed for a moment.

"Come on, girls!" Freddie roared to the two middle-aged ladies. "Hop into that Mozart."

There were gay sophisticated Broadcasting Commission laughs, the gurgle of cheap claret being poured from a hand-flung pot and some preliminary throat-clearings from Fantasia.

"*Rugiadose odorose*," she sang delicately, making Freddie look foolish. People everywhere put on music faces. George took a long deep swig at his claret to get cultural strength and —tititi—ti-ti-tititoto sang the piano under the plump not always accurate fingers.

240

Arrested groups held glasses awkwardly.

"Go won!" teased Scotty's voice from the corner into an unspeakable pianissimo. But he was too obscenely drunk to be aware of fifteen outraged faces even if he could have recognized them.

After the Scarlatti, Fantasia was coaxed into singing Faure and after the Faure someone played a violin so badly no one bothered to shush Scotty when he lurched across the living-room in full cry after a model. It was splendid to have a lawful reason for laughter.

At eleven the groups were re-organized about supper. George, in agony at having to avoid Sadie Klein in such a small space, was contemplating going home when a statuesque blonde, the latest crush of their daughter, strode in with her Brünnhilde locks dangling to her waist and rose-bud breasts smaller than their counterpart exhibitionistically displayed over the neck?- waist?-line of her dress.

There were welcoming bays everywhere. Hope sprang eternal from one of the bedrooms to cry "Darling!" once in a strangulated voice and reeled away again to her *chaise longue* pleasures. Millie Lamb called gaily to everyone, "Like my dress? I'm late because Nigel only just finished it. But just . . .!" She beamed at the delicious boy with her.

"He forgot the top, Sweetie," Fantasia crooned.

"No! It's all there. Like me?"

"Those falsies are terrific, darling," Hope said maliciously, reappearing. She tried another door. "Whoops! Wrong room! But what an ee-normous house!"

Struggling for a hearing, a record sobbed away at a four-voice fugue. Scotty overturned a demijohn of claret. There were moans and cries of "Someone drive him home," "Empty the dirty old nonsense out the back."

"Take me home, George," Lissie whispered pitifully from the chair-arm on which she was perched. But George, fortified by the vision of Millie and Hope, toping steadily at a poisonous punch concocted by his host and joyous at having found a dumb brunette receptacle for anecdote on his right, merely nodded, while keeping his head averted from his dear wife. He was jolted, however, by the appearance of Jockel and Sadie, pouncing from a doorway at his left. Mrs Jockel and Mr Brewster measured each other against a photograph at least thirty years old.

"Why, Harry! Sadie!" George said with every false expression of surprise and delight. Jockel grinned or grimaced into his glass.

"You've changed," Sadie said abruptly. George introduced Alice to fill in the clumsy gash of such a statement.

"I knew George years ago," Sadie said. Grotesque coquetry fluttered across the scena of her face and vanished forever into the wings. "Perhaps even before you."

"That would be very likely," Alice agreed. She contemplated the bitter face of the woman standing in front of her. And wondered. George had only mentioned Sadie as an afterthought—the girl who was waiting and left so. Her saintliness could not repress the tiniest sense of elation. She gazed fondfoolishly up at big comfy George with his curly mat of brown hair, saw that he had forgotten brunette and was being winning and engaging to the newcomers. Dreadful George, she thought lovingly. He's a naughty old boy! Meanwhile Sadie inspected all the demolition work of time through her own permanently twenty-five-year-old eyes and shuddered in her turn. Still hated, of course, for it is hard to give up the pleasure of a life-time, but felt a certain indescribable joy at the fifty-inch waistline that was almost a joke.

"It's remarkable," George was saying to Sadie, fixing her with a look out of habit rather than desire, "that we haven't run into each other before this."

"I drink mainly at the club," Jockel explained. "We're not

great party goers." (Various vistas opened thereupon of evenings in the home, of gardening manuals, slipcover patterns,
build your own workshop.) "But now I can't even drink much
with my ulcer and Sadie has had to pamper it. Tough, eh?"

"I hate parties," Alice said unexpectedly. "George nearly
always gets sick and I'm the one who has to look after him."

"Oh, Lissie," protested hurt small boy George. "Surely I'm
not as bad as all that."

George could not believe what time had done to Sadie Klein
of the bouncing curls and giddy eyes. Behind this sour face and
the snapped-shut look there was the faintest phantom of Sadie,
rain-streaked after the concert with tram lights glistening on
the wet shadowy skin. Too much powder now. Lipstick run
into grooves along the mouth in the smallest of tributaries.
Hair almost white, curls less lively. Delicate curve of cheek
had receded. The chin and nose protested far too much. You
cannot believe it, he was telling himself. You'd never think it
was the same woman. Thank Heaven time has dealt more
kindly with me. They meandered through difficult waterways
of smalltalk. When Jockel was called away for a moment to
arrange transport for a couple who lived near them at Palm
Beach, Sadie suddenly realized that after all this time she had
nothing whatever to say to George and that she never had.
Kisses are a poor substitute for lack of ideas. Realization came
too late. She excused herself and followed Harry; while,
warned of her late victory, George followed, idiotically
attempting to resurrect something from that forgotten relationship; but all he could do was wave bleakly at the rearlights of
their car, get caught up with Hope and a plate of bolognaise
and forget about everything, even Lissie, who fell asleep in her
chair.

At two someone woke Alice by falling on top of her. As
she thrust up against a stinking mountain of flannelette the
peculiar emptiness of studio and livingroom struck her the

sort of blow she remembered from years back when on looking round at parties she would realize her husband was no longer there nor that particularly good-looking woman in the red— Ah yes! There she was! Then that fair . . . It was like being young again. Just as horrible. But the fear dribbled away and, wandering dazedly to the kitchen, she found him talking endlessly to Fantasia and Millie who had compensated for the failure of her grand entrance by turning down three improper suggestions from her host. Alice's thin mouth stretched into a yawn that exhaled the entire evening—gins, clarets, girls, artists—all vanished stalely into a Sunday sobriety fished out of an hour's doze that made the coming day's routine swell like a bursting bud.

"My little girl's tired." George dropped the tea-towel thankfully. "Darling," he said, "I was just telling Fantasia about Sadie. I thought I carried it off fairly well. You know she used to be crazy about me, poor girl. Goodness, how she's aged! It's amazing, but I'd never have known her if it hadn't been for Harry. Not for a minute."

"None of us ever would," Fantasia said brightly, still vital at two-thirty. She hummed Schubert and broke into dulcet phrases, used her pot-scourer vigorously and literally throbbed across the empty plaster rooms. "*Mein herz, mein herz!*"

They were very nearly the last to leave. The half-shut eye trembles. There is the groped-for thanks. The goodbyes protract themselves through kitchen, passageway, livingroom, studio. The front door opens into urban drizzle and tenements sulking under the oily street-lights. The cruellest evening ends its purple blaze in washed-down apricot tentative fingering along the mind's horizon.

They drove home in miserable dampness, George shuddering beside Alice with his jaws clenched against the spasms of shivering that clutched him. Along Point Road in the pre-dawn dark, the trees were distressed by an unexpected wind that was fretting the harbour. Into this dark green leafy sodden place of plane-tree and elm, of sandstone and slate, Alice, as if by an association of colour, would find at moments like this the simple air "Greensleeves" patter a minor rain across her mind. "Alas, my love, you do me wrong to cast me off discourteously, and I have loved you so long delighting in your company." Over. And over. Sudden squall caught them getting out of the car after easing it into the street-level garage. They were drenched under the umbrellas of the elms. By the end of the week the cold which George caught that night had developed into pleurisy and bronchial pneumonia.

Teeth out and the consequent pleating of his melted face made him look shockingly old. A tube ran into his nostrils and a drip-tube fed into his upper arm. Private rooms fostered remoteness from life but his blurred sight discerned a shock of colour where one of the sisters had arranged a bunch of calendula that Jeannie had brought him. They were the sun rising and the sun setting for nearly a week of babblings, strange dreams and a death-tussle in which he was a half-hearted participant.

Sometimes he was aware of Lissie's voice and the outlines of half-known faces staring at this exhibit of congested lung. Nurses and sisters alike coddled him during the first four days when death seemed close enough to cough warningly and deprecatingly of its presence. Faces and calendulas entangled, bent their petals of charity about him, sponged, hovered, changed tubes across, recorded temperature and pulse rate, spoke softly, became part of a deft and many fingered machine that seemed to be continually attending him. At one stage the timbre of English changed to the dramatic rhythm of Latin and the whiteness that secured him was shattered by the peace of black alpaca. This colour-change was grasped by a final strength in him with such evidence of balm, such thankfulness,

245

there appeared to be nothing more to do except let eyelids screen eyes, the mouth drop open into the perplexed wonder of childhood, and the soul drift away like a puff of air.

A day later he was sufficiently better to recognize his wife, but refusing to return, negating life with all his strength, he mumbled weakly,

"Marry some nice old buffer, Lissie, with scads of dough."

His family, gathered about the bed, smiled tolerantly and then laughed with relief. He was going to get better.

So better that within three days his conscious charm began to win over the nurses. One dark boyish girl of about eighteen he particularly liked.

"Move over, Mr Brewster," she would order pleasantly, deftly tucking the sheets around. And in the jargon, "Have we drunk our medicine?"

The skittish plural. But he loved the fondling sound of it; and, luxuriating, sank back in his cool pillows and captured her vivid eyes.

"You remind me of someone."

Enigma merely smiles and does expert things to the bed-clothes.

"It worries me."

"Well, we mustn't have that, must we?"

"But you do, you know. Do remind me of someone."

"Do I?"

"Yes. I can't think who."

"I hope she's a film star."

George would have hoped so too if he had not been so weak.

He lay there, all primped up for visiting time. There they were. Lissie's face had the devout capitulation of a nun's. In black the resemblance was startling, especially when she sat with Jeannie who had now dyed her hair flamingo and shadowed her eyes with iridescent green mascara. They fussed lovingly and although George's voice was barely audible,

246

he talked endlessly. From where he was lying he could not see Jeannie's black-stockinged legs but she waved one at him just as they were about to leave.

"Don't worry him, darling," Lissie said. She laid mild remonstrations on another's soul like strips of adhesive plaster.

"Late beatnik manifestations," Jeannie giggled and shrilled happily.

"Please," whispered George. "Please." She had interrupted his story.

Nuns rustled along the hard polish. One, a tall athlete who had hovered over George day and night when he was dangerously ill, came in, took his temperature and patted his shaggy head.

"Thank you, darling," he whispered, the small boy.

Everyone laughed.

"The old boy's back on form," Jeannie said with wistful sentimentality to her friends later. "Flirting with the Mother Superior, even in front of Alice. And she dotes, does Alice. Isn't it odd?"

"Not really." Millie Lamb was running an electric razor skilfully over her shins. "He's a selfish old bastard but he's not malicious. That's something special. You don't take after him."

"Beetch!" Jeannie said good-naturedly. "The truth is he never takes time off from thinking about himself in order to be malicious. Malice does imply giving thought to another and Georgie isn't capable of that." She leant her long face on her hands and looked sideways at Millie. "But you really should see the cookie with the lambent eyes who brings him Akta-vite and bikkies. George says bikky. It's more lovable."

"Mmmm. Would she not be a little young for your poppa?"

"Oh, of course. Although he never really sees himself past it, poor darling. They'd have to slice it off before he'd believe he was incapable."

247

"Well, do tell. Who is she? Make it dramatic."

Millie dusted off both legs and slipped back into her slacks.

"Do you know Nancy Harrington? Oh, you must have seen her around Hope's place—she used to be Nancy Whosit—Reardon."

"The handsome one you always call Mrs Red Setter? The one with the gorgeous voice and no behind?"

"No behind. Only a past."

"Ooooh—ever so! Hand me a Kleenex, old girl."

"Well, Lambent Eyes is Red Setter's daughter. Isn't it a scream that she should be washing Daddy's bot.?"

Speculation gobbled George up whenever he saw her, so much so that he mentioned it next visiting day to Alice and Jeannie. Without compunction for her mother, Jeannie told him, explaining how they had left the hospital one afternoon together, Lambent Eyes in her civvies—turtle neck sweater and skin-tight jeans—and they had got talking on the bus going in over the bridge. George's eyes popped as he absorbed the fact and then agreed she was a chip off the old block. He wondered in an idle way who the father might have been and later that night when she brought him his supper, he managed to drag the scabby past into the present.

The soft indrawn smile wavered on the beautiful blurred Renoir face.

"I know you knew mother."

"You know?"

"Yes. Your daughter told me anyway, but when I saw your name on the wall chart I wondered. Mother often speaks of you."

"So you have been in touch all these years?"

"Not all. For the last couple. It was an accident, the way we met—but it's a long story."

George watched the youthful hands, the mobile lips.

"So she often talks about me?"

"Oh, yes."

"Oh." His lower lip jutted its dwarf doubt.

"Nicely," she said, helping or relieving him. "Always kind things."

"Well, that is lovely of her." The blood flowed. He smiled. "That *is* nice. Do give her my regards."

"Oh, I will."

They appraised each other awkwardly in the consciousness of their secret knowledge while his mouth crumbled busily away at a biscuit. Memory cut into him viciously and an elderly unstanched tear wobbled down his cheek in his ash-grey world of regret. Snug beneath pillow, wrapped in a monogrammed hanky, were the rosary beads he brought back from Notre Dame one September afternoon five thousand, six thousand years ago. Settling back below the coverings he groped for them. The hardness of each bead transmitted confidence to his hands and when the girl had gone away he cried quietly and happily and mumbling a Hail Mary went to sleep peacefully without examining his conscience.

Miss Red Setter woke him at five. The charming asymmetry of her face stared its unintended accusation the length of the bed. Hazily he said "Nancy," closing his eyes again to focus this surprising apparition in his mind—and shuddered. The cot shuddered. Renewed, flowers on the chest of drawers vibrated sympathetically and his reopened eyes explored reality, bringing him peace for the moment, in the encompassment of a hospital sterility that made him more like a faulty machine than a broken male body. During that day he was scolded twice for complaining by his favourite nun, but recovered some self-respect when the Bishop visited him in the evening. This was a privilege proper to a prominent figure of Catholic laity and it did George good to notice the fawning accompaniment of the nuns at his side.

Beckett was still a slender gradual man who approached his statements, his friendships, even his God, circumspectly. But once the meeting had taken place and his certainty was established, from that moment his dependability was a miraculous shining thing. On the edge of the chair, his bony haunches dug into the support, the Bishop clasped sanctified hands slowly on his sparse knees and contemplated the flaccid face against the pillow.

"And how are you?" he asked at last.

An irrepressible religious amorousness flooded George. His *savoir-vivre* demanded constantly changing interests. Diversion fluttered its scarlet emperor wings and alighted on this next blossom, this clerical shrub.

"One must not complain. These sacrifices are demanded of us. It's extremely kind of you to come, your Grace."

"No. No, it isn't kind," his Grace said with the thoughtful honesty that made him unpopular with his flock as well as those grazing beyond the fold. "I had a spare morning and suddenly thought of you."

"It's still very kind," George murmured, unwilling to release his misconception.

"You've been here quite some time," the Bishop continued, ignoring him. Each retina, transparently glimmering with hazel light seemed a tiny lake. He fiddled with his coat buttons in a pointless sort of way, fastening and unfastening, while his eyes, mildly observant surveyed George's propped-up body.

"A fortnight. An indescribably long and ghastly fortnight."

"When—er—when do you think you will be going home?" the Bishop asked.

"I don't know exactly. Another week. Two. They enjoy mystery in the medical profession. A hangover from witch-doctor days. I get the impression there was more to my illness than they say, but of course all questions are diverted. I really took a knocking about, you know."

Beckett nodded. "I am sure you did. I am sure. You must have gained much grace therefrom."

"Well, frankly," confessed candid George, "Sister Cepheus said I behaved like a child of three." (He was still mortified.)

"Indeed?"

"Yes. I couldn't believe that she would be so hurtful." Snide wavelets of pain that were not purely of the mind plashed about his heart. He gasped for breath and tensed his body, but they passed in a few seconds and he felt he had been deceived by physical manifestations.

"Perhaps you misunderstood," the Bishop was saying meanwhile, "and she was merely joking." He bent forward, his now wispy white hair fringing and fluffing over the beaked face that trembled on the brink of a smile. "She's a very capable woman."

"She saved my life," George admitted. "And I thanked her from the bottom of my heart. But why this?"

"This?"

"Yes, this."

"This what?"

"This being compared with a child."

"Oh, yes."

"Don't you think it was uncalled for?"

"You must put it out of your mind, my dear Brewster. It's really not important, you know. Fancy letting a trifle like that upset you. But I suppose you are still far from well." George lay silently. He had felt so terrible after he awoke, and he hadn't meant to complain, but the words had been pumped out of him by a visiting stranger agony that had crept all over his chest. It was only momentary the first time, but the second and third occasions had extended their visits beyond the bounds of reasonable politeness. He could feel the murmur of this enemy even now, distant, warning and horrible. He could hear Beckett faltering on.

251

". . . must understand the fullness of her day. Perhaps she also was not well. There are a dozen reasons why she did snap. Can't you see?"

George nodded. He moved slightly in the bed and the visitor moved within him, came closer, more dreadfully close, and said again, "Lie still."

"I liked those articles of yours on the young people," said the Bishop. He groped for topics. "They appeared about a month ago."

"Yes, I remember," managed George.

"Forceful and honest. They created a great deal of discussion among some of the parish workers I see at Guild, you know. There was even—hmmmm—heated debate."

If he did not move, not even by an inch, he could hold this thing back. Only his lips traced outlines of words.

"Well, that is very satisfying, your Grace, very satisfying. Oh, you make me feel much better."

"I'm a skilled social worker myself." The pallid face allowed some mirthful creases to form. "Those figures you quoted. Were they exact?"

"Oh, yes, indeed."

"Really. How dreadful. Mr Quarmby who works in the Newtown area felt perhaps you had overstated the case. Still— it was a jab in our social consciences."

He shifted his lean flanks on the hard chair and after a protracted foraging removed his watch from an inner pocket. Examining the position of the hands seemed to occupy quite a time for it was done with a benign calculation that removed all offensiveness from the act.

"I've brought you a little book. It's an analysis of Newman's letters. You might frighten Sister Cepheus with it next time she is high-handed!"

He shook silently with dignified mirth. A gong boomed. The violet shadows on the coverlet dissolved and formed new

252

arabesques as the Bishop opened up his brief-case on the bed and took out the book.

"Goodbye," he said, cutting through George's gratitude. "Goodbye." He held his fingers close to the other man's lips and for a silly bizarre instant George wondered if anyone had ever seized it and kissed it passionately.

"God bless you," said the Bishop. "Say a prayer for me."

Which is all I have ever done, thought George, prayed or begged, selfishly and exuberantly for myself. God or girls. Who was it had said that? He tried to remember but gave up, acknowledging some truth in it. And in some wishy-washy way his prayers had been answered, he supposed, there having been divinities of all kinds. Begging and pleading for himself. It was a disgusting thought if examined too closely but he was in no condition to examine anything except the smooth surface of words, unhollowed by secondary meanings. The Bishop had asked him also to pray, to beg selfishly on his behalf. It was understandable. Every soul for itself.

The psychological cunning of it!

Comforted, suppliant George, his plump freckled hands clasping God, fell into dream-streaked sleep that lasted until two in the morning. The lightly beating heart, intolerant of heavy darkness, frightened him awake. There had been a dark lane in his dream, a narrow place walled in with fearsome unknowns that tried to take him as he pelted its length. At the far end a gate. He was longing and dreading to go through.

Sweat ran down his cheeks. Sitting up in the twilight of this prophylactic room he cried out.

"Was that nice?" Nita asked, petulant and brown, the darling, as she lay beside him in the long grass. "Was it?"

But no words came and as he fought to answer, Lissie said "No" very firmly and took away his fishing-line where he kneeled on the breakwater in the middle of a sunny schoolday. "You are treating me like a child!" he complained sourly, the bile in his mouth; but she said nothing, her nun-like gravity severe under the nurse's veil. "You act like one!" spluttered Jeannie, batting her spikes of lashes at him. . . . *"Liebling!"* He was cold on the breakwater, despite the golden light that seemed to pour everywhere without warmth. The tide had swung in farther up the river so that he was able to look back across the splendid reach of water to the houses along the road and the mountain's finger held warningly against the sky's lip. Foot-scuffing the dust Nita wandered past the houses in her scarlet costume, leading an enormous red setter that circled and scented and cast around along the turf and darted behind the ugly blackboys growing near the water. He scrambled to his feet, hitching up his old khaki shorts and, gathering his sandshoes and bait-tin in one hand, started to run towards her shouting her name. But no amount of running seemed to bring him closer. The calloused surface of the breakwater probed his yellow grubby soles, and once, stubbing his toe on a jutting rock, he had to stop, hopping and yelling to relieve pain that flickered away to an unexpected nausea which emptied itself in a gush of brown bile. "Nita," he said weakly, so softly that only he could have heard, and at once she turned, whistling the dog to heel and sauntering across the road to him. He was sick again before he reached her and when he looked up she had gone and there was only the immense curve of the river and himself wrapt in a spacious silence, snappily clad in a corker suit, the shoulders padded just enough, the hips *assez étroit*. Stained glass of incredible blue towered all round him; he could not remember being in a church of such lucency before with sunlight lemon as spring pulsating gently across the chancel and aisle down which now he felt he could walk more firmly. Lissie was waiting by the rail to receive Communion, so he tiptoed past her and in the daylight outside, just as lemon-flowered as the luminous church, he discovered Hilbery and Mrs Red Setter lying on

254

rugs with a picnic lunch spread out between them, a riot of jellied madrilenes in cups and small bottles of chilled wine that repeated the stained glass effect. Mrs Red Setter put her fingers to her lips, the lovely mountain, and said: "Sshh. Don't make a noise or you'll wake mother. Don't. Please don't." And Hilbery said, "Why not write her a letter, old boy? You know you're a dab at that." George smiled with dream pride and watched them tolerantly as they ate. "Lissie will wash up," he said after a while. "She is the embodiment of kindness." Raising his voice he shouted for her again and again, but the syllables battered against the towering blue walls to bounce back over and over, so that he began to move away from the others to the southern transept where interlacing arcades of lilac and cerulean sprang away from corbels, each face of which he knew, he knew. Some smiled. Some frowned. He could still see Lissie through the wonderful glass walls but his shouts could not pierce this immovable blue and he began to stumble along its polished sides, searching for the doors he knew must be there. Unexpectedly they opened before him and at last she turned her head, at last, as he waved through melting glass, waved and called and waved, until the night sister came running down the corridor in time to find him pitching from his narrow cot towards the glossy floor.

Hoisting and heaving in the panting silence she managed to raise him to the gothic tangle of bedclothes and then her palpating and inquiring fingers found the very last beats of his pulse like the tiniest of brum watches, hesitant and apologetic, afraid even at this stage to be too dogmatic.

## ALSO BY THEA ASTLEY

### Girl with a Monkey

Elsie is a school teacher, clever young and eager for life. Harry is older, a council road-worker, uneducated and inarticulate. He is of interest to her; she is his obsession. Elsie realises she must escape – from the small, steamy north Queensland town, and the stifling relationship which threatens to trap her.

### Hunting the Wild Pineapple

Leverson the narrator, at the centre of these stories, calls himself a 'people freak'. Seduced by north Queensland's sultry beauty and unique strangeness, he is as fascinated by the invading hordes of misfits from the south as by the old-established Queenslanders.

Leverson's ironical yet compassionate view makes every story, every incident, a pointed example of human weakness – or strength.